Awakening

Chronicle of Pip of Pandara
Book One

Originally published as
Child of the Flame

Charles Ray

Uhuru Press
North Potomac, MD

Originally published in 2010 as *Child of the Flame* on CreateSpace Independent Publishing Platform, ISBN 1456439197

For information about this and other works of this author, contact the author at charlesray.author@gmail.com.

Printed in the United States of America

Cover art and design and interior illustrations by the author.

DEDICATION

To fans of fantasy, whether it be sword and sorcery, or urban fantasy, if you like to journey to make-believe worlds, I hope you will enjoy your trip to Pandara and its environs.

Author's Note

This book was first published in 2010, under the title *Child of the Flame*. While I was not at all unhappy with that version, I've always felt that it could be better, that it needed more color and character development. So, after more than seven years, and a lot of thinking about what I needed to change, here it is, with a new cover, new interior illustrations, and some new content.

One of the things I struggled with in writing the original, was the language used by the various peoples, in particular, the form of 'you.' Knowing when to use 'thee' and when to use 'thy' bedeviled me for the longest time, and after a few years of distance, I noticed some inconsistencies. I'm still not sure when one or the other is proper, but I think, now, I'm at least consistent, even if I've used the incorrect form. I can always say, that's the way the people in my make-believe world talk.

I also had fun doing the new illustrations. If they look familiar, that's because I am from the Marvel Comics school of art, and was an editorial and magazine gag cartoonist in another life. While these won't win any art awards, I do believe they illustrate the story better.

If you're reading this a second time, thanks for reading the first version, and I hope you'll find this one even better. If you do like it, please take the time to leave a

Charles Ray

review—even a few words would be nice—on the site from which you acquired it. For any author, but especially for independent authors, reviews help draw reader attention to books, and being read is why we write.

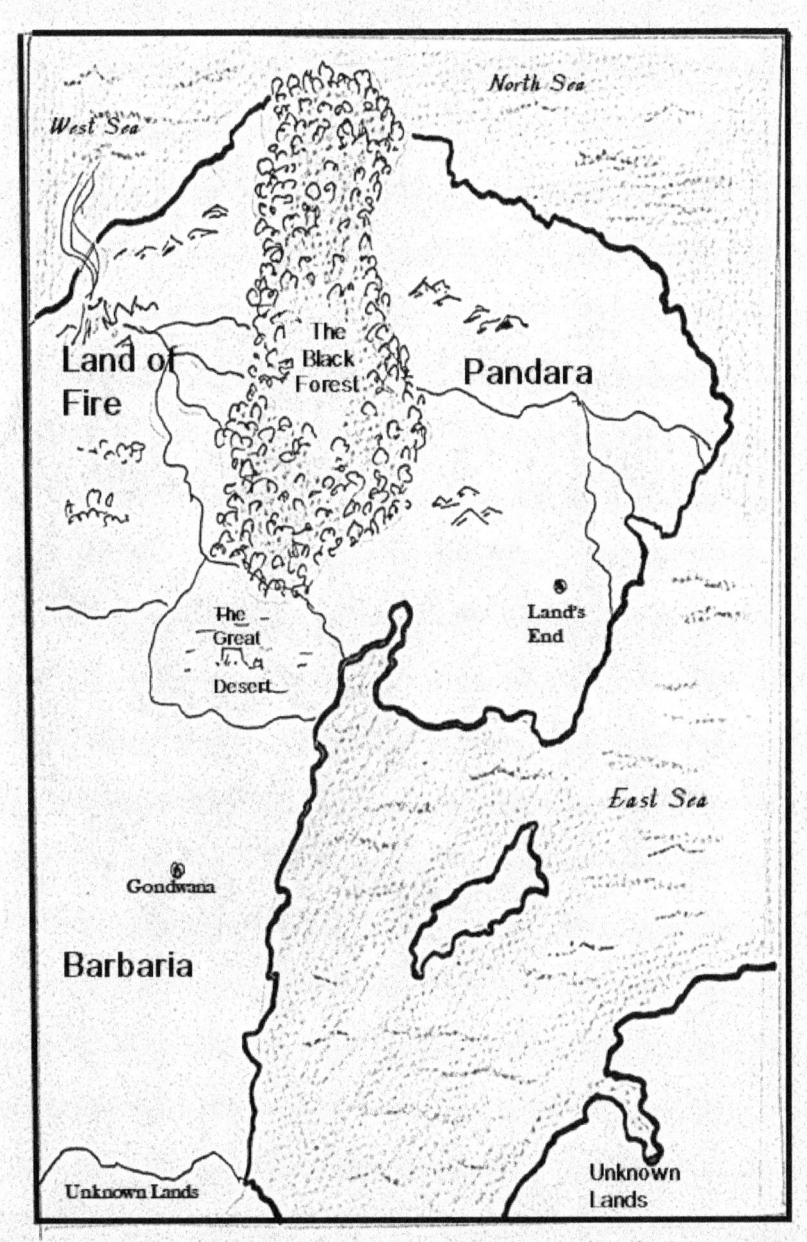

North Sea

West Sea

Land of Fire

The Black Forest

Pandara

The Great Desert

Land's End

East Sea

Gondwana

Barbaria

Unknown Lands

Unknown Lands

Prologue

1.

The hulking, dark building crouched on and around the hilltop, like some giant beast lurking in wait for prey. Constructed from black stones, mined in the nearby mountains by unwilling villagers who labored under guard, it was so black that, in moonlight and sunlight, the highlights were blue. Imposing by day, and terrifying by night, the castle had four large towers at each corner, with firing slits on all sides, and a large, looming tower in the center, with an onion-shaped dome at its top. Covered passageways, suspended above the courtyard, connected each of the corner towers to the central one, and covered passages along the top of the wall allowed guards to move from tower to tower around the entire circumference unobserved.

At the base of the hill, scattered like the bleached and broken bones of the dragon's meals, were the shops and hovels of the common folks. It cast dark shadows over the community for half the day, and stood menacing and dark, like some malevolent spirit for the rest. Merchants and shoppers alike averted theirs as they went about their business, as if in hope that if they didn't look at it, its occupants would ignore them.

Charles Ray

Three men met in a torch-lit room on the second level of the central tower. One of them, an immensely fat man with a bulbous nose and thin hair, his obese body straining against the gold-trimmed tunic that barely contained him, sat on a high-backed wooden throne, the arm rests of which were carved in the shape of gape-mouthed serpents. Standing in front of him, the other two men were quite different, different from him and equally different from each other. One was tall and slender, with sunflower-colored hair, a vulpine face, and a small, triangular tuft of blonde hair under his lower lip. His eyes, though, were his most prominent feature; cold and lifeless as little balls of ice, they gazed out at the world with complete disdain. At his waist, he wore a sword with a bejeweled hilt. His tunic and pants were as black as night and bore no decorations. He stood at ease, with a look of boredom on his narrow face. The other man was small, with a flat yellow-brown face, almond shaped eyes that were as yellow as his face, and a head that was devoid of even the hint of hair and glinted under the light of the torches set in sconces around the walls of the room. He lacked even eyebrows, giving him the appearance of an under-ripe pumpkin sitting on the shoulders of a beheaded corpse. He wore a simple gray robe and cloth slippers.

The fat man held a piece of parchment in his fat hand. He looked down at the parchment with a sour look on his florid, sweating face.

"I do not fancy having to appear as if I am begging this wench," he said. Twin streams of spittle flowed from between his fleshy lips and down the sides of his stubbled jowls.

"B-but, celestial majesty," the small man in gray said. "If you are to achieve your goal of building a mighty army, one large enough to defeat the devil spawn, it would be wise to seek her cooperation."

"I disagree," the man in black said, tapping his long fingers on the hilt of his sword. "It would be a trivial matter to defeat the small force she keeps to guard her castle and fend off the occasional bandit raid. After that we could draft as many of her people as you might need to build our, your army."

The fat man chuckled. "You make an excellent point," he said. "Why should I have need to ask for anything of anyone?"

"B-but, beneficent one, if we attack her, it might alert the real enemy of our intentions," the bald man said. "Defeating the devil spawn requires surprise."

The fat man turned to the man in black. "He makes a valid point. What say you?"

"As much as it pains me to have to agree with the little toad, he does have a point." The man in gray winced. "Very well, majesty, if it is your wish I will deliver this request for you."

"It is good to see my two trusted advisors in agreement for a change. Good, deliver the damn letter and see what she says. You are not to take no for an answer, though . . . do you understand?"

"Most certainly, majesty. I will take ten of my best warriors. That should encourage her to be . . . cooperative."

"And if she is not?"

"Then, she shall live only long enough to regret it, and the question of whether or not she agrees will be moot." The man in black stood, and slammed his left fist against his chest. "You have my sworn oath, majesty, you shall have your army. The gods will have much blood spilled in their honor."

The fat man's porcine eyes shifted to the little gray man, his gaze boring through him like a hot knife through suet. "What say you?"

Shoulders slumped in defeat, the little man nodded. "I . . . agree, beneficent one, if she refuses your most gracious offer, then . . . I suppose there is no other alternative."

With a stabbing motion of his pudgy finger, the fat man pointed at the tall man in black. "So be it," he said. "Do not fail me."

His right hand over his chest, the target of the pointing finger bowed. "It will be as you wish, majesty." Neither the fat man, nor the man in gray, could see the look of venomous hatred in his icy eyes.

2.

Two men sat in a shaded amphitheater, set in quiet woodland in the shadow of the great Mountain of Fire. They sat facing each other, eyes on the same level, on the grass in front of a chair-shaped mound of dark brown earth and lush green foliage.

One was short and muscular, clad in tunic and trousers of forest green. He had flame-red hair and eyebrows, and a long straight nose. At first glance, his eyes would appear light brown, but upon closer inspection, one would see that they were actually a light shade of red. The second man was taller, and thin to the point of looking emaciated. His complexion was pale and his hair so white that at a distance and with the light striking it in a certain way it looked silver. He wore a robe that was light gray, almost silver, that was hard to distinguish from the rest of him from a distance.

"I sense tension in the forces of the air and earth," the redheaded man said. "Portentous events are about to unfold."

"Aye, I have felt the same as thee," the pale man said. "There be trouble brewing in the lands to the south and east. I believe it to be the time foretold by the prophecies."

"But, the child foretold by the prophecies has not yet grown to manhood. He knows not yet of his power or origin. I fear that thee might be too optimistic."

"Thee speaks truth." The pale man nodded his agreement. "Our reports indicate that he still be unaware, and has yet to develop to the point where he can be prepared for his role. And yet, I feel that the prophecy is about to become reality."

"Thee art usually correct in thy feelings. We must only hope that if thee are right the child can be made ready."

They lapsed into companionable silence; two old friends comfortable in each other's presence, without need of the intrusion of words beyond what had been said. The silence went on and on, until the man in gray sighed.

"*I have faith in the prophecies.*" The pale man formed the thought in his head.

The redheaded man nodded. "*As do I.*" he thought.

They nodded at each other, each aware of what the other had thought, for they were a people who could, when they wished, communicate without spoken words. "*But, thee must never forget, the gods help they who help themselves. Those found wanting, or who refuse to prepare, are left to their fate. This thee knowest well.*"

"*Aye, I do know well. We shall not be found wanting, and I have no doubt that the chosen one will be up to the task before him when the time comes. Thee must have faith in the prophecies.*"

Awakening

Charles Ray

Chapter 1

Lands End

He was on his way back to his uncle's tannery, after delivering a bundle of cured hides to the saddle maker at the far end of Millwood Lane, when Pip encountered trouble, trouble in the form of a group of four young men idling near the bakery, engaged in some conversation that would only appeal to young men of their ilk. Pip had sensed their presence, by what means he could not be sure, before he saw them. He had that sense of foreboding, an itch that nagged at his mind, a feeling that spelled but one thing—trouble.

They were all about his age, but taller and heavier of body and limb. As he neared them, their conversation ceased and they all eyed him closely.

The biggest of the group, and its undisputed leader, was Sandrin, son of the richest farmer in Lands End if not all of Pandara. Sandrin nudged the boy standing to his left.

"Well, if it ain't the little girl who lives in the tannery," he said. He snickered as if he'd just told the funniest joke. The three others laughed along with him.

Pip kept walking, his gaze on the street beyond the smirking boys, and his heart in his throat. He felt his face burn with a mixture of anger and shame. It wasn't his fault that he was small for his age, or that he had yet to begin sprouting the scraggly hairs on his smooth chin like these boys, hairs that would someday grow into the full, luxurious beards favored by many of the men of Lands End. Maybe it was his small size, but the boys in town seemed to delight in taunting him, and on occasion, physically assaulting him.

He moved as close to the edge of the uneven wooden walkway as possible, to put as much space as he could between himself and the four boys, but with Sandrin prodding them, the three boys with him spread out so as to block his forward progress. He had to either stop, or walk into the cobbled street. Neither seemed desirable.

"Where be you goin', little girl?" Sandrin asked. His face was contorted in a smirk, and he had an evil gleam in his eyes.

Pip stopped and stared up at his tormentor. Although Pip knew that the boy was only a few months older, he stood a full two hands taller, a dozen pounds heavier, and already had several strands of dark hair sprouting from his square jaw.

"I be not a girl, and you well know it Sandrin," he said. "I be a boy the same as you."

"Well, now, you certainly do not look like a boy, and you certainly be not like me. Your hands and feet be small just like a girl, and your face be as smooth as a baby's bottom."

That, Pip could not argue. As the boys laughed he felt his cheeks get warm, and knew that his ruddy complexion was redder than usual.

"I have to get home," he said. "My uncle be waiting for me. I have other errands today, and he will not be happy if I be late."

That was not true. The hide delivery had been the last his Uncle Auric had given him. His hope was the ingrained respect for elders and the special regard that most people of Lands End had for Auric the tanner would cause them to allow him to go on his way.

When Sandrin poked him in the chest with his forefinger, he feared that it hadn't worked. His hopes began to fade. Apparently, this crew of ruffians had no fear of offending elders by interfering with the commerce of one of the community's most respected tradesmen. They seemed to be standing their ground, feral grins creasing their dirt-stained faces.

Then, Sandrin stepped to the side. The other boys followed suit, leaving the walkway clear for Pip.

"Go ahead, runt," Sandrin said. "We wouldn't want to be interfering with old Auric's plying his trade. It be no matter anyway. We will get at you tonight at the audience."

Pip shot through the gap the group made, not looking back. He dashed toward his uncle's tannery some two hundred paces distant, hearing the mocking laughter behind him fading somewhat as he neared the safety of his uncle's shop.

He dashed into the tannery, where his Uncle Auric was working on a new piece of leather, and flopped down in the corner near the window. Dejected, he hung his head between his knees. He was conflicted. Ordinarily, he didn't bother telling his uncle when the other boys bullied him, but then, thought better of it. Normally a cheerful lad, he knew that Auric would notice his gloomy mood, and while he was not so blunt as to ask outright, Pip knew that he would wonder and worry, and would be disappointed if he didn't share his sorrow. He called the man uncle, but in truth, they shared no blood. Auric, and his goodwife, Ludmilla, had fostered Pip when he was still an infant in swaddling, a foundling whose origins were unknown. He often thought of them as parents—they were the only parents he'd ever known—but, Auric had insisted that he call them aunt and uncle, for reasons that he would never elaborate.

Pip sniffed and looked up at his uncle, who was bent over the leather, but watching out of the corner of his eye. "Why do they hate me so, Uncle Auric?" His face was contorted in a painful grimace. "I've never done anything to any of them, yet they treat me as if I have the pox, or worse."

Auric looked down at Pip, frowns of worry creasing his broad forehead. He placed the leather on the workbench and crossed the room to stand before him.

"Now, lad, I be thinking you worry overmuch," he said. "I think mayhap you be misunderstanding them. Surely, no one could be hating a fine lad like you. They be just boys of high spirits, and at that age, they be getting up to mischief, that means nothing."

Auric sighed heavily. Since Pip turned seven summers, this was a conversation they'd had on a number of occasions, and truth be told, he'd noticed that a fair number of the residents of Lands End appeared to go out of their way to avoid the lad now that he was on the threshold of his sixteenth summer, the beginning of manhood, and a time when young men of Pandara began searching for a mate.

He attributed a large part of it to jealousy, especially on the part of the young men. Pip was handsome, some would say, too handsome, with a beauty that was almost, but not quite, feminine, Auric thought. Slender, with long, graceful limbs, he bore no resemblance to the barrel-chested, bandy-legged Auric, with his muscular arms, and the beginning of a pot belly that bulged his pants out like a small melon. Auric's hair was thin and blacked, streaked with white at the temples, while Pip's was lush and a russet color like flames in a fireplace in winter, with thin strands of black threaded through the red like tendrils of smoke from a coal fire. Auric and his wife Ludmilla had dark brown eyes. Pip's eyes were amber.

No, Pip resembled neither of the people who had raised him from a swaddling. That, however, had not kept them from loving him with every fiber of their being. They'd fallen instantly in love with the quiet, unblinking infant, who had been brought, wrapped in a silk blanket, in the middle of the night. Unlike other infants, Pip never cried. He lay quietly in the crib Auric had built for him, taking in everything with his amber-colored eyes.

Auric and Ludmilla hadn't gotten a clear look at the man who brought Pip to them. He'd stayed in the darkness just outside the door, and his face was covered by a thick scarf, which had disguised his voice as well as his visage. Not that it mattered. Ludmilla had never been able to bear a child, so Pip, as they decided to call him, filled a void in their lives, becoming the son that Auric had feared he would never have. Why Auric had decided to tell Pip that he was *not* his son, but a nephew, he could never say. It just seemed at the time something he had to do.

The sad look on Pip's face told Auric that their conversation was not ended.

"But, I do think they dislike me greatly," Pip said. "Look how they avoid me at the audiences. Everyone else mingles and has fun, but no one will share so much as a word with me other than you, Aunt Ludmilla, and Galen."

"Ah, lad, mayhap it be because they be jealous of your uncommon good looks." Auric had said this many times, and many times it had failed to convince Pip.

"No, Uncle Auric," he said with adult finality. "It be just because they do not like me."

Auric shrugged, a sad look creasing his face. Pip recognized the expression; he'd seen it often enough. His uncle wouldn't argue further. He would let Pip sit in the corner and fret over the fact that the people of the town treated him as if he was some alien being. He would stew and worry until something distracted him, or he came to thinking that maybe the people were right. The fact, that he had to admit even to himself, was that he *was* different. He didn't even resemble his uncle and aunt.

And, the difference was more than just appearance. There was, for instance, his fascination with fire. Not setting them, but an attraction, as if the flames were calling out to him. He had never, like so many young ones, been tempted to put his hand in the fire—it was as if he knew it would hurt—but, he found the hearth seemed friendlier whenever he sat and gazed into the flickering flames.

Soon, he was distracted. A ladybug was making its way through the dust on the workroom floor. He watched it, fascinated by the way it made wiggly lines in the dust, but always in the direction of the small hole at the base of the wall. He was wondering what the small bug was thinking, where it was going, when Auric's voice snapped him out of his reverie.

"Pip, lad, you know tonight be the castle audience. Queen Daphne be opening the castle to all the town folk, and there will be food, drink, and music. You know how you love to listen to music." Auric's round face lit up in a smile.

Pip could not resist Auric's infectious mood, and returned his smile. "That be true. Audiences at the castle do be fun." Then, his smile wavered. Everyone in Lands End would be present at the castle, and that included Sandrin and his friends. If his evening was to be pleasant, Pip knew he would have to find a way to avoid them.

The door to the workshop swung open with such force it hit the wall with a loud thud. Ludmilla, a broad smile on her round face, strode in. She stopped just inside the room, her hands on broad hips, and looked from Auric to Pip, her brown eyes twinkling. She cocked her head to one side, and brushed at her light brown hair, which was pulled back into a small bun, exposing her pink, shell-like ears.

"Well, what be my two men up to this fine afternoon?" she asked.

"Nothing," Pip and Auric said in unison. "We be just waiting for you." It was a lie, and she knew it. But, she loved hearing them say it.

Pip's worry over being disliked by the rest of the village, and the prospect of being bullied by Sandrin and his friends, faded into nothingness. In Ludmilla's presence, it was impossible to remain morose. Her smile was even more infectious than Auric's. She could find joy in any situation, and even in the dark, cold days of winter, when the clouds covered the sun and the wind whistled down the chimney, she could find a reason to laugh and smile. She brought brightness and happiness to any room, and, Pip thought, cleanliness too. Ludmilla was forever cleaning and rearranging things in the household, and only in the shop, where Auric and Pip worked on the leathers, did she allow any clutter, and only that because Auric had pleaded, complaining that whenever she tidied up, he was unable to find his tools easily and it slowed his work. She grumbled and frowned—something she rarely did—but agreed not to touch his workshop.

"What be we waiting for, then?" She walked over, leaned down, and tousled Pip's red hair, then stood and poked Auric's ample belly. "We be wanting to get good seats up front se we can see the dancers and musicians, don't we?"

"Of course, we do, my dear," Auric said, as he gently caressed her cheek. "I know how much you and Pip like the music."

She leaned into him. "As if you don't as well, husband of mine? I saw you at the last audience, gawking at that pretty young dancer, and your feet were tapping in time with music even more than mine."

"Well, I must confess, I do like a lively tune as much as the next now and then."

Pip enjoyed watching the two of them together like this. His fondest wish was that someday he would have such a relationship; could find someone other than his aunt and uncle who could find joy in his presence.

Ludmilla turned to him. "Now, Pip, you must go and wash up. We can't have you appearing before Queen Daphne looking like a common street urchin."

"But, Aunt Milla, I washed good at midday."

"Land sakes, boy, you not be thinking that last all day, do you? You have dust on your face, and I be betting that your hands are all dirty from delivering those skins for your uncle."

"She be right, Pip," Auric said. "Those leathers been on the shelf a full seven day, and I know they was dirty. You want to be presentable at the castle, do you not? We will not have the people thinking Ludmilla is not keeping a neat house."

Ludmilla slapped Auric's shoulder. "And, so shall you. You be even dustier than Pip."

Auric made a face as if he had been sucking on the minty grass that grew in the high meadows. Pip laughed.

"Now, you be not laughing at your uncle, do you boy?" Auric said. He twisted his mouth as if angry, but only succeeded in looking like he had stomach gas, which only made Pip laugh harder.

Ludmilla reached down and pinched Pip's ear. "Now, you stop that, boy. Your uncle works hard, so it only be natural he be a bit unkempt. You apologize this instance."

"I'm sorry Uncle Auric," Pip said. "I mean no disrespect, but it just looks so funny when you twist your face like that."

"So, you think I be funny, do you?" Auric took a playful swipe, which Pip ducked. "Well, let us see how funny it be when I take a rough cloth and lye soap to your face."

Pip made a dash for the door.

"No, no, I can wash my own face. I be not a baby, you know. I will soon be a man."

Auric made as if to chase after him. "Maybe so, but you still be a baby to me, and you be remembering that."

Watching them, Ludmilla smiled contentedly. She waggled a finger at them as they tumbled through the door.

"Goodness gracious," she said. "The two of you be as noisy as a tree full of howlers." She referred to the long-tailed, arboreal creatures that inhabited Pandara's forests, famous for their eerie laughing sound when the moon was full. "Now, go on the two of you and get yourselves clean. We have only one hour before the audience starts, and I will be very cross if we arrive late and do not get good seats. And, do not forget to wash behind your ears, the both of you."

Chapter 2

Knowing full well that for all her cheerfulness, Ludmilla was very serious about arriving early at the audience, they wasted no time in cleaning up. They also changed into clean trousers and tunics, along with vests made from the finest leather by Auric himself. With their matching brown vests, they made a fine pair, and Ludmilla looked pleased as she beamed at them, one slender and beautiful, one rotund but sturdy. They knew she thought of them as the pride of the town.

Now that they were cleaned and dressed to her satisfaction, she nodded, and they set off for the castle, north of their cottage. She walked between them, her arms linked with theirs. She was only a hand-span taller than Pip, but every bit as rotund as Auric.

By the time they arrived at the castle gate a crowd had already gathered. Everyone in Lands End looked forward to the weekly audience, as the gathering was called. It gave them a chance to bring any grievances they had before the queen and the court, but more importantly, it provided grand food and entertainment, which was why most came. Audiences were held in the castle's courtyard, a broad square, paved with large stones worn smooth by generations of feet that had trod upon them since the castle was built. In the center of the end of the courtyard opposite the gate a stage was erected in front of the great wooden doors of the throne room. On each side of the stage were two large trestle tables laden with food enough to feed an army. Pandara, however, had no army, for the land had been at peace for as long as the oldest among them could remember. Only a small royal guard, about twenty men, whose duties consisted mainly of standing sentry duty at the castle, and on occasion patrolling the borders to the south, where only the Great Desert separated Pandara from the southern kingdom of Barbaria, a dark and forbidding place from which bandits on occasion crossed the desert to raid small farms near the border.

No one remembered why the gathering was called an audience, since rarely did anyone submit a complaint or request of Queen Daphne, just as few had ever done so to her father before, or his father before him. Instead, they descended upon the tables, filling hands, baskets, or even pockets, with as much food as they could carry, before finding a place to sit in front of the stage.

Ludmilla clutched the bottom hem of the apron she always wore, creating a makeshift container, which Auric and Pip filled with their favorite foods. They then made their way through the milling crowd, finally finding an empty space at the front centered on the stage. The missions were just beginning to tune their instruments as they arranged their food on the cobblestones of the courtyard.

Pip glanced around. The courtyard was jammed with people of all ages. Some, like Pip, were looking around, but most were busy with their food. Pip was elated to note that Sandrin and his gang of bullies were not present, thinking that maybe, just maybe, he would be able to enjoy the music and dancing without being molested for once.

The musicians finished adjusting their instruments and began playing 'Maiden on the Green,' a lively tune about a girl who liked to dance on the village green; one of Pip's favorites.

All conversation ceased as the first notes from the mando, a stringed instrument made from a gourd with a handle made of flame tree wood and strings of woven silk, wafted across the courtyard. There were two mando players, accompanied by a young woman playing a tindal, a brass bell suspended in a wood frame by silk threads, and a drummer tapping on a water-bucket-sized drum which was a flame wood frame over which was stretched a leather hide made of cured goat skin. Pip's heart swelled with pride when he noticed from the maker's mark on the hide that it was one of Auric's. His uncle was known as one of the best makers of drum covers in all of Pandara.

Pip was no longer interested in the food. He sat back, bracing himself with his hands, and let the music wash over him.

After finishing 'Maiden on the Green,' the musicians began playing a popular dance tune. Food was forgotten as people began pairing off and dancing around the courtyard. Ludmilla chided Auric, poking his ample belly repeatedly, until he shrugged and finally agreed to dance with her. Despite their ample girths, and *his* reluctance to take the floor, they were both excellent dancers. Pip, on the other hand, as slender as he was, was one of those people who never seem to get the right and left foot to move with one accord, and more often than not, when he tried dancing, they became entangled, and he wound up on his backside. Watching his aunt and uncle, though, was like magic, and Pip stood, and tried mimicking their movements. Sure enough, he very quickly ended up stepping on a man's foot, getting his own feet entangled, and falling, face down, into the lap of Ramona, wife of the baker, who laughed and patted his cheek.

Red-faced, Pip struggled to his feet. Then, a voice from behind sent shivers of fear through his body.

"Well, if it ain't the tanner's little girl." Sandrin's voice, all too recognizable to Pip, was full of menace.

He turned and saw Sandrin and three of his friends, standing in a semi-circle, their fists clenched, and knew all too well that he was in trouble.

His first thought was to turn and run, but there were too many people, and it would be rude to run among the dancers; Ludmilla would never forgive the havoc that would cause. Breaking through the line of bigger boys, all of whom had expressions that told him they were intent on having some fun at his expense, was also out of the question. His only hope was that the only fun they had in mind for him on this night would be limited to taunting.

Sandrin moved in and leaned until his face was only inches from Pip's. "Time to pay the piper, squirt," he said just above a whisper.

Pip took a step backwards.

"Look at her," one of the boys said. "Looks about to wet his trousers." He so amused himself and his friends, he didn't notice the mixing of genders.

Pip kept his mouth clamped shut, hoping they would find his lack of response boring, and move on to other amusement. Unfortunately, luck was not with him. They were not dissuaded.

Sandrin knelt and took one of the sticky buns from the food leftover from Pip's family's meal. Smiling like a feral cat playing with a crippled bird, he dipped the bun in Auric's flagon of ale, ruining both in the process. Pip remained silent. Dissatisfied with Pip's lack of reaction, he stood and grabbed his wrist with a work-hardened hand.

"Come on, Little Pip," he said, his voice dripping with menace. "We be continuing today's conversation outside the castle walls." He started for the exit, pulling Pip along.

Pip wanted to pull away, but feared that the ensuing commotion would spoil the evening for Auric and Ludmilla. The decision was then taken from him, when the other boys closed in, surrounding him and Sandrin.

They moved in a tight group toward the exit, looking like a gang of boys up to some mischief. This earned them a few frowns from adults they passed, but most of the revelers paid them no mind. Once through the great archway, they turned left, walked to the corner of the wall and then around it, stopping at a small copse ow willow trees that grew near.

They still formed a circle around Pip, their shoulders pressed together, leaving him nowhere to run.

"Now," Sandrin said. "We be playing a little game."

"What k-kind of game?" Pip asked, and instantly regretted doing so. The fact was, he didn't want to know, because he was sure he would not like it.

"Oh, I think you will be liking it." Sandrin had a mocking tone in his voice. "This is how it works. You try to get out of the circle. If you get out, you win, and whoever lets you out must take your place."

Pip did not like the menacing tone in Sandrin's voice, nor did he like the situation he was in. All of the boys were bigger and much stronger than he, and there was no way that he, with his light frame, would be able to break through the circle they'd formed around him. Of course, he thought, that was the whole idea.

"When I say 'now', you try to get out," Sandrin continued. He looked around at his confederates, a feral grin making him look even more dangerous than usual. The boys grinned back at him. "Now," he said, and his fist shot out, slamming Pip's chest and sending him reeling against one of the boys.

The boy pushed Pip back to the center of the circle.

His chest felt like it was on fire, and he had to struggle to pull air into his lungs. Just as he was beginning to breathe normally, Sandrin hit him again. This time, he fell to his knees.

"Oh," Sandrin said. "I forgot to tell you, that we keep hitting you as long as you be in the circle." He hit

Pip again, a solid blow to the side of his head that sprawled him on his back. He immediately rolled to his side and curled into a fetal position with his hands up in an effort to protect his face and head.

"He seem not to want to play." One of the boy's voices, coming, it seemed to Pip, through a thick cloth.

His chest was on fire, his head hurt, and there was a loud ringing in his ears. He lay curled up on the ground, struggling to breathe.

"If you do not stand, we be unable to hit you with your fists," Sandrin said, as if from far away. "So, we be having to use our feet."

And, they began kicking him. The kicks were not too hard or painful at first, but as the bloodlust took hold, they began kicking harder. Pip twisted in an effort to take most of the blows to his shoulders and buttocks where he had a bit more padding, but it was only marginally less painful. He felt waves of pain radiating out from every part of his body.

Then, as suddenly as it had begun, the kicking stopped.

"Why do you boys not pick on someone your own size, or someone who can fight back?"

Pip didn't recognize the voice, could only tell that it was female, and young. His vision blurred from the pain that had been inflicted upon his body, at first, all he could see were indistinct shapes. He squinted, and as the scene began to come into focus, he could see that Sandrin and his friends had all turned in the direction of the voice.

Pip could make her out now, a girl who was not much taller than he, dressed in a green calf-length skirt and a green, collarless blouse with long sleeves that hugged her arms. Her hair was flame-red, an even darker hue than Pip's, that framed an oval face. Her eyes, reflecting the light from the torches on the castle walls, were the color of her hair, but so bright, they seemed to be lit from behind. She was not much shorter than Sandrin, about the same size as other girls in the town of Sandrin's age, but the swell at her bodice and the flare at her hips made Pip think she might be a bit older.

She stood, hands on her hips, her feet shoulder width apart, glaring at the boys, who had now broken the circle around Pip and were now standing shoulder to shoulder facing her.

"And, just who might you be?" Sandrin asked. He stepped out in front of his companions, demonstrating his leadership of this pack.

The girl—woman—Pip was still not sure, didn't flinch. "That is of no concern." She didn't use the common patios of the townsfolk, nor did she sound like the high-born of the castle, like Galen. "I am telling you to leave the boy alone. Go find a cat to set aflame or something."

Pip had never seen anyone go up against Sandrin and his gang of bullies, least of all a girl, but this one stood her ground, and through the haze of pain, he could see that she showed no sign of fear.

"I suppose you plan to make us?" Sandrin said, his voice a growl. He took a step toward her.

"If I must," she said.

Pip's body pulsated with pain, and his head throbbed. His vision was still blurred, and he had trouble concentrating. He felt hot stabs of pain with every breath, and their voices seemed to be coming to him from a great distance.

From where he lay, though, he could see the wicked grin on Sandrin's face as he turned to his companions. He saw him spin around and lunge at her, his outstretched hands like claws, reaching for her shoulders. What happened next, was a blur. As he watched, he thought it must be the effect of the beating he'd received, because such a thing couldn't be happening.

One heartbeat, Sandrin was reaching for the girl's shoulders. She seemed to blink out of existence, only to pop back a step to her right, and she raised her left hand, and Sandrin lying on his back on the spongy earth, moaning in pain. She stood over him, hands on hips, her lips curved up in a slight smile.

As Sandrin lay writhing upon the ground, his cronies looked nervously from him to the girl who had put him there, unsure whether to rush to his aid, or to run away. Pip lay curled up, peering at the scene through one eye, the other now swollen shut from Sandrin's blow. He heard groans, but couldn't be sure if they came from him or from Sandrin. As if through an early morning mist, he saw Sandrin push himself slowly up, first bent over, then finally, to an upright position. He glared at the girl standing there with a mocking smile on her face. He raised a fist, but it was a weak gesture.

"Boo," she said, and took a step toward him, her right hand raised, a finger pointing at him.

Sandrin, bully that he was, paled. As her finger drew nearer, he helped his friends make up their minds on whether to stay or go, he ran to his left, giving the girl a wide berth, and ran off into the dark as if he was being chased by some denizen of the Black Forest. His friends were close on his tail, running like the little furry darters that lived at the edge of the forest.

The girl came to where Pip lay and knelt beside him. He could see but dimly, for now his good eye was beginning to cloud over, and he was having trouble breathing. He felt her hand on his forehead. It was warm, but not uncomfortably so.

"Do not worry, little one," she said, her voice gentle. "You will be fine in a few moments."

He felt both her hands, their warmth flowing, first over his face, and then down his body, spreading out into his limbs. The pain seemed to lessen. He thought he heard her softly humming, but didn't recognize the tune. Then, the darkness descended upon him.

Awakening

Charles Ray

Chapter 3

When he finally awakened, Pip had no idea how long he had slept, but the fact that he still heard music playing, in fact, still playing the song they'd been playing when Sandrin hit him in the face, told him it must not have been very long, unless they were playing it again at someone's request, which was just as likely. He lay on his back on the spongy earth, in the shadow of a tree that grew near the castle wall. He remembered being beaten and kicked, but felt no pain. His vision, which he remembered being blurred, was now sharp, and all about him was clearly discernible.

He vaguely recalled being knocked to the ground and being kicked, and there was . . . a girl. She had come to his rescue. Had knocked the bully, Sandrin, to the ground, and chased him and his gang away. She had then touched him, hadn't she? He seemed to recall warm, soothing hands, and the pain evaporating, but he was not sure. He did know that, after the beating he'd taken, he should feel pain, but there was none. She must have had some kind of special medicine, but he sniffed the air, sniffed his arms, and smelled nothing but his own sweat.

He pushed himself to a sitting position, and looked around. There was no one near. No sign of Sandrin and his cronies, or the girl, whoever she was. He searched his memory for her, but nothing came. She must, he thought, come from of the outlying villages, probably in town bringing crops to market, for he couldn't remember ever seeing her before. Even though Lands End was Pandara's capital, it was still a small town, and Pip was familiar with every face of every resident. In addition, even though her words had come to him as if she'd spoken through a cloth, because of his pain, he remembered that she didn't sound like anyone else in Lands End. She was such a beautiful lady, and despite her apparent age, Pip could not help thinking of her as a lady, there was no way he could have missed her if she'd ever walked the streets or visited the markets of the town. He would have seen her as he made deliveries for his uncle.

Lands End didn't have much. The castle, an imposing structure of light gray stones strapped with iron bands, towers that rose some fifty feet to pierce the sky, was the most visible structure. There was a small monastery and square in front of the castle. Beside the monastery was the barracks building that housed the palace guard. To the south of these structures were the houses and shops, modest structures mostly of stone of a lighter hue than the castle's stones. And, Pip knew on sight the resident of each structure.

No, he decided, as he rose and brushed the dust from his trousers, the mystery girl was definitely a stranger to Lands End. But, that left a question in his mind; why had she helped him? Never before had anyone intervened when Sandrin and his friends picked on him, often in plain view of other adults, who merely turned their heads and walked past as if nothing was happening.

That last act, helping him, marked her as a stranger. Other than Auric, Ludmilla, and Councilor Galen, no one else in Lands End had ever shown much concern for his welfare. That, of course, was other than Queen Daphne, It would be the height of arrogance for him to think that someone like him, a mere foundling adopted by a leather worker and his wife, would ever have crossed the queen's mind.

He arrived back at the spot his family occupied just as the musicians finished playing, and Auric and Ludmilla, flushed, sweating, and smiling returned.

Ludmilla tousled his hair. "Pip, be you having a good time?" she asked.

"Wonderful, Aunt Milla," he replied.

He never told either of them about the frequent thrashings he'd received at the hand of Sandrin and his friends, and fortunately, whatever balm the strange girl had used had removed all traces of the latest encounter.

He worried, though. They often pummeled him, but this night had been different. There had been a level of anger and violence like never before. He'd been bruised before, but never like this.

Well, all that is past now, he thought, so I might as well enjoy the rest of the evening. "The music is really nice," he said. "And, you and Uncle Auric are the best dancers in all of Lands End." He forced a smile, which made his face relax, making him feel better, and soon, his smile was real. "After so much dancing, you must be famished. Would you like me to get you some more food?"

"Thank you, lad," Auric said. "That be nice of you. I would not mind a bit more of that fruit bread." He patted his ample belly and smacked his lips.

Ludmilla poked him in the belly with her pudgy finger. "I think mayhap you have already had a sufficient quantity of sweets."

Auric pouted like a child, looking as if he would cry. "I be not all that stout," he said. "And, besides, I need all the strength I can get to work the animal hides as I do, and you know that. But, even more than all that, my dearest, I need a lot of strength to keep up with you and your dancing every week. You know that you be the best dancer in all of Lands End, and I be not wanting to shame you by not keeping up."

Ludmilla smiled and blushed. "Oh, very well then. Pip, you can bring him one very small bun." She held up a hand, making a semi-circle with her thumb and forefinger. "No bigger than this, mind you."

Pip knew that she jested. She denied Auric nothing—Pip either for that matter. And, truth be told, his Uncle Auric, his slightly rotund shape notwithstanding, was stronger than men in the village half his age. Nevertheless, he could not resist a jab at him to make up for Auric's threat to scrub him with lye soap. "Okay, Aunt Milla," he said. "I will get him a very, very small piece . . . promise."

As he turned to go to the food table, Auric swatted his backside. "You had best be jesting, boy. You be bringing me a big bun, or I be taking me a piece of your hide. Now, off with you to do your duty."

Pip smiled as he walked to the table, not so heavily laden with food now. He waited for old Kerwin, the baker, to finish filling a straw basket from the food that remained, and then picked up three of the largest fruit buns he could see.

Returning to his family, he handed the largest of the three buns to Auric, who beamed a smile at him, and immediately bit off a huge chunk, chewing lustily. He handed another to Ludmilla, and took a bite off the third. The sweet tartness of the fruit, pears from orchards along the coast, rolled over his tongue. Ludmilla held hers and watched the two of them gulping down the tasty treat. She then took a bite, much smaller than either of theirs, and smiled as the taste hit her mouth.

Pip plopped down next to them and began idly nibbling at what was left of his bun, while Auric, his own finished, looked hungrily at the one in Ludmilla's hand, only a small morsel missing. After frowning at him, Ludmilla took another small bite and handed the rest to him. He began attacking it immediately, which caused her to laugh.

Paying them no notice, Pip's attention was drawn to two jugglers who had replaced the musicians at the center of the stage. They tossed two torches back and forth to each other while juggling three clay plates each. Pip noticed that, like him, the crowd was mesmerized by their performance.

When the jugglers finished, a grand finale, with one juggling two torches and six plates, while the other stood at the edge of the stage and urged the audience to cheer him on, they left the stage to wild applause and cheers. Two young castle attendants, boys a year or two younger than Pip, came out with brooms to clear the stage, brushing away the pitch that had fallen from the torches, and polishing the wood until it shone like glass.

A hush fell over the crowd, a quiet so intense, Pip could hear his uncle and aunt breathing. Everyone present knew what came next. This was the signal for the arrival of their beloved Queen Daphne.

When the stage was clean, with not a speck of dust in evidence, the two boys withdrew through the large doors. A few minutes later, they came back, along with four others, bent under the weight of the smaller throne that the queen used for courtyard audiences. Made of light weight carved brown wood and inlaid with gold leaf on armrests and back and an inlaid gold star on the high back, it was used whenever the queen appeared outside the castle. The five-pointed star, with golden rays extending out from between the five points, was the royal seal of the monarch of Pandara. Some in the crowd 'oohed' and 'aahed' as it was brought out and placed carefully in the center of the stage, well back from the front edge, giving Daphne the opportunity, should she desire it, to watch performers on stage and still be seen by her subjects. After a few final adjustments to the placement of the chair, the boys withdrew.

A figure emerged from the shadows behind the big doors. Tall, and gaunt almost to the point of looking emaciated, and dressed in a simple brown robe, he had a narrow face, with a long nose as straight as a knife blade, thin lips that covered crooked, slightly brown teeth, and an unruly mop of white hair that stuck out in all directions, almost, but not quite, covering his large ears. Galen, the queen's privy councilor, and the second most powerful person in the kingdom, walked in a slightly stooped shuffle to the front center of the stage. His hawk-like eyes scanned the crowd. When his gaze fell upon Pip, sitting in the front of the crowd, his normally glacial expression became a touch warmer—a compassionate look in his eyes.

After what seemed to Pip to be an overly long pause, and still with his gaze locked with Pip, Galen raised his right hand, exposing a skinny arm covered with wiry white hair.

"Citizens of Pandara," he said in a deep, resonate voice, completely out of character with his mousy, scholarly appearance. "Her Majesty, Queen Daphne."

He stepped to his right, turned, and bowed low.

Through the doorway emerged the most beautiful woman Pip had ever seen. At each audience, to his young eyes, she seemed to grow more beautiful. A bit shorter than Galen, and just as slender—though, on her it did not look like emaciation—because of the way she carried herself, her regal bearing, she looked taller. She wore a flowing gown, off-white in color, high at the neck and with long sleeves that cuffed at her delicate wrists. The dress flowed downward to the floor, stopping the thickness of a fingernail from touching it, giving her the appearance of floating as she moved to stand near Galen. Her hair was brown, with golden highlights, framing a perfectly oval face that looked as if had been carved from a piece of flawless marble. Her eyes were golden brown, and twinkled when she smiled, which was often, and she had just the barest hint of color in her cheeks. Hers was a face that was often in Pip's dreams.

Daphne, queen of all Pandara, moved slowly to the front center of the state, a step away from the very edge, and even more slowly looked from right to left, making eye contact with every individual in the audience, acknowledging each of her subjects. Her lips, full and rosy pink, smiled faintly but warmly, but there was mirth in her eyes.

She gazed out over the crowd.

And, when she spoke, her voice, though soft as a rose petal or a gentle spring breeze, carried over the crowd, and could be heard clearly by those in the back of the crowd. To Pip, her voice was like the musical sound of the shallow springs that crisscrossed the farms that surrounded Lands End.

"People of Pandara," she said. "Welcome, one and all. I do hope that you have found the evening's entertainment to your liking."

There were murmurs of agreement from the crowd. Someone from behind Pip shouted, "Long live, Queen Daphne."

Daphne smiled, and inclined her head slightly in acknowledgement, and acceptance of the love and admiration emanating from the crowd. And, loved she was, for she ruled with a light hand, in fact, seemed to hardly rule at all, for she never ordered or commanded. Instead, she requested in a soft, polite voice that fell like music upon the ears of those receiving such requests.

"I have a special treat for you this night," she said. "I know how much everyone here loves a fine-woven tale, especially one told by a master storyteller." She paused, then turned and faced Galen, who was standing at her side. "Tonight, Master Galen will entertain us with one of his stories."

The privy councilor's eyes widened, and he frowned, holding his hands up in a placating gesture. "But, your majesty, I'm sure they do not want to hear my boring stories."

Pip laughed, and then quickly clapped his hands over his mouth. The queen and Galen acted out this little play at each audience; her announcing him, him demurring, but then giving in. Even though he'd seen and heard it many times, Pip was always amused.

"Now, friend Galen," the queen said. "We shall have none of this. Your queen has commanded." She frowned, but everyone could see the twinkle of amusement in her eyes.

Galen frowned once more, and bowed low as Daphne withdrew and sat upon her throne, a mischievous look in her eyes.

"As your majesty commands," he said, bowing once more. "If I must, I must."

Even though everyone in the audience knew Galen's protest for what it was, a pretense only, many nonetheless mouthed pleas that he please tell them a story. The man often used stories to teach the boys and girls who studied at the small school housed in the monastery, where the five bald monks provided basic knowledge of words and numbers. Before becoming privy councilor, Galen had been headmaster and senior monk, and now, when his royal duties permitted, which was often since the demands upon the castle from the people of Pandara were few, he still taught classes, mostly those about the history of the kingdom. He served as privy councilor because he felt a duty to serve his young queen, but he taught because he loved it. Queen Daphne was not a monarch to place undue burdens upon her servants or advisors, and the monastery was but a short walk from his offices within the castle.

Pip loved his studies, and he enjoyed Galen's classes most of all. When the other boys age were on the town square playing warrior, Pip could most often be found sitting beneath a tree reading one of the books lent to him by the gray-haired councilor, or from among the hundreds of volumes in the monastery's library. That he was the only student allowed to remove books from the library was, along with his small size and difference in appearance, yet another reason the other boys picked on him. Never, of course, when he was reading, for fear they might damage a book, something that would earn harsh punishment from the sour-faced monks. But, as soon as he no longer had a book in his hands, the taunting and beating would begin.

But, not this night. Sandrin and his bully boys had been chased into the night, and Galen was about to tell one of his wonderful stories.

Galen raised his hand, and the crowd went quiet.

"Citizens of Lands End, attend closely, for I am about to tell you a story that was told to me when I was a lad, no older than this one here." He pointed a bony finger directly at Pip, drawing amused laughter from the crowd, and causing Pip's face to redden. Even though he didn't like being the center of attention, Pip's eyes were raptly focused on the older man. He'd heard the story Galen was about to tell many times, often in classes at the monastery, but he never tired of hearing it.

"Once, long, long ago," Galen continued. "There was a kingdom much like Pandara. The people of this kingdom lived in peace, the crops were bountiful, and the herds provided meat for all. The sun rose and the sun set, and the rains to nourish the land with as much regularity as the sunrise and the sunset.

The stories that Galen told were favored by everyone, young and old alike, but none liked them as much as Pip did—of this, Pip was sure. He sat enrapt, his head against Ludmilla's shoulder.

"Peace had prevailed in the kingdom for so long," Galen continued. "the people had forgotten the art of war. Except for a few castle guards to keep the king safe, and to keep wild animals out of the fields, or to forestall the occasional thief, there had been no need for men at arms for many generations. It was thus when the armies of the dark lords, led by a golden-haired warrior, fell upon the kingdom. The kingdom was unable to defend itself.

Galen's voice took on a raspy quality, and he looked as if he would cry.

"The dark warriors laid waste to the land, despoiling the crops and slaughtering the herds." His eyes blazed with anger. "Most of the men and older boys were slain, and the women, the most elderly, and the children taken captive to become thralls to the dark warriors and their lords.

He paused, and asked a nearby townsman to bring him a flagon of the berry wine from the nearest table. After slaking his thirst, he wiped his lips on the sleeve of his robe, and continued his tale.

"Just when the people of the kingdom feared that all was lost, and they would spend the rest of their days in bondage, there came a child to save them. The child was half of the human world, and half of the world of magic, and he had the power to control fire. At the head of an army of human and, let us call them fairy creatures, the child faced the dark warriors. After a terrible battle, those dark warriors who were not slain by the magic of the fire child, or by the emboldened combined army, fled in terror back from whence they came, and the kingdom was restored to peace and prosperity."

Galen ended his tale, his arms hanging limply at his side. He gazed out over the crowd for a heartbeat, then two, then half a dozen more. Then, the audience erupted in cheers and applause. "Well told, Galen!" "Your stories are the best." Cheers such as this came from every corner of the courtyard. Galen accepted the adulation in silence, as was his habit and as was his due, for he knew that he was indeed the most accomplished teller of tales in all of Pandara. He beamed a friendly smile down at Pip, who cheered loudest of all.

The tale of the child of the fire, someone who was of the human world and the worlds of magic, and who could command the allegiance of the creatures of magic, who came when needed, and in a heroic battle, saved the kingdom, was his favorite of all Galen's stories. And, even though, he'd heard it many times, he never tired of hearing it. He often fell asleep at night, listening to Auric's snoring from his cot in the corner of their tiny cottage, and quickly drifted into dreams where he was such a hero.

As usual after one of Galen's stories, his heart was racing and his face was flushed. The councilor never told mundane tales of mundane events in the lives of mundane people. Oh, no, not him. Galen's stories were always fantastic narratives of magical events that happened to, or were conducted by, people with magical powers, people who were bigger than life. In Lands End, in all of Pandara in fact, where everyone knew that magic didn't *really* exist, the tales were greeted with joy and amusement, because they told of world that did not exist, beings who had never been born, and things that could not happen—great entertainment for an evening's merriment. Or, so everyone thought.

"Yes, Galen, your stories are the best," Pip said. "Please, tell another." Pip snapped his mouth shut as soon as he'd spoken. His face turned a darker shade of red. It was not like him to speak up in public thusly, and he was as surprised at his effrontery as were Auric and Ludmilla. Worse, it was not seemly for a child to speak out so in the company of adults.

Ludmilla pulled him against her ample bosom. "Hush, Pip. The councilor is famished after his story, and now we must give him time to recover himself." She pinched his ear as she spoke. He clamped his lips tighter to keep from squealing and causing further embarrassment.

Galen beamed down at him.

"No, dear lady," he said. "Let the child speak. He is, after all, one of my best pupils, and always wants to hear more, to know more." To Pip, he said. "And, I suppose the story you want to hear is the one about the adventures of the Child of Fire in the Land Beyond?"

Galen was referring to the mythical land rumored to lie in a region far beyond Pandara, beyond the rugged hills and steppes of Barbaria, the uncivilized land to the south, inhabited by warlike people who occasionally raided the farms in Pandara's south, near the Great Desert and the dreaded Black Forest. The land was a legend, that everyone believed did not exist, but it was a riveting tale nonetheless.

But, Pip had been chastened by Ludmilla, so he only nodded meekly.

"Perhaps at another audience I will tell that tale," Galen said. "But, for now, as the good lady Ludmilla has said, I must have food and drink, or I will surely swoon, and believe me, lad, that would not look good. Think what my students would say on the morrow if they heard that their teacher fainted like a young maiden at her betrothal, and all because he could not tell two tales."

This caused laughter from the crowd, and a few whistles, for none there thought of Galen as maidenly or weak.

Galen then left the stage and went to the nearest food table, where he helped himself to large quantities of everything there, and despite the gauntness of his frame, began consuming an amount of food that would have staggered a man twice his size. He washed the food down with flagon after flagon of the strongest ale made in Lands End, and even after three flagons showed no signs of inebriation. People crowded around him as he ate, praising him for his storytelling and asking his advice, which he freely dispensed around a mouth full of food, spewing crumbs as he spoke.

Unable to get through the crowd around Galen, Pip picked at the remnants of his own food. His thoughts were on Galen's promise for the next audience. Waiting would be difficult, as difficult as waiting for Winterfest, when the adults prepared gifts for all the children to be opened at the rising of the sun, when days crawled by as slowly as the snails crawled across the stone walls that encircled the fields. He wanted the days to race, to fly as swiftly as the fork-tailed Ratcatcher bird swooping down on a field mouse. He knew that each night he would go to sleep thinking of the tale that Galen would tell, creating in his mind different scenarios involving each of the fantastic creatures that myth said inhabited the imaginary worlds that Galen created.

Charles Ray

Chapter 4

Just as Pip had thought, and feared, the days until the next audience crept by with agonizing slowness. Each day, he went about his chores, delivering cured hides to various merchants and residents of Lands End, or when not busy, sitting quietly in his special corner of the tannery, reading near the fireplace, or just sitting, gazing into the flames and making up his own stories in his mind.

Sandrin and his cronies regarded him through narrowed slits of lids, glaring with hatred, each time he neared them. Though their lips curled in anger at the sight of him, they left him alone. The mysterious girl, or woman, in green had obviously made an impression. Pip had not seen her again, and wondered where she had gone. He knew the truce with Sandrin and his bullies would not last forever. Someday, they would regain their courage, and the torments would resume.

The possibility of their physical torment and verbal taunts, though, bothered Pip far less than the agony of having to wait for the next installment in Galen's story.

But, the day did finally come.

As usually happened, he and Auric were herded from the workshop into their cottage by Ludmilla who supervised the selection of their wardrobe, fussed over Pip's hair, and observed the washing of his face and hands, making him do it twice to make sure he was clean to her satisfaction. "No one from this household will appear in public looking like a beggar," she said when Pip complained. Her stern voice and fierce demeanor sent both Pip and Auric scurrying to wash yet again, finally after a third time, passing her inspection.

They arrived at the castle early, and were able to get prime seating in the front at the center of the stage. The better, Pip thought, to hear Galen's story. Auric, on the other hand, was more interested in the items displayed on the food tables off to the side than any of the entertainment, although he did dance a turn or two with Ludmilla between attacking with vigor several mounds of the choicest viands.

The musicians, as usual, were in fine form, even better than usual, Pip felt. The other entertainer, a fire eater from Neuport, drew 'oohs' and 'aahs' from the crowd as he put flaming torches in his mouth, apparently unaffected by the fire.

After the pages had positioned the throne, Galen came forth and introduced Queen Daphne to the crowd. She stepped out onto the stage, and there were gasps from many in the audience. She wore a green gown, as dark and lush as the leaves of the flame tree. It had mid-length sleeves and a high collar, and Pip thought he'd never seen her look so lovely. Daphne spoke a few quiet words to Galen, greeted the crowd, and then they went into their usual act, with it appearing that she was having to force him to tell a story to the assembly. Though it was all an act, and everyone knew it, they never seemed to tire of it, and those in the audience loved it.

Galen then took center stage, while Daphne sat demurely upon her throne. He bowed deeply to the queen, and then turned to face the waiting crowd. He stood for the longest of times, staring out over their heads, his eyes peering through narrow slits as he swept his gaze from side to side like a Ratcatcher Bird in search of prey.

Just as Pip thought he would burst with impatience and blurt out something that would earn his ears a pinch from Ludmilla, Galen began speaking. "This story begins some months after the magical child had come to the rescue of the kingdom." His voice rang out across the courtyard, carrying to the far corners. "The child was made head of the royal army, and came to live in the castle."

He paused and surveyed the audience.

What comes next, Pip thought. What exciting adventure awaits this magical creature? He was fairly bursting with anticipation.

"What comes next," Galen said, as if reading Pip's thoughts. "Is the stuff of legend. Word came to the castle that, in a faraway land, there existed a grave danger to the kingdom, greater even than the previously-defeated dark army. A danger that would pose a challenge for the magical child and his army of magical warriors."

Pip found that he was holding his breath, sitting cross-legged on the hard cobble stones of the courtyard, his chin cupped in his hands, his attention riveted on Galen. Galen's words seemed to enfold him in a magical haze where time stood still.

"It was foretold that the child must take an army and subdue this far land, or the kingdom would be in great peril." Galen paused, looking out over the audience. "It might, should he fail, even be destroyed."

This was a new twist on Galen's story of the magical child. So, there was a challenge even greater than the dark armies. Pip was fairly bursting to know what great quest awaited the child.

But, before Galen could continue his story, there came a loud clatter from the entrance to the courtyard. Galen looked over the heads of the audience, and his eyes narrowed to slits. His mouth twisted into a frown. All heads turned to see what or who had so rudely interrupted him.

Standing framed in the arched doorway to the courtyard was a tall man. He had a swarthy complexion and a lithe, but strong-looking frame, his blond hair was swept back on his head, exposing a high forehead. His angular face, hooked nose, and piercing blue eyes gave him the look of a bird of prey. Standing at least a head taller than Galen, who was the tallest man in Lands End, he was the tallest man Pip had ever seen, and he was dressed in black from head to foot, tight fitting pants that hugged muscular legs, and a black tunic open down to the middle of his chest which was covered in a mass of dark blond hair. A tuft of hair, the same color as that on his chest, sprouted just beneath his lower lip, ending in a taper above a jutting, pointed chin. Over his tunic he wore a black leather chest protector, and a wide leather belt encircled his waist. Attached to the belt was a scabbard as long as Pip was tall which contained a sword with a carved black hilt.

Two men flanked the stranger. They, too, were dressed all in black. One was short, with bow-legs and broad shoulders, but with muscular thighs like the tall man. He had an oval face, almond-shaped blue eyes, and a blond mustache, the ends of which hung well past the point of his chin. He walked with his back bent and his shoulders hunched, giving the impression that his head rested directly upon his shoulders without benefit of a neck between them. The other, of about the same height, was as thin as a fence rail. His face was narrow, almost pear-shaped, and his wide-set eyes were round like little tea saucers. He had no facial hair, and his face was pock-marked and scarred, giving him an appearance even more menacing than the other two.

Behind them was a group of shorter men, ten in all, with dark, almost black, hair, some with skin the color of sunbaked brick, others with skin only slightly lighter than the black uniforms they wore. They were armed with spears, and they arranged themselves in two rows of five, with the men at the end of the front row facing outward, and the back row facing the exit to the courtyard. The spears were held loosely, but there was no doubt from the rigid cast of their facial muscles and the tension in their forearms that they were ready to wield them at a moment's notice should it become necessary. The three men in front kept their right hands lightly on the hilts of their swords as they advanced in measured steps toward the stage.

Galen stood at the front of the state, his body quivering and his face contorted in a stormy expression. "Who dares come before Her Majesty, the Queen, under arms?" His voice rang out across the courtyard, echoing off the stone walls.

The three men, walking with the square-shoulder posture and swagger of warriors, their eyes scanning the crowd, continued to advance upon the stage. The clink of their weapons, and the dull slaps of their boots upon the stone floor, were the only responses to Galen's demand.

At five paces from the stage, the tall man raised his hand in a quick gesture, and the group came to an abrupt halt, the two men flanking him suddenly standing as still as carved wooden statues, except for their eyes, which continued to scan the crowd around them.

After several heartbeats, the tall man inclined his head ever so slightly in Galen's direction, and then lifted it to fix the queen's councilor with an icy, arrogant stare. "I am Tenkuk, son of Ghengu and Weya, Champion of My Lord Prince Ostro, Sovereign of Gondwana, capital of the Kingdom of Barbaria, and commander of the army of Barbaria," he said in a loud, somewhat high-pitched voice. "I come at the command of my prince, bearing a message for Daphne, Queen of Pandara. And, who might you be to make demands upon a subject of Prince Ostro, old man?"

Galen's eyes blazed. He drew himself up to his considerable full height, and in the regal voice he used when angry, said, "I am Galen, and I am Privy Councilor and Chief Advisor to her Majesty Queen Daphne, and I make demands because my duties demand that I do so." He paused and glared down from the stage. "You good sir, are quite out of order. *No* one but the royal guards bears arms in the presence of the queen."

Tenkuk returned Galen's glare with a stony gaze, and laughed, but there was no mirth in his laughter. "Well, Galen, Privy Councilor and Chief Advisor, the customs of Barbaria are quite different. In our kingdom, only death separates a warrior from his weapon. Not even when we sleep do we part from them."

"I am familiar with your . . . Barbarian customs," Galen said. "In your kingdom, to sleep with a weapon at hand is to invite death."

Tenkuk tightened his grip upon his sword, so hard that his knuckles paled. Galen continued to glare down at him, giving him stare for stare, despite being armed with naught but his considerable wit and his regal bearing.

Then, the black-clad warrior eased his grip, threw back his head and laughed. This time, there was a tinge of humor in the laugh. His companions, though, continued to grip their weapons, as they looked at him with puzzlement all over their faces. The spear-carrying guards, back by the entrance to the courtyard, gripped their weapons tighter, and maintained their stony-faced vigilance.

"Well said, friend Galen," Tenkuk said. "I like a man who is unafraid to speak what is on his mind. I had heard that you Pandarans were a soft lot, given to . . . well, let us just say, you are a refreshing exception to what I had been led to expect."

Galen continued to stare down at the man, his gaze icy and piercing.

"Very well," the warrior said. "I will have my men wait outside the courtyard. But, I will *not* give up my own sword. It is too much a part of me, and I would feel naked without it. I can assure you, however, I offer no harm to none but he who threatens to harm me."

"Pandaran custom is—" Daphne silenced Galen's protest with a slight wave of her hand.

"That is okay, Councilor Galen," she said. "In Pandara, we welcome strangers, and do not insist that others follow our customs. If our visitor believes so strongly about keeping his weapon, and he means no harm, I will grant him leave to keep it."

Galen's brow furrowed, and he frowned, but bowed his head in acknowledgement of the queen's command. "As you wish, your majesty," he said. Turning back to Tenkuk, he said, "You said that you have a message for her majesty from your master. What is it?"

Tenkuk ignored Galen, his eyes on Daphne. "So, the stories I have heard are true. The queen of Pandara, in addition to being beautiful, is also wise beyond her years."

"The message," Galen said, his tone more insistent.

"The message, friend Galen, is for the queen's ears alone."

"In Pandara," Daphne said. "We have no secrets from the people. You may deliver whatever message you bear here and now." Her tone said, deliver it here, or deliver it not.

"As you wish, my queen." Tenkuk reached inside his tunic and withdrew a rolled parchment wrapped with a red ribbon. He removed the ribbon and unfurled the parchment. "This message is from The Lord Prince Ostro of Gondwana, High Prince of Barbaria and Conqueror of the Western Tribes, to Her Majesty Queen Daphne of Pandara, daughter of Cedric and Freda."

At the mention of her parents' names, Daphne blanched, but quickly recovered her composure. Tenkuk, however, had seen the expression of pain that crossed her face. He lowered the parchment. "Continue, good sir," she said. "What message does your prince with the very long title have for me?"

"Honored Daphne, daughter of Cedric and Freda," Tenkuk read. "I, Prince Ostro of Gondwana, High Prince of Barbaria and Conqueror of the Western Tribes, send my most humble greetings. It is my most fervent wish to unite all of the tribes of Barbaria under one sovereign, and to that end I desire to have, no indeed, must have a suitable consort to share my throne. In the hand of my loyal deputy and champion, the warrior, Tenkuk, I do submit to you my proposal, to wit; that we join our two houses, families, and thrones into one. As my queen, you will join me in ruling all of Barbaria, and in time, perhaps, even the whole of the world. I await your acceptance of my proposal. Yours in sincerity and everlasting friendship. Ostro."

Finished reading, Tenkuk refolded the parchment, stepped forward, and proffered it to Galen. The councilor took it as if it was something that had just been picked up from a stable floor. He turned and raised his eyebrows at the queen. She reached for it, and a bit reluctantly, he handed it over. Daphne, after taking the parchment, held it one way, then another, idly fingering the remnants of the was seal, but not opening it. Finally, she dropped it into her lap, and looked down at Tenkuk.

"My lord Ostro would like your answer upon my return," he said. "What say you?"

Galen's eyes blazed again, and he whirled around, but Daphne silenced whatever he was about to say with a wave of her hand.

"You shall have my answer when you return to your master," she said, in a quiet, steely voice.

"I shall give you until sunrise," Tenkuk said. "My men and I will encamp on the green facing the castle."

Daphne's delicate nostrils flared. "That will not be necessary," she said. "You can begin your return journey to Barbaria tonight, for I will give you your answer now. My answer is, no. I have no desire to be the queen of Barbaria, or be the consort of your master, or of any other for that matter."

Tenkuk took a step back, a look on his face as if he'd been slapped. Then his eyes narrowed to tiny slits, and his hand went to the hilt of his sword. "Take care what you say, Daphne, daughter of Cedric and Freda. My lord is not accustomed to taking no as an answer to his royal requests."

"Then, it would appear that his request is not a request, but a command?" Daphne's voice was steady. She looked down at the black-clad warrior, an expression of iron resolve on her face. "Be that as it may, my answer remains the same. No."

Still gripping his sword, Tenkuk took a step forward. His companions also tightened grips on their own weapons and turned their heads to face outward.

With their brows furrowed, and with menacing looks on their faces, they stepped forward to remain beside their leader. Galen sprang from the stage and placed himself in their path.

"How dare you make aggressive moves toward the queen," he said in a thunderous voice.

Tenkuk and his men stopped. His gaze bored into Galen. "And, just who among you would dare to try and stop me?"

The men in the crowd looked down at their feet. Only Pip kept his head up, glaring daggers at the strangers who would dare to show such disrespect to his beloved queen. After so many generations of peace, there were none left among the Pandaran men to stand up to the Barbarian warrior but Galen. The two royal guards who had been standing at the entrance found themselves surrounded by spear-wielding warriors, and the rest of the royal guard was among the crowd unarmed, or in the barracks beyond the town square. Galen, however, showed no fear, despite being a scholar and not a man of war. "I would dare," he said.

Tenkuk laughed. He removed his hand from the hilt of his sword. Standing face to face, the man's height was apparent. He stood a half head taller than the councilor, and now looked at him down his nose as Galen was nor more than a dung beetle that he was about to smash beneath his boots. Then, his hand shot out, his fingers together and stiff like a spear head, striking Galen in the center of his chest. Galen made a wheezing sound, and collapsed.

Pip, who during the confrontation, had been standing between Auric and Ludmilla, burst from the crowd, and launched his small body at the warrior.

Momentarily caught off guard by the suddenness of Pip's attack, Tenkuk reeled backwards, bumping into his two companions. Pip slammed into him, his small fists pounding away at the warrior's midsection. Unfazed by the blows, Tenkuk recovered his balance, grabbed Pip by the collar of his tunic, and lifted him off the ground as easily as he would've lifted a small basket of fruit. He held him at arm's length, leaving Pip's blows no place to land but his arm. He laughed.

"So, good Daphne," Tenkuk said. "We do have a warrior in Pandara. Two, in fact. And, they would dare challenge the mighty Tenkuk. What shall I do with your young champion, eh?" Holding Pip easily in his left hand, he reached for his sword with his right.

"No," Daphne cried. "Do not hurt the child. Was it not enough to strike poor Galen down?"

"Oh, do not worry about the old man, my queen. He will recover after a while, though, I fear he will be a trifle stiff and sore and his breathing will be uncomfortable for a few days." He stared into Pip's eyes. "Now, young warrior, as you can see I have not slain your old friend, so if I put you down, will you give me your oath that you will not attack me again?"

Pip sputtered. "I will do to you what you did to Galen, you beast," he said, punctuating his threat with a futile swing at Tenkuk's face.

"Well, in that case, you leave me no choice," Tenkuk said, drawing his sword, a large weapon with a sharp, wicked-looking blade that made a swishing sound as it came from the scabbard, and glinted in the light from the torches set in the walls surrounding the courtyard. "I will have to defend myself against you."

Pip kept swinging his fists. Ludmilla grasped her ample bosom and fainted, falling back into Auric's arms. Queen Daphne rose from her throne, her face pale.

"No," she said. "You cannot mean to harm a child?"

At that moment, Galen groaned, opened his eyes and surveyed his surroundings. At the sound of his teacher's voice, Pip stopped struggling, while Tenkuk, with a wicked smile, continued to hold him away from his body with his left hand, while the sharp edge of the sword he held in his right hand was less than an inch from his neck.

"Oh my," Galen said, clapping a hand to his head.

"Teacher Galen, be you all right?" Pip asked.

"I believe so, lad, though I do feel a bit of pain in my chest where that brute struck me."

"So, you see," Tenkuk said. "I have not slain your teacher. So, there is no reason for you to continue to try to kill me, is there?"

Pip's eyes narrowed in thought, as he contemplated the sharp steel so close to his neck. "I-I guess not," he said in a small voice.

"Then, surely you can release him now," Daphne said.

Tenkuk fingered the little triangle of hair beneath his lower lip, and cocked his head to one side. "I think not, milady," he said. "This little rooster is the only person here with the spirit of a warrior in him. I think therefore, he might be of value." He swung Pip around to the tall warrior on his left. The man grabbed Pip by his shoulders, holding him off the ground. "Madong, take care of our little warrior, but take care. I think he me might bite as well as scratch."

Away from the shiny blade, Pip was finally able to breathe. He tried not to show that the pressure of the warrior's fingers digging into his shoulders was painful.

Tenkuk didn't bother to wait to see if his orders would be obeyed, so unaccustomed was he to even the thought of disobedience. He turned back and faced the stage, staring up at Daphne, still grinning his wicked grin. "I think I will take him back with me. He might provide my lord some amusement while he awaits your reconsideration of his proposal. We might teach him warrior skills and make him part of our army." With his left hand free of Pip, he continued to play with the tuft of hair on his chin. "Then again, mayhap my lord will remind you if you tarry too long in responding, by sending a piece of him back to you each day that you keep him waiting."

Auric, who had been holding Ludmilla up, opened his mouth, his eyes wide, and then fainted, collapsing in a heap next to his still unconscious wife. Daphne's hand flew to her mouth, but she remained silent, eyes narrowed to slits, her lips set in a grim line. Galen, who by this time had managed to push himself up into a sitting position, made as if to rise, but was unable to get enough strength and coordination in his arms to complete the move. He settled back on his haunches and glared up at Tenkuk. The rest of the assemblage, men, women, and children, stood mute, looking on as this strange performance played out. Unaccustomed to any conflict more violent than a good wife hitting her spouse over the head with a broom when he came home late, reeling and reeking from drinking ale in a local tavern, they had no clue what to do, and having experienced no war for generations, didn't possess the required skills to be useful even if they had a clue.

His threat delivered, Tenkuk bowed insolently in the general direction of Daphne's throne, and backed slowly toward the opening in the courtyard wall. His men, weapons held menacingly, formed two lines outside the entrance to the courtyard, and when he and the two warriors who had accompanied him inside, along with Pip, exited, flanked them and began marching smartly away.

As he was led away, Pip looked from side to side, but none of the adults, many of whom were parents of children who had tormented him, would meet his gaze, looking instead down at their feet. Auric and Ludmilla, being tended by two neighbors, were still unconscious near the stage. Just as he was being taken through the courtyard archway, he saw Sandrin and his friends near the front of the crowd. Unlike the adults, they did look directly at him, and Pip was taken aback by what he saw. In their eyes he saw fear, but also something else; he thought it might be grudging respect. Pip, the undersized boy who they tormented endlessly, the boy with features too fine for a male, was the only one present besides Galen who'd had the courage to confront these warriors from a faraway land. Pip also felt fear, but strangely, not as much as he would have expected. Mostly, what he feared was not knowing what would happen next. At the same time, that thought also excited him. He'd always dreamed of adventure, and now he was in the middle of an adventure, unlike anything he could ever have dreamed of. He stared back at Sandrin and his bullies, stared with the steady gaze of a warrior, and when he did so, their gazes dropped to their shoes like everyone else. This made Pip feel better.

What he did not see, nor did anyone else, was a slightly built young woman with flame red hair and slightly reddish eyes, dressed in green, standing just inside a pool of shadow outside the courtyard walls. Her red eyes blazed, but the rest of her face was as still as stone.

Slowly, ever so slowly, she backed deeper into the shadow, and then, as if she'd never been there, she vanished.

Awakening

Charles Ray

Chapter 5

Once they were well outside the castle walls, Pip was tossed onto the back of one of the pack mules the Barbarians had brought with their convoy. His hands were bound with a leather thong, and that was secured to the animal's halter, with just enough give in the bindings to allow him to grasp the coarse hair of its mane.

Tenkuk mounted his horse, a magnificent black stallion with a white blaze on its forehead, and waited while his men assembled behind him, with men armed with spears in front, behind, and to each side of Pip. Once they were assembled, Tenkuk, with a wave of his hand, ordered them to move out.

They moved at a canter, to allow the mules carrying their supplies to keep pace, but the animal Pip was riding still had to stretch its shorter legs to keep up with the horses. Every few paces, one of the spearmen riding alongside, would poke the mule with the butt of his spear, causing it to jump, sending arrows of pain up Pip's spine. His bottom began to ache from the constant slamming against the animal's bony back, and the insides of his thighs burned from rubbing against its rough hide. He held the mane in a death grip, which caused his fingers and arms to ache. This was only the second time in his life he'd been on the back of an animal, usually riding in Auric's cart whenever he accompanied him to the villages to buy hides from the farmers, hunters, and trappers.

Even at a canter, though, they were soon past the nearest villages, clusters of wooden cottages with thatched or tile roofs, dark and quiet in the dark of night, with only the occasional barking of a curious dog to mark their passage. After two hours of riding, which to Pip's aching body seemed to have been a full day, they passed the last settlements, and entered the lightly wooded area that stretched for miles to the Great Desert. To the east, the land sloped down gently toward the coast and the blue waters of the East Sea, and to the west, standing like an obsidian wall against the night sky, loomed the forbidding presence of the dreaded Black Forest.

The Black Forest was a vast expanse of tall conifers and broadleaf trees, trees that pierced the sky like giant lances, and got its name from the fact that they were so interlaced at the tops they blocked most of the light from reaching the ground below, or so it was rumored. No one from Pandara had ever, to Pip's knowledge, ever penetrated more than a few paces into their inky depths, for it was also rumored that strange and bloodthirsty creatures lurked within the deep shadows, waiting for foolhardy enough to enter. Pip tried not to look in that direction.

"When can we stop?" he asked the soldier on his left, earning a poke with the butt of the spear. "I really need to stop." Another poke, this time, a bit harder, accompanied by a glare that said, 'be quiet, or the next time it will be with the sharp end.'

Pip clamped his lips tight and tried to squeeze the muscles of his stomach and lower belly, but his bladder was pressing against the walls of his abdomen so hard it hurt. The jostling of the mule had stirred the liquid he'd had at the castle, and his bladder felt like it was about to burst. If they didn't stop soon, he greatly feared that he would embarrass himself, and soak the mule's back, which would make for a very uncomfortable ride.

Just when Pip thought he could not hold his water in another minute, Tenkuk raised his right hand, and the procession came to a stop.

"Now that we are well away from Lands End, and in no danger of an ambush from these Pandaran jackals, we will make camp here and resume our journey on the morrow," he said. "We are a full day's ride to Gondwana, and I wish to be fresh when we arrive tomorrow night."

As soon as the bindings on his hands were loosened from the tether and he was lifted from the mule's back, Pip made a dash for the nearest bushes. The soldier guarding him gave chase, but stopped and laughed when he saw Pip undo the front of his trousers and began splashing the bush with a golden stream. Pip ignored the man's snickering as he emptied his bladder with a hissing gush that left him faint, and left his legs as limp as the flour noodles that Ludmilla liked to serve at special family meals.

When he'd finished and refastened his trousers, the soldier roughly pushed him back into the encampment. He was shoved down against a rotting tree trunk, and his hands and feet were lashed tightly. Another rope was tied around his chest, binding him to the trunk.

Wriggling, Pip shuffled his body into as comfortable a position as he could manage with both hands and feet tied up, and tried to shrink into a small ball in the hopes that the guards would ignore him. Even though his arms and legs felt like they were on fire for a while, and then went numb, he bit his lip to keep from moaning, fearing the spears that the guards held menacingly across their shoulders. After a while, despite the pain and discomfort, exhaustion overwhelmed him, and he fell into a sound sleep.

The smell of grease and overcooked meat, the whinnying of the horses and mules, and the clatter of weapons and equipment jerked Pip from a sleep that, though sound, he felt was too short. It was if he'd just closed his eyes, but the gray light filtering through the trees told him that it was dawn. Though wide awake, he kept his eyes tightly shut, hoping that it was all a dream, and he would shortly wake up, open his eyes, and find himself at home, on his pallet in the corner near the fireplace.

The clatter didn't die down, and even though the meat smelled burned, it made his stomach growl and his mouth water. He opened his eyelids the tiniest of cracks. He was still where they had left him, tied against the old tree trunk, curled up and leaning to his right side, with his heels digging into his buttocks. Opening his eyes the rest of the way, he blinked. There were tree trunks just inches from his face. When he blinked again, the tree trunks resolved themselves into large, black leather boots, dusty from much use. He moved his head and his eyes followed the lines of the boots, up a pair of stocky, cotton-clad legs, up past a slim waist, around which was a black leather belt, which held a long sword. His gaze shifted from the sword, over the flat belly, up to a large chest, and then up to a pointed chin, and a triangular tuft of yellow hair just below the lower lip, then on up to Tenkuk's eyes, cold and unfeeling, like a snake or lizard sizing up its prey.

The warrior chief looked down at Pip. His lips turned up in an amused sneer. "Ah, I see our little fighter is finally awake. He slept so soundly, I feared he might have died of fright during the night."

As Pip awakened fully, the pain returned to his hands and feet, in fiery stabs that caused him to wince and groan. He quickly stifled his groan, and looked up at Tenkuk, summoning all the courage left in his small body, and refusing to look away. But, the pain was almost more than he could bear. His face contorted, and tears leaked from the corners of his eyes.

"The bindings are painful, are they not?" Tenkuk fingered the tuft of hair beneath his lower lip. "Well, we are far enough away from your home now, so I suppose it would be okay to take them off." He motioned to the warrior standing nearby, and indicated that Pip's hands and legs were to be freed. "But, heed me well, young warrior. If you try to escape, I will have my warriors put you on a spear like a pig on a spit. Do you understand?"

Pip's throat was dry, and not just from thirst. He could only nod weakly. He had no doubt, no doubt at all, that Tenkuk spoke the truth.

When the bindings were loosened, the rush of blood into his fingers and toes brought, not relief, but a fresh stab of white hot pain. Pip doubled over in agony, much to the merriment of the rough men standing around the fire. Though curled up on the ground, feeling as if his whole body was engulfed in flames, Pip fought the urge to cry out. He endured the pain until it subsided to a manageable level, whereupon he sat up, rubbing his ankles and flexing his fingers to restore circulation.

This seemed to impress Tenkuk. With a sharp wave, he silenced the laughter of his men.

"Bring the little warrior some food," he ordered. He then turned and walked over to his horse.

A warrior, a man with hunched shoulders who appeared only slightly older than Pip, but much more heavily muscled, took a gourd from a pack on one of the mules. Made from a dried gourd cut in half lengthwise, it served as both plate for food and dipper for water. He dipped the gourd into an iron pot suspended over the fire, and filled it with a grey, mushy substance, which he thrust under Pip's nose.

The mush looked as grey and unappetizing as the paste the scribes of the monastery used to bind their books. It had dark brown lumps floating in it, which from the way they glistened in the light of the morning, Pip recognized them as pieces of meat, and the whole concoction smelled like the polish Auric used to treat hides, but Pip's stomach growled, overcoming his initial revulsion. He snatched the gourd from the warrior's hands. He hadn't been provided a spoon, but then noticed that none of the others had either, so he copied them, scooping the mush into his mouth with his fingers, chewing quickly and swallowing. The mush had a taste similar to the library paste—Pip had once had a lump of it forced into his mouth by two of the older students. After the first few mouthfuls, though, the rancid taste ceased to bother him, and it barely occurred to him that he'd not had a chance to wash after relieving himself the night before. But, his stomach hardly cared. He kept shoving the lumpy paste into his mouth until there wasn't more than a few grey streaks left in the gourd.

His meal finished, Pip placed the gourd on the ground. The hunch-backed warrior, who had stood by silently with a slight smile on his face while Pip ate, cuffed him on the back of the head with a hard and callused hand, causing Pip to see stars before his eyes and hear a loud ringing sound in his ears.

"Every warrior cleans up for himself," the man said. "I might have to bring you the food, because my commander ordered it, but I will not clean up after you."

Pip picked the gourd up. "How do I clean it?" he asked. Other than the drinking water in the leather bladders strapped to one of the mules, there didn't seem to be any water in the camp.

"You are the . . . little warrior, you figure it out. And you better be quick about it. We leave soon." He turned and walked away chuckling to himself.

Cleaning eating utensils without water, Pip thought. Such a ridiculous notion. Ludmilla always washed their utensils thoroughly with harsh soap and hot water, and would have launched into a storm of complaint and remonstrations had anyone suggested she use utensils not so cleaned. Observing the soldiers, though, Pip learned something new—revolting at first, but new nonetheless. Each soldier partially filled his empty gourd with dirt and, using his fingers, scrubbed the interior. After tossing out the dirt, the soldier would then scour the inside of the gourd with leaves or tufts of the wiry grass that grew in profusion. Having no soap or water at hand, Pip copied them, hoping the journey would reach its end before he had to again eat from one of the gourds cleaned in this manner.

When the soldier was satisfied that Pip had cleaned the gourd adequately, he snatched it from him and put it away, giving Pip a nasty look as he did so.

After eating, Pip felt the urge to relieve himself, and told the hunchback so. The man accompanied him to the area outside the encampment that had been designated as a latrine, and, holding his nose against the stench, Pip did the necessary, using the wiry grass afterwards to clean himself as best he could.

The meal and morning ablutions complete, they set out, Pip was now unfettered, but still clung tightly to the mule's mane as it almost ran in a bone-jarring tempo to keep up with the horses. The animal seemed to resent Pip's presence upon its back, and occasionally reached back to nip at his leg.

They rode until the sun was high in the sky, and Pip's stomach was starting to growl again. He thought surely that they would stop to eat, and as much as he hated the thought of eating from one of the dirt-scoured gourds, his stomach didn't seem to care.

But, they didn't stop.

As they rode on, Pip noticed that the warriors seemed to be glancing fearfully at the towering dark trees on their right. Even Tenkuk seemed to be wary. A few of the soldiers even made strange motions with their hands as they looked at the Black Forest.

"When do we stop to rest?" Pip asked the soldier who rode on his right side.

The man didn't growl at Pip, or frown at him, as they had done in the encampment. Instead, he looked at him, with creases of worry furrowing his brow.

"We reach the border of Barbaria soon," the man said. "And, well away from this accursed forest. Only then will we stop for the midday meal and mayhap rest for a spell."

The naked fear on the man's face and in his voice puzzled Pip. "I know there be animals in the forest that can eat a single man or child." He'd also heard stories of hunters who, while chasing game had wandered into the fringes of the forest and been set upon by packs of wolves, but these were rare occurrences. "But," he said. "Surely there be nothing that a band of warriors armed such as you be cannot handle."

"Pah, boy, that just shows how ignorant you are." The soldier spat and made the strange sign with his hands again, drawing his thumb across his chest and then up to his shoulder. "There are things in the forest that are much more dangerous than a pack of wolves. Beings of the mist who appear and disappear like smoke, and who can wither your soul with a glance. There are even rumors of creatures that can burn a man to a crisp with a glance and a wave of the hand."

Pip kept his expression impassive, but he mentally laughed. *And, you think I be ignorant.* Everyone knew that magical beings were but creations of the imaginations of fanciful storytellers. He thought of telling the soldier this, but remembered the sharp jab of the spear butt, and decided to remain silent. If the people of Barbaria wanted to believe in magic, it was not his place to point out their mistake. Even the children of Pandara knew that magic did not exist, and that it was only stories for their entertainment.

These Barbarians might be might warriors, but they were not as wise as Pandarans. Mayhap, he thought, there was hope.

Chapter 6

The Black Forest

The sun had passed its highest point in the sky, and begun its descent, and they still had not reached Barbaria's border. Nor had they once stopped, not even to allow the men to relieve themselves. Pip felt the pressure of his bladder, and his stomach growled so loudly he hardly heard the clopping of the animals' hooves.

Suddenly, without any forewarning, the column stopped, and everyone's attention was drawn to the towering trees on their right. Weapons were held at the ready. Even Tenkuk looked nervously toward the forest.

Pip craned his neck and squinted his eyes in an effort to see what had so spooked the warriors, but except for the waving of the tall grass at the edge of the road, he saw nothing.

The soldiers had all crowded in, facing the forest, their spears pointed at the trees. Tenkuk had wheeled his horse around, and now paced nervously back and forth behind them. The mule upon which Pip rode made whimpering noises and scuffed nervously at the ground, as did the other animals.

"Stay alert," Tenkuk said in a commanding voice. "Mayhap they will see that we are a well-armed and ready force, and will allow us to continue our journey unmolested."

All eyes were on the forbidding forest. Pip had been forgotten.

Despite his hunger, and need to relieve his bladder, Pip's mind worked furiously. With no one paying him any attention, he realized that he finally had a chance to get away. The soldiers' fear of whatever imaginary creatures were in the forest might give him the advantage he needed, an advantage that would be lost once they crossed the border. He had a healthy fear of the forest creatures, especially the wolf packs, but decided that he'd rather take his chances with them than end up in a strange land, prisoner of the beast Tenkuk and his master.

Slowly and quietly, he slid his leg over the back of the mule and dropped to the ground, holding onto the hope that his captors, with their attention focused on the dreaded forest, wouldn't notice him. He rubbed the animal's neck, hoping that would keep it quiet. Finally, he began to creep toward the animal's rear.

Peering past the animal's twitching tail, he saw that everyone was still staring at the forest.

Turning to the side, he took a few steps, and then began running as rapidly as his legs would carry him, in the direction of the towering trees.

He was only a few paces from the first line of trees when he was noticed.

He heard Tenkuk shout. "Get that boy! You two, go after him."

"B-but, my lord, he's going into the forest," a nervous voice said.

"I do not care," Tenkuk said. "Go after him. Surely you can outrun a mere stripling."

Pip heard the clatter of weapons and the slap of boots against the earth, but didn't dare look back. He continued his headlong flight, and was soon beneath the trees and in the dim shadows. Still, he did not stop. His lungs were on fire, and his legs had begun to ache, but he kept running. He heard the footfalls of his pursuers, and they seemed to be getting closer.

He darted, first left, then right, between the trees, trying always to keep moving in the same general direction so that he could find his way back to the road after he evaded the men pursuing him. The muffled curses of the soldiers, as they came after him, seemed to be coming closer and closer.

Suddenly, he pitched forward, his left foot caught in the tangled roots of a large tree that he'd almost run headlong into, and he ended up with his face almost buried in the soft, black earth.

As he pushed himself up, he looked back over his shoulder. The soldiers, triumphant grins on their faces, were less than twenty paces behind him.

"Hah, got you now, you little devil," one of them said.

Pip sighed, knowing his bid for freedom had failed. Then, as if they'd run into a stone wall, the two soldiers stopped, their triumphant grins replaced by expressions of astonishment and fear.

"If thee wishes to leave this forest alive, thee will turn around, leave the boy alone, and depart forthwith," a familiar voice said.

Pip's gaze swung around to his front. Standing there, not five paces from where he lay, was the strange girl—woman—who had saved him from Sandrin and his bully friends. She was now wearing a dark green tunic and pants that were so similar to the green of the forest, if not for her red hair, she would have merged with the background and been virtually invisible. Standing next to her was another woman, wearing similar clothing, only hers was brown. Her skin, hair, and eyes were the same color as her tunic and pants.

The two soldiers, eyes wide, gaped at the two women. The older and larger of the two finally found his voice. "Begone, girl," he said. "Our master will have us drawn and quartered if we do not bring the boy back to him. I think that it is you who should leave, or forfeit your lives." He began drawing the short sword at his side.

"I have given thee fair warning," the woman said. She turned to her companion. "Tamara, wouldst thee give our . . . friends here a wee taste of what might befall them should they not heed us?"

The brown-haired woman lifted her hands, and waved them in the air.

Pip gazed, open mouthed, at what happened next.

The roots of a tree behind the two men lifted up from the soil like snakes, and crawled slowly over their feet, writhing and winding in and out and around their legs.

The younger soldier screamed and tried to jump away, but the tendrils tightened, holding him in place. Fear contorted the older man's face, but he stood his ground. "I have warned you," he said. "We cannot return without the boy."

The redhead sighed. "Oh, you mundane can be such a bother." She lifted her right hand, palm facing the soldiers, and uttered words in a language that Pip did not understand.

A wall of flame appeared in front of the two soldiers. Pip could feel the heat where he lay, but noticed that the ground the flame remained unscorched.

The wall of fire was more than the older man could take. He screamed, dropped his weapon and fell to his knees. His young companion knelt beside him. Their clothing was beginning to smolder. The flames reflected off the sweat that coated their faces.

"Please, oh creature of the forest," the older man cried. "Spare us. We will leave as you ask."

"Very well," she said. "But know ye this. If thee should go back on thy oath, thy lives be forfeit."

She waved her hand again, and the flames disappeared. The brown woman waved a hand, and the roots withdrew into the earth. Pip could feel a cool breeze caress his cheek. The only sound was the harsh breathing from the two soldiers.

Still on their knees, the two men brushed at their clothing and faces. They had looks of shock on their weather-beaten faces. "Do we have your leave to depart?" the older man asked.

"Be gone," the redhead said. "But, look not back, and tarry not, lest I have a change of heart."

Before she had finished speaking, the two soldiers stood, and whirled around, running like the devil himself was behind them, back toward the road.

When the sounds of the fleeing soldiers had faded, Pip pushed himself up to a standing position and faced the two women.

"Who be you, and how come you to be here?" he asked.

"That is not for thee to worry about, Pip of Lands End," the redhead said. "Come and stand thee next to me. We have a long journey, and we must not tarry. Once they get back to the others, they might recover their courage and return. Though our power be great, it would be difficult to defeat such a large band, and we must not risk injury to thee."

"Where be we going?"

"Thy questions will be answered in good time. Now stand ye next to me and take my hand."

Pip brushed the twigs and dust from his trousers and stood to the redhead. "I be not a baby, I need no help to walk," he said.

"Thee speaks truth, Pip," she said. "I saw how thee confronted the Barbarian at the castle. But, thee must take my hand, for we have far to travel, and we will not be walking."

"I do not understand," he said, as he reached for her hand. "How be we—" His words were cut off by the darkness that surrounded him as their hands touched.

Awakening

Charles Ray

Chapter 7

The Land of Fire

The darkness was complete. Not just the absence of light, but the absence of sound or feeling. I be dead, Pip thought. But then, he thought, how can that be. The dead surely do not know that they are dead, do they?

When the light returned, Pip found himself standing in a glade, surrounded by trees of the brightest green, flowers covering the soft green grass, and a babbling brook meandering into the glade from his left.

The two women stood flanking him. He was still holding the redhead's hand.

"Thee can release my hand," she said. "We are here."

Pip looked around, his mouth agape. 'Here' was clearly not the Black Forest, at least, not the Black Forest that he knew. In that forest, the trees towered toward the sky, and were gnarled and twisted, and the ground beneath them was brown and devoid of all but the hardiest of scraggly looking weeds and thorn vines.

The trees surrounding this place were tall, but not as tall, and instead of being bent and twisted, they were stately, and the land beneath them looked as well kept as a farmer's field.

"Where are we, and how did we come here?" he asked when he'd finally found his voice.

"Thy questions will be answered in the fullness of time," the redhead said. "Now, must we hurry. King Valdun awaits us."

Pip stood his ground. "No," he said, stamping his foot. "I will not move one step until you tell me at least who *you* be."

"Thee did not tell me this mundane would be so stubborn," the woman in brown said. "Tell him, please. I wish to go home."

"Very well," the redhead said. "I am Vera of the Fire Folk, and my companion is Tamara, of the Folk of Earth and Wood. Now, may we go?"

Pip had never heard of Fire Folk, or the others, and his head was filled with questions. Where was this strange land, and how had he been brought to it? How, in fact, had Vera and Tamara been there in the Black Forest just when he needed them? So many questions with no answers, but he'd implied that if she told him who she was he would go with her to wherever it was she wanted to take him. He shrugged and fell in behind the two women as they headed for an opening in the trees, an opening that looked a lot like the archway to the castle courtyard in Lands End.

And, an archway was what it was. They walked through it into a large open-air amphitheater, the walls of which were formed by trees that grew so close together they formed a barrier that could only be accessed through the archways. Open to the sky, it was well lit. At the end opposite the main archway, the tree branches formed a smaller archway. The surface was soft green grass that seemed to support Pip on a cushion of air. Next to the smaller archway, the ground curved upwards, formed into a shape that to Pip looked a lot like Queen Daphne's throne.

The trio walked across the amphitheater, stopping a few paces from the throne.

Through the small archway came a man, or at least to Pip, he looked mostly like a man. He was slightly taller than Vera, and muscular, with the same red hair and reddish eyes, and wore a simple green tunic and pants. He carried no weapons.

The two women dropped to one knee. Vera pulled Pip down so that he knelt next to her. The man walked to the throne, and, after looking down at them, sat.

"King Valdun," Vera said. "We have brought the boy, Pip, as thee instructed."

"Thee has done well, my daughter," the man said. His voice was deep and, even though he did not speak loudly, it echoed off the surrounding wall of trees. "Did thee encounter any trouble?"

"None that we could not handle," she said.

"Very well then," Valdun said. "Please, thee may stand. This is not a formal court." The three stood. "Good. Tamara, thank thee for aiding my daughter in this quest." The brown girl bowed her head. "Thee may go, and please give my thanks to thy good parents."

"Thank thee, King Valdun," she said. "I will do so."

Tamara bowed again, and left through the main archway.

"And now, daughter," Valdun said. "I imagine that it is thy wish to refresh thyself after such a long journey. Please, thee may absent thyself. I have much to discuss with our young guest."

"As thee wish, father," Vera said. She inclined her head slightly and departed.

"Now, young Pip," Valdun said. "Come thee here and sit beside me. We have much to discuss, and I wager thee hast many questions."

Pip hesitated, shuffling from one foot to the other. Sit next to this strange person, and a king no less? How could he even dare, he but a commoner, the foundling of a tailor's family? In Pandara, even though Queen Daphne was a gentle and understanding monarch, none but the ladies in waiting who helped her dress, or Galen her trusted councilor, would dare get so near her, because it was just *not* done. Yet, here was this man, and Pip saw that he did indeed have the bearing of a king, and Vera and Tamara *had* given him the deference one would give a king, here he was *inviting* Pip to sit next to him—on his throne. Pip could neither move nor speak.

Valdun chuckled at his discomfort. "Come lad," he said. "Though I be a king, I do not bite. Well, only my enemies, and then not often, and thee art not my enemy. So, come . . . come and sit here beside me, for I have a tale to tell thee."

The voice was deep, but gentle, and for reasons that he could not understand, Pip trusted this man, and he felt compelled to do what he asked. Even though, he could not even be sure that this *was* a man. He was in a strange land, brought there by means he did not understand, a land with people, the beautiful Vera included, who could do things he could not previously imagined possible, things that he had hitherto only thought of as fanciful imaginings in the tales told by Galen and other storytellers. He moved slowly, his body seeming to move at some outside command, and he stepped up onto the hummock where Valdun sat, and sat beside the king, careful to keep his distance and not touch him.

Valdun chuckled again, and laid a muscular arm over Pip's shoulders, pulling him closer, and ruffling his hair. His body was considerably warmer than Auric's or Ludmilla's, actually almost hot, but to Pip, it felt quite comfortable.

"Now, lad, doest thee have questions, or should I tell thee a tale?"

Pip took a deep breath. Did he have questions? Only a thousand times a thousand questions, and more, but he didn't know where to start.

"Y-your majesty," he said, when he felt that he could control his voice. "I have many questions. How came I to be here? What did the Lady Vera do in the Black Forest to cause flames to spring from the earth, and then disappear so quickly? How did the Lady Tamara make the roots of the trees move like snakes? I be mighty confused and scarce know what to think, or where to begin."

"Ay, lad, it must be confusing for thee. I tell thee what; let me tell you a story," Valdun said. "And after I have told my tale, if there remain questions, then I will assay to answer them."

Pip nodded, and the king pulled him closer. Pip could smell the forest in the man's muscular body, and feel a pleasant, warmth that reminded him of the hearth in his foster parents' cottage. He wondered, as he nestled against the man's shoulder, if he would ever see Auric and Ludmilla again.

"Once, many summers past," Valdun began his tale. "A young princess went into the Black Forest to hunt for the sweet berries that were reported to grow in its dark recesses. She had been told that the forest was a dangerous place that she should avoid, but she was headstrong and willful, and went anyway. She took with her only two retainers and promised her sister, a twin who never disobeyed their parents in anything, that she would only go in two hundred paces, pick a basket of berries, that they would share for the evening meal. She swore that she would be back in on time.

Pip found Valdun's voice soothing, and his storytelling style as captivating as Galen's, and was quickly swept up in the tale.

"True to her word," Valdun continued. "And, after the urgings of her retainers, she did, in fact, only go two hundred paces into the dark and forbidding woods. With luck, she found a spot where the bushes upon which the berries grow were abundant, and heavy with ripe, black berries. Her retainers, nervous at being even such a short distance into the forest, kept watch while she filled her basket with the succulent fruit, and were relieved when she announced that she had enough, and they could leave the forest, get into their carriage, and return to Lands End and the castle."

Valdun's cadence had picked up as he spoke, and Pip sensed that he was getting to an exciting part of the story. And, in this, he was not disappointed.

"They had gone but fifty paces on their back trail, when they were set upon by a pack of wolves. In the confusion, the princess was separated from her retainers, and she ran into the forest to escape the wolves. Two she-wolves from the pack gave chase, and after a mere thirty or so paces, overtook her.

"The two wolves set upon her, and but for a man of the Folk, who happened to be wandering and was nearby, would have torn her to pieces. But, using his magic, he slew the wolves, and brought the seriously injured princess back to his home here in the Land of Fire.

Valdun paused and rubbed Pip's shoulders.

"Her healing took many risings and settings of the sun, and all the skill of the best healers in the Land, but recover she did. And, during her illness, and the period of recuperation, the man of the Folk never left her side, but to eat and take care of certain bodily functions that must never be done in the sight of others. When the princess had recovered enough for conversation, the two would sit for hours and talk; her telling him of her life in the castle, and he of the ways of the Folk.

Pip looked up to see that the king's eyes were glistening, and his expression was sad.

"They were of an age, seventeen or eighteen summers, when the sparks that fly between a man and a woman can be exceptionally strong, and as often happens under such circumstances, the two fell in love."

"Did they marry?" Pip asked.

Valdun laughed. "Ah, I see that thee are also impatient, and want to get to the end of the story without taking the journey in its fullness. Be patient, lad, for I will soon come to that part." He patted Pip's head. "Now, we of the Folk seldom interact with mundanes, which is what we call the people of thy land, and there was strong resistance to their relationship. In particular, this particular young man of the Folk was the son of the king, and he was expected to marry another of his own people to carry on the royal line. In like manner, the princess was expected to marry another of royal blood from among the mundane. But, both were headstrong, and were very much in love.

"The young man went to his father, and said that he would relinquish his right to the throne and allow his younger brother to reign in his stead, if only his father would give him leave to wed the princess. On her part, she vowed to learn the ways of the Folk, and remain in the Land of Fire, never to see her home again. The king was moved by their ardor and sincerity, and after much soul searching, allowed the union."

"So, they did marry," Pip said, smiling.

"Yes, they did, and it was a wedding to be remembered. Even though the bride could not exchange magic tokens with her betrothed as is the custom of the Folk, she had, through her efforts to master our customs, insofar as a mundane is capable, she had won the hearts of everyone. There was a ten-day celebration, after which they settled down to a life of married bliss."

"And, they lived happily ever after?" Pip asked, for he liked stories with happy endings.

"Thee must have patience, young Pip, for the story is not finished. After a year, they had a son, and this further endeared her to the Folk, for the son was the first of his kind, a union of the Folk and the mundane, something that had been thought not possible.

"One day, when the child was still a swaddling, not yet able to walk, the man and his bride were taking a family stroll through the forest when they were attacked by a band of brigands from the kingdom far to the south. They were badly wounded, but managed, through the husband's magic, to escape. The princess, unfortunately, was the more seriously wounded and died from her wounds after two sunsets. But, the man recovered. Or, I should say, his body recovered. But, his spirit was fatally wounded, he was desolate. The wound to his heart would never recover.

"After he had healed enough to travel, he announced that he would take the child to his mundane people, the family of the princess, where he could grow up knowing the other half of his heritage."

At this point, Valdun stopped speaking, and bowed his head. He sighed and wiped a tear from his eye.

Pip, too, had been saddened by this tragic story. "Your majesty," he said. "What happened next?"

"Alas, young one," Valdun said. "I can only tell thee part of what happened, for on his way back to the Land, the prince was attacked by Barbarians and in his depressed state, his magic was not enough to save him. There are those among the Folk who say that he allowed himself to be slain so that he could be with his beloved."

"I be taken by the Barbarians," Pip said. "They be worse than the animals of the forest. If not for Vera and Tamara, I might also have been slain."

"Yes, I now. I cannot tell thee exactly what the man of the Folk did, but there is more that you need to know."

"More? Your majesty, please tell me."

"The man of the Folk of which I spoke was my brother, Valcan, and the princess was Daria, the twin sister of your Queen Daphne, queen of Pandara."

"I know that Queen Daphne once had a sister," Pip said. "The story is told that she was lost in the Black Forest, and eaten by animals."

"That is true, in a way. The Barbarians are like animals, except that most animals only kill when they need food, or are threatened, while the Barbarians kill for conquest, or for pleasure."

Pip nodded. "What happened to the baby? Can you tell me?"

"Aye, lad, I can," Valdun said, a smile creasing his face. "The baby has grown into a fine young man, one of valor and intelligence."

"He lives in Lands End, or some other town in Pandara?" Pip wondered who the mysterious baby might be.

"He lived in Lands End," Valdun said. "At this moment, though, he sits here, talking to his uncle."

Chapter 8

Pip was stunned. His mind was racing, and his heart pounding. His mouth opened and closed like a beached fish, and his eyes refused to focus.

Valdun laughed and again tousled his hair. "What is the matter, Pip? Thee looks as if thee hast seen a spirit from the lair of demons."

"B-but, that means that I be . . ." Pip could get no more words to come. He felt as if his brain was frozen and some giant force had clapped a hand over his mouth. One moment, he'd been Pip, the foundling of Auric and Ludmilla, living in Lands End, and running errands, attending the town school run by the queen's privy councilor, and on more occasions than he cared to remember, trying to dodge the taunts and physical abuse of the older boys, and enduring being ignored by the girls, and the next . . . to be told that he was the son of Queen Daphne's sister and a man who could do magic, who was also the son of a king, was more than his young mind could absorb.

"I understand. It must be difficult for thy mind to take all this in so quickly. I fear, though, that I must add more to the confusion. When thee was born, you were given a name that I fear thee doest not know. Thee were christened Valdar, which is a combining of the names of thy father and mother."

"V-Valdar? My name is Valdar?"

"Aye, it is our custom to name the male child thus. Thee art Prince Valdar. Prince in both the land of the Folk and of the mundane. What say thee to that?"

Before Pip could answer, Vera walked back into the amphitheater. She had changed into fresh clothing, this time, her tunic was a lighter green, overtopping dark green leggings. Her red hair still glistened with moisture.

"Well, father," she said. "From the bemused look on Pip's face, I guess thee has told him of his heritage.?

"I have, and I fear that it has rendered him speechless. Speaking of speech, daughter, I think thee must teach him proper speech. We cannot have a prince of the Folk speaking like a common peasant."

Vera frowned. "If I must," she said. "I find the speech of the mundane grating to the ear, but I am the only one of the Folk who speaks it fluently."

"We must also enlist others to teach him all else that he must know."

"Thinkest thee that he has power?"

"Of that I have no doubt. I can feel it," said Valdun. The question is, what are his powers, and in what strength. As he is a result of a union of Folk and mundane, there is no forecasting what he can do. One other thing, daughter, as long as he remains with us, thee and all others must address him by his true name, Valdar, son of Valcan and Daria. Of course, since he is thy cousin, I suppose thee may be allowed the liberty of a pet name for him."

Vera turned to Pip. "Well, Prince Valdar, what say thee? Do I address thee as Prince Valdar, or should I continue to call thee Pip?"

Pip, his mind still wrestling with his new status, snapped his head around to gaze at her, as if he'd just awakened. "Uh, I suppose Pip be fine," he said.

"Good," Vera said. "And thy first lesson—no, I think I should teach you the proper speech of the mundane first—your first lesson begins now. Repeat after me, "I suppose Pip will be fine.""

Pip looked wide-eyed at her. "I suppose Pip be, uh, *will* be fine," he said.

"Good. Starting from now, Cousin Pip, each time you speak like a peasant, I will pinch your ear."

Pip rubbed his ear. He could imagine that before he learned to speak in what she considered a proper manner, his ears would be quite sore.

Valdun smiled indulgently at his daughter and his nephew. It was clear that Vera actually liked the younger boy, and in truth, he had his mother's personality. He was easy to like.

"And now," he said. "I think the two of ye, before getting too involved in the lessons, should get Valdar refreshed and in proper garb. I also reckon that he could use some food right now. Am I right, young prince?"

"Y-yes, your majesty. I do be hungry." He saw Vera's hand streaking toward his head, and didn't duck fast enough. "Ow," he cried. You never told me how to say anything really, so it be not fair for you to punish me for that."

She pinched him again. "It will make you remember. The correct way to say that is to say, 'I am hungry,' and 'it is not fair.' Now, repeat it."

"Yes, your majesty, I am hungry." He turned to Vera. "It is not fair to punish me for that."

"That's much better." She massaged his wounded ear, and nodded. Then, she took his hand and led him away. As they left the amphitheater, Pip could hear Valdun chuckling.

She led him to a sheltered cove on the banks of a stream and instructed him to remove his clothing and bathe thoroughly. He hesitated, red-faced. "There is nothing to worry about, Pip. I will leave and allow you privacy."

"B-but, how be, no, how am I to wash, with no soap?"

Vera plucked a large leaf from a vine that overhung the stream, and handed it to him. "Use this," she said. "It will clean better than that harsh soap your people use in Lands End, and it smells better. I will return shortly with new garments for you. And, do not forget to wash behind those dirty ears of yours."

When he was sure she was gone, Pip removed his tunic and pants and dropped them on the grass. Taking the leaf she'd given him, he waded into the stream. The water, rather than being cold as he'd expected based upon his experience with streams in Pandara, was pleasantly warm.

He dipped the leaf into the water and rubbed it across his chest. It made a foam thicker than any he'd ever seen with the soap Ludmilla made from animal fat, and as Vera had said, had an odor as pleasant as a field full of newly-bloomed flowers.

For the first time in his life, Pip actually enjoyed bathing. The sweet smell of the leaf and the warmth of the water was unlike anything he'd ever known. When he was completely clean, including his red hair, he climbed out of the stream and pulled on his pants. He was just about to put on his tunic when Vera returned.

"No, no," she said. "We must get rid of those filthy things. Here, you wear this." She handed him a tunic and a pair of pants.

They were deep green, and as smooth as silk cloth fresh from a weaver's loom. After handing over the clothes, Vera discretely disappeared into the trees to allow him to change. They fit as if they'd been made special for him, he thought, and the clothing was as soft against his skin as Ludmilla's touch when he was ill with fever. At the thought of Ludmilla, he felt the sting of tears in his eyes, and wiped them away.

"Okay," he said. "You can come back now."

She stepped through the bushes. "Well," she said. "You do look handsome. More like a prince now, except for those horrid shoes. Here, give them to me, and take these."

She handed him a pair of green shoes that looked like they were made from leather, but the smoothest leather he'd ever seen, with green laces and brown soles. Like the clothes, when he slipped them on, they fit perfectly.

He whirled around and smiled at Vera. "These be, er, are the finest clothes and shoes I have ever seen. How come they to fit me so well?"

She frowned at his effort to get the grammar right. "We of the Folk know many things. Things that you, too, shall know in time, Pip. Now, come with me. Food awaits."

He followed her through the trees to an open space wherein sat a table made from the bough of a tree, around which were four stones shaped like backless chairs. On the table were fruits, vegetables, and a flagon of something that looked like the red wine that the men of Lands End drank.

They sat facing each other as he ate. "I know you are accustomed to eating the flesh of animals," she said. "But, we Folk do not take the life of an animal without cause, and we never consume flesh. We received everything that we need from the plants of the forest."

He had noticed the absence of meat on the table, but had been so hungry, and everything had tasted so good, he hadn't bothered. He had to admit that it was probably the best meal he'd ever had, and that was saying something, for Ludmilla was the best cook in Lands End. He mumbled around a mouth full of food, causing Vera to laugh. Then, he swallowed, and looked at her. "This is wonderful," he said. "I have never eaten anything this wonderful." He felt a small pang of guilt at rating this food higher than Ludmilla's, but had to admit that, in truth, it was.

"Good," Vera said. "But, I advise you to eat a bit more slowly. No one is going to take your food away from you."

Pip dropped his head in apology. He hadn't realized that he was eating so fast. He had been hungry, and the sight of so much food had overwhelmed his table manners. He then resumed eating more slowly.

When he had finished eating, Vera said that it was getting late, and after his long journey and adventures, he should get some rest. She showed him a small structure made of boughs and leaves, and informed him that this would be where he would sleep.

Inside the shelter, he found the floor covered with ferns and leaves, and the ground beneath as soft as his bed at home. He had barely settled his body on this soft bed, when he fell into a deep and dreamless sleep.

Charles Ray

Chapter 9

The sound of Vera's voice woke Pip from the best sleep he'd had in a long time.

"Wake up, lazy one," she said. "Do you plan to sleep from the first of the sun until it goes to sleep itself?"

He sat up and stretched. He had no idea what she meant, other than he'd slept later than he normally did. Surprisingly, considering that it was his first time sleeping on the ground, he was completely rested. In fact, the foliage upon which he'd slept was even more comfortable than his bed at home, and the warmth of the earth beneath it had cradled him like a mother's arms.

"Good morrow," he said. "How long did I sleep?"

"The entire dark cycle," she replied. "I looked in on you once or twice, and you slept like a swaddling baby after feeding. Would you like to join me for the morning meal?"

At the mention of food, his stomach made a gurgling sound. Because he'd slept in his clothes, having fallen asleep before he thought to disrobe, there was no need for delay. He stood. "Yes, I would, but first I must wash my face, brush my teeth, and . . .

well, you know. Is there a plant that I can use to clean my teeth?"

"Of course. A twig from the mint plant will leave your mouth as fresh as a field on the first day of planting season, to use your mundane people's way of reckoning the seasons."

"Oh," he said. "You mean as fresh as spring."

She sniffed at him. "Is that not what I said?"

Jerking her head around, causing her red locks to swish in front of her eyes, she turned and led him to the stream, where she showed him the mint plant, and how to find and break off the proper size twig. Then, she left him to his morning ablutions, informing him that they would break fast at the same place they had eaten on the previous evening.

After brushing his teeth with a twig that indeed taste like fresh mint, and left his mouth tingling, he disrobed and took another bath in the warm, soothing waters of the spring. Refreshed and redressed, he found his way to the table that was again laden with all manner of fruits and vegetables. There was also a flagon, only this time instead of the red liquid, it contained a frothy white liquid. Vera stood at the table, her plate already full. Pip pointed at the flagon.

"That is milk that we get from the mountain goats that inhabit this region," she said. "We get milk and butter from them, given freely because we do not eat their flesh."

She lifted the flagon and poured some of the liquid into a carved wooden cup that sat near a similarly carved wooden plate, which had already been filled almost to overflowing with berries, a round green fruit that looked like an apple, but which Pip had learned from the previous evening, had a minty flavor, and some bulbous items that looked like onions, but tasted like mutton.

Remembering the chiding of the evening before, Pip took care to eat slowly, chewing each mouthful and savoring the combination of tastes; washing each mouthful down with a sip of goat's milk, which was creamy and had a combination sweet and salty taste that he found not at all unpleasant.

When the morning meal was finished, Vera took him to another spot on the bank of the stream and showed him how to use the soap plant to clean his plate and cup, which she told him he could keep in his dwelling if he wished. Of course, as a prince, he could have someone bring him food, but Pip agreed that having them in his possession was a good idea. Besides, he had not yet quite adjusted to being a prince, and wasn't ready to be waited upon.

Pip was accustomed to doing things for himself, and he decided that, for the time being, he would continue to do so. In addition, other than Vera, Tamara, and King Valdun, he had not seen another creature since his arrival in this strange land.

"Vera," he said. "Before we leave for wherever it is you are taking me this morning, may I ask a question?"

"Of course, you can, cousin. Since I am your teacher for most things anyway, you can ask me anything at any time."

"My first question is mayhap strange, but since arriving here, I have heard this place called the Land. Is that its name?"

"Ah, yes. We call it the Land, but the full name is the Land of the Fire, so called because of the Fire Mountain, which is the source of our warmth, and according to legend, is where our people sprang from."

Which, Pip thought, would explain Vera's ability to manipulate fire the way she did.

"Where be, er, where is the Fire Mountain?" he asked.

Vera gave him a playful pinch on his left ear, not to hurt, as he *had* corrected himself, but as a gentle reminder. "It is a day's walk from here, at least for a mundane. For us Folk, and mayhap for you, it is a mere thought away. You will see it soon enough, I warrant, but first, there are many things you must learn."

"Do you mean that I must go to school?"

"Yes, in a manner of speaking, that is what you will be doing."

Pip enjoyed school, especially the lessons on Pandaran history taught by Councilor Galen, but he hoped that his lessons here would go fast. He was anxious to see the mountain of fire of which Vera spoke. "Very well," he said. "but, I have one more question, please. I have only seen three people, if you are people, you are, aren't you, since we arrived. Where are the others?"

She frowned at him, and her brow furrowed. "Of course, we are people," she said sharply. "In many ways we are like the mundane, except that there is more variety, and we have certain . . . abilities that mundane do not possess. You will learn more of this in your lessons. As for where the others are, here in the Land of Fire, we tend to keep to ourselves unless there is an assembly, or someone is in need of assistance. You will meet others as the need arises. Now, no more questions. We must get to your first lessons."

He had a thousand times a thousand more questions, but her expression was set, and he knew more answers from her. As she turned and walked away, Pip followed.

They walked nearly one hundred paces along a winding path among the trees. All manner of colorful flowers grew along the path, from large red flowers that looked like roses, but whose bushes bore no thorns, to tiny yellow flowers that hugged the earth. Large moth-like insects flew from blossom to blossom, picking up and depositing pollen as they traveled. The air was warm, but pleasant, and a gentle breeze blew through the leaves and needles of the many species of tree that grew in thick, but neat groupings. The ground beneath his feet was soft, but not mushy like a bog. It was like walking on a feather-filled mattress.

They came at last to a clearing. In the center of the clearing, sitting cross-legged on the grass, was a being, the likes of which Pip had never seen or imagined. He, she, or it—he could not be sure—was thin without appearing gaunt, and the skin was the color of a polished silver flagon. The hair, a thin covering plastered to an oval skull, was as white as the first snow of winter season. The face was narrow, with prominent cheekbones and a straight, thin nose over thin lips. The creature; no, Pip reminded himself; the person, had eyes that were as blue as the midday sky on a cloudless summer day.

As they neared, Pip was still unable to ascertain the gender. The person wore a white tunic that covered the thin frame. They stopped, and the person bowed from the waist without rising.

"Good morrow," the creature said. "Thee hast refreshed, I pray."

Vera inclined her head politely. "Good morrow, Hermes. I have brought thy pupil." To Pip, she said, "This is Hermes. He is of the Water People. He will instruct you in the history of your lineage, at least, insofar as the Folk are concerned, and mayhap test for signs of any power that you might possess. I will return for you before the midday meal."

With that introduction, she bowed once more, turned, and disappeared down the trail.

Pip stood looking down at the man; he had at least learned that much; although, he was at a loss as to what Water People were.

"Sit thee here next to me," Hermes said. "We shall begin if thee art ready."

"Yes, Master Hermes," Pip said, and sat down cross-legged on the soft grass, but facing Hermes rather than beside him. "I am ready."

Hermes smiled, his eyes seeming to glow. "There is no need for such formality. Thee art, like me, of royal blood. I am Hermes, and thee art Valdar."

So, even this stranger knew Pip's birth name. Not that it really surprised him. It seemed that many people knew more about him than he knew about himself. Just another of the strange things about this strange place. "Yes, Mas-, er, Hermes," he said.

"Very well, then. Let us begin. I will begin at the beginning, after which, if thee wish, thee may ask questions."

Pip nodded his acquiescence, and Hermes, in a voice that was amazingly deep and resonant for someone so thin, related the history of the Land of Fire. His account was full of details, but somehow, Pip was able to follow along without strain.

In the far, far past, before the memory of any living being, even among the Folk who are very long lived, Hermes related, the Land was one. Beings of all types lived in peace and harmony. Some had special powers, some had none. For a long time this did not matter, but finally, those without powers, who came to be known as the mundane, became jealous of the Folk, who possessed what the mundane called magic, and separated themselves and refused to have any contact with them. The mundane then further separated, from others of their own kind, with those of a peaceful nature settling in what is now Pandara, and the more militant mundane crossed the Western Desert, a desolate place of sand, rock, and stunted, spiny plants, to a place of rocky soil which they called Barbaria, which, in their tongue, means 'warrior.'

At first, the three lands coexisted in relative peace, but the mundane of Barbaria, being aggressive and warlike by nature, began to raid the outer settlements of Pandara, and on occasion, would even gather up enough courage to sage forays into the Land of Fire, wherein dwelt the Folk.

Unlike the mundane of Pandara and Barbaria, the Folk were more varied, but they still lived in harmony and cooperation. Some, and Valdun and his half-brother Valcan were among them, in addition to other abilities, had mastery over fire, one of the main elements of the world. Others, and Hermes jabbed his chest with his bony thumb, controlled water, and yet others, like Tamara, had a special affinity with the earth and its products, the trees and other plants.

Also living in the Land of Fire, lived the original inhabitants of the World, the trolls, gnomes, and ogres. They, too, possessed special powers. The trolls worked underneath the earth, digging out its treasures, which they shared with the Folk through trading for things the Folk produced, such as clothing made from plant fiber. The gnomes had the ability to disguise themselves as any element of the solid earth, be it stone or dirt, and they served as the sentinels along the borders to warn of brigand incursions. The ogres, largest of the creatures of the Land, were master fighters, and they defended the Land against some of the wilder creatures of the Black Forest who occasionally wandered into the Land of Fire. One ogre was known to be able to soundly defeat a pack of ten wolves without becoming tired.

Each had his or her own place, and most kept to themselves. They did, though, share their powers and skills for the mutual benefit of all the Folk, for that is how they were known, including trolls, gnomes, and ogres, just Folk, different in appearance and skill, but inside, at the very core, the same.

When Hermes finished his tale, his shoulders slumped, and he closed his eyes.

To Pip, who, prior to the arrival in Lands End of the Barbarian Tenkuk and his band, had only known the people of Pandara, the knowledge that there were so many people who were so different from each other, struck him like a gale-force wind off the East Sea.

"So," he said. "Except for my father and mother, and the Barbarians, who seem to enjoy bringing pain to others, there has been no contact between the different people for a long, long time."

Hermes sighed. "Until tragedy brought the noble Princess Daria to the Land of Fire, barely alive, and the rare hunter who became lost in the forest, who we helped with an unseen hand to escape the ravenous wolves, there has been no real commerce between our people. There are the rare few on both sides who have had infrequent contact. My brother Valcan was one such. He knew someone in Lands End, which is how he was able to deliver thee there after thy mother died. But, the name of that person died with him, and since, we have had no contact."

"But, I saw Vera in Lands End. She saved me from a gang of bullies."

"Ah, yes. Thy birth presented a great challenge. When it was decided that thee would grow up among the mundane, it was also decided that someone would look out for thee. Vera is but the latest. She has been watching over thee for three summers, since thee started thy growth into maturity. The watchers are not usually seen by anyone, but in that particular case, thee sorely needed help, so she had no choice but to allow herself to be seen."

I appreciate that she saved me from being kicked to death, Pip thought, but it would have been better had she saved me from some of the other beatings.

"Nay, young Valdar," Hermes said. "Thee hadst to find thine own way as much as possible. Vera had only to make sure that thee survived to be able to do so."

"I suppose that makes sense. Wait! I spoke not. Can you hear my thoughts?"

"Aye. And, I think thee also, with the proper training and concentration, can do the same. I sense in thee a power stronger than in any other of the Folk."

"You mean that I am able to hear the thoughts of others?"

"Aye, young one. If I sense correctly, the power within thee, with proper guidance, it is possible for you to see what others wish to hide from thee, and mayhap even more."

Pip could only shake his head in wonder. It went on like this, one shock after another, until the sun was directly overhead. Just as Pip was about to ask yet another question, Hermes held up his pale hand.

"What be—no," Pip corrected himself. "What is the matter? There is so much more that I want to know." Need to know was more like it, he thought. All this time I have been living as one person, when I was actually another person entirely.

Nothing is wrong, Valdar," Hermes said. "It is nearing the midday meal, and before we stop, there is one more thing I must do with thee."

Pip's face creased in a puzzled look. "What must you do, Master Hermes?"

Hermes searched around in the grass until he found a small, dry twig about the size of Pip's thumb. He held it up inches from Pip's face.

"This is a simple test. I want to test thy powers." He gave Pop a stern look. "Thee must listen carefully to what I say, and do precisely what I tell you to do. Doest thee understand?"

"I, I think I understand." Though, in truth, he had no idea what Hermes was doing, or was about to do. He could, however, follow instructions, and he would endeavor to do exactly as Hermes instructed.

"Good. I want thee to concentrate on this twig. Remove all other thoughts from thy mind, and focus *only* on this twig." Pip stared at the little piece of wood. "No, no," Hermes said. "Do not strain thy mind. Merely look only at the twig, and think only of the twig, while thee listens to the sound of my voice."

Pip's face relaxed, and he tried to block out all else, letting his mind center on Hermes' pale hand and the twig which it held. After a while, a haze seemed to move around the twig, blocking the sight of Hermes' face, his body, and the glade in which they sat. Only the twig remained in sharp outline.

From what seemed like a great distance, he heard Hermes' voice. "Now, Valdar, I want to imagine this twig engulfed in flames."

Pip thought of fire; for a heartbeat he could see in his mind the hearth in Auric's workshop, but, remembering Hermes' instruction, he brought his thoughts back to the twig. Pip had always found the fire in the hearth comforting, so it was no problem seeing flames beginning to flicker around the twig. As he thought of fire, the mist, which had been gray, began to darken until there was naught but blackness surrounding the gray-green piece of wood, that seemed to float before his eyes.

Suddenly, the twig moved sharply to his right, out of his range of vision. "Oh my," he heard Hermes' voice say. "Thy powers art strong. It took but four heartbeats for thee to summon flame."

Hermes and the glade came back into focus. It seemed as if hours had passed but only a moment had passed at one and the same time. Pip felt somewhat disoriented. On the ground near his feet lay the twig, a few small flames still flickering at its tip. Hermes was waving his left hand over his right, the first two fingers of which were red. The red began to fade as he waved, and was soon gone, and his fingers were again pale. Hermes sighed.

"Are you in pain, Hermes?" Pip asked. Then, the thought hit him. "Did I hurt you? Did I cause that?" He pointed at the now smoldering twig. A look of astonishment was on his face.

"Aye, thee did. The power of the flame is strong in thee. Do not worry, though," Hermes said, holding up his hand. "I am fine. I warrant, though, that thee also hast other powers that are just as strong as that of the flame. It is as the ancients foretold. A child of two worlds, a child of fire, shall be born, and he shall bring the worlds back together."

Pip's mouth gaped open. This sounded a lot like Galen's story of the fire child. He wondered if there were other stories from Pandara that had their counterpart in the Land of Fire. He felt a pang of regret as he thought of his old teacher. Except for his pale skin, and his magical ability, Hermes was a lot like Galen; he was patient, and he seemed to enjoy imparting knowledge. But, he was also much, much more than Galen. The privy councilor could not heal a burn the way he had just seen Hermes do, and he had never once indicated that he knew what was in someone else's mind. He had also, Pip remembered, never even hinted to Pip that he was special, other than as a good student who, unlike the other boys, never acted up in class and who enjoyed learning. *The Fire Child!* Wouldn't Galen and everyone else in Lands End be amazed when they learned that it was more than just a story to entertain people at the audience. It was real, and even more amazed would they be when they learned that the runt, Pip the foundling, who other boys taunted, girls rejected, and adults ignored, was that child.

Until that moment, Pip hadn't given much thought to how, or if, he would get back to Pandara and Lands End, but his heart swelled at the thought, and he was determined. He would somehow get back to Auric and Ludmilla, maybe he also had Vera's power of transport, or he could get her to take him. When he returned, though, he would be a different person. Just let the other boys try to beat him again, he thought. He would show them something they would never forget.

Thee must not think such thoughts, Valdar. He heard Hermes' voice clearly, even though the man's lips had not moved. *Thy powers are not for vengeance. They must be used to protect the weak. We of the People do not make war on others. We use our powers to save others, or when necessary, for defense.*

Pip lowered his head in shame, but also amazement. Not only could Hermes read his thoughts, he could send his thoughts to another mind. *No, Valdar, I am not projecting. Thy art sensing my thoughts. Alas, I have not the ability to project, but I warrant that thee might have such power within thee, though.*

You mean, I am able to hear what others think, and mayhap can send my thoughts to them? Pip thought hard, in an effort to see if Hermes could 'hear' him.

Aye, that is what I mean. And, it is not necessary to think so hard. Thy thoughts are powerful, and when thee thinks so hard, it causes a pain in my head. Forsooth, thee art most powerful, the most powerful I have encountered in my many summers.

Pip's world, which until that time had been limited to the cobblestone streets of Lands End, and the nearby farmlands, had expanded immensely. He felt excited, and, at peace, at one and the same time.

"Is the lesson over?" Vera's voice, behind him, startled him. "It is time for the midday meal," she said. "I pray that I am not disturbing anything important."

"No, not at all," Hermes said. He smiled broadly. "I have just been testing young Valdar, and I must say, the prophecies are correct. He has powers beyond my imagining. We have this day only touched the surface. I believe that with the proper training, he will be the most powerful of the Folk."

Vera smiled and patted Pip on the shoulder. "If I know Hermes, he has worked you hard, and you are starving. Let us go and eat." In response, Pip's stomach growled. "After midday meal, you must start your other training, and you will need your strength." She smiled at Hermes. "He will be yours from the rising of the sun until the midday meal. From the completion of the meal he will be in the hands of . . . others. I hope this meets with your approval."

Hermes nodded. "Until the morrow, Valdar," he said. "Think thee on all that we have discussed today. On the morrow, we will do more tests of your powers."

"Thank you, Hermes. I look forward to our next meeting."

Pip and Vera left the teacher sitting cross-legged in the glade, and went to the eating place.

After a meal that seemed to Pip to taste even better than the two previous one, Vera took him to an open field that was several minutes' walk away, at the end of a serpentine path through the woods.

A wide expanse, shaped like a large serving platter, it dipped toward the center and was surrounded by tall, stately broadleaf trees. In the center of the field was a large circle of bare, packed earth. In the center of the circle stood two creatures unlike anything Pip had ever seen before.

Had he been able to stand upon his own shoulders, his head still would not reach a level with theirs. They had broad shoulders and long arms that hung lazily at their sides, and they were covered from head to foot with gray, tangled hair. Their brows were low, like shelves over small red eyes that peeked through the matted hair covering their faces. As Vera and Pip neared them, their mouths opened, revealing two rows of sharp teeth, made more dangerous looking by two prominent canines that curved like the tusks of a wild boar. Pip slowed his forward pace.

"There is nothing to fear, Pip," Vera said. "They look fierce, and in battle they can be, but they are your teachers for the next phase of your training." She waved at them. "Walu, Wera," she said. I have brought you your pupil. This is Prince Valdar, also known as Pip. He comes to us from the land of the mundane."

Their mouths stretched into what Pip assumed were smiles of welcome. But, had he been alone, and encountered them with such expressions, he would have turned and fled for his life.

"Welcome, Valdar," the slightly taller of the two said. "I Walu. This my mate Wera. We teach you fight with hand."

Walu stretched out a hairy paw, a hand three times the size of Pip's. Taught to always be polite, Pip placed his hand in Walu's. He was surprised at how soft and gentle the grip was.

Walu and Wera are ogres," Vera said. "They look fierce, but they are really the most gentle of creatures, unless provoked or threatened. They will teach you how to defend yourself when it is not convenient or wise to use your weapons or other powers. They were my teachers when I was a stripling, and I can promise you, they will teach you well."

Pip remembered how handily Vera had dealt with Sandrin and his bully friends back in Lands End. If these two could teach him such skills, along with his powers, whatever they were, he would be afraid of no one ever again.

"Vera come back evening meal," Walu said. "Valdar be ready eat then."

Vera laughed. "I warrant he will also be ready for a long soak in the stream. See you later, Pip." She was still laughing as she walked away.

Pip stood facing the two ogres, unsure of what he should do next. He need not have worried. The decision was made for him.

"We begin easy," Walu said. "First, Wera teach you how to use hands."

Pip was unsure about fighting with a woman, even one as imposing looking as Wera—or, perhaps, *especially* one as imposing looking as Wera, even though the two mounds on her chest clearly marked her as female. Actually, he was anxious about the prospect of fighting *anyone*, having only been accustomed to being the one being beaten. He had never struck anyone.

Wera approached him slowly, bent slightly at the knees, and with her large hands held up in front of her body. "You hit me," she said.

Pip hesitated. "I do not know," he said. "I have never hit anyone before."

The ogres laughed, deep, guttural sounds from deep within their chests.

"Not worry, little one," she said. "If you hit, not hurt."

He could see the logic in that. Her hide looked as tough as an ox's hide. He swung his right fist at her.

He found himself on his back, staring up at the blue sky, all the wind gone from his lungs.

"Now," Wera said. "I show you what you do wrong, and how to do right. Get up."

Pip spent the remainder of the afternoon being alternately thrown, knocked down, or pushed back several paces. By the time the sun was nearing the horizon, his body ached all over, but he had managed to learn a few of the ogres' tricks, and on one occasion had even sent Wera flying across the practice area, which seemed to have delighted Walu.

Despite the pain, Pip learned much. He learned which parts of the body, from the are just in front of the ear, or the point of the wrist behind the thumb, to the joining of the body to the legs, and the kneecaps, were most sensitive to pain, and how to use the weight and force of a larger opponent to drive him or her off balance. He learned how to avoid blows while maintaining his balance, and to focus on his opponent to find on opening to attack.

Walu was just congratulating him on his progress when Vera walked out of the tree line.

"Well, how has our young student on his first day of training?" she asked.

"Valdar do good," Walu said. "He knock Wera down. First time that happen with new student."

"He be good fighter when finish train," Wera added.

Vera looked at Pip with something akin to respect in her eyes. "So, you have talents of which I was not aware. Mayhap the prophecies were correct."

Pip rubbed his chest, which felt like someone had laid hot coal on it. "I know not what the prophecies be for sure," he said. "I do know that now I have not a bone or muscle in my body that does not ache. And, I think Wera allowed me to knock her down to make amends for the hundred times she ground me into the earth."

"Aye, mayhap. But, you are standing, which is more than can be said for most of their first-time students. After my first lesson, I could not walk for two suns. Worry not about the ache." Pip noticed that she'd ignored his partial reversion to commoner's speech patterns, probably out of sympathy for his discomfort. "A time in the stream with a special plant that grows nearby will ease your pain. And, I warrant that you are as hungry as a fire bear after a winter of hibernation."

Pip's body hurt so, he had scarcely noticed that he was famished. But, first things first, he thought. If she had something that would take the pain away, food could wait.

He thanked the two ogres, and said he looked forward to more training on the morrow.

"No," Wera said. "Next train in two suns. Next, Valdar train with Nork the troll. One sun with Nork, one sun with Wera and Walu. Then you learn all ways to fight."

He looked at Vera, his expression puzzled.

"On the morrow, you will begin weapons training under the tutelage of Nork. Nork is a troll, and trolls, when they are not deep within the earth seeking gold and other precious minerals, are the best at using club and sword in all the Land."

He shrugged, and immediately regretted it. His body ached with every movement of each part other than his mouth and eyelids. He nodded again at the ogres and followed Vera to the bathing stream.

She showed him the plant, a low growing fern-like plant with broad leaves, that grew in the shadow of the trees along the banks of the stream. The dark green leaves had spikes around the edges and glistened when he pulled one off and held it in the sunlight.

"Do I rub this where it hurts?" he asked.

"No, as you soak your body in the warm water, you chew on the leaf and swallow the sap. Be careful, though, not to swallow the leaf itself."

"Is it poison?"

"No, it will not kill you, but if swallowed, it will plug up your nether orifice for many suns. Believe me, that is an experience you do not wish to have."

She then discretely withdrew, leaving Pip standing on the edge of the stream, bemused and almost overwhelmed at all the information that had been poured into his brain in one short cycle of the sun. When she was well out of sight, he removed his dusty clothes, picked another one of the spiky leaves and carefully put it into his mouth. The taste was a combination of sweet and tart, and he felt his lips pucker, as he chewed. He eased into the warm water, sliding down until only his nose and eyes were above water.

In a short while, he felt his body start to relax. Moreover, his mind, which had been whirling with everything he had seen, heard, and done, began to calm. Facts, names, techniques; all sorted themselves into neatly arranged categories, and began to make sense. The aches in his body began to lessen.

When the pain was completely gone, he stood and spat the chewed-up leaf into his hand. He then waded over and tossed it onto the grassy bank, to allow it to decompose and add nutrients to the soil as he'd seen the Pandaran farmers do with the chaff from harvests. He then plucked one of the soap leaves and returned to the water, where he scrubbed thoroughly, enjoying the sweet smell of the plant and the soothing feeling of the water on his body. As he washed, he noticed that his hair, usually tangled after washing, was smooth and lay plastered against his skull.

When he felt clean, he left the water and lay on the soft grass to let the air dry his body. He then shook the dust out of his clothing as best he could and dressed.

When he arrived back at his shelter, he found a fresh tunic and pants laid out on his sleeping mat. He pulled off the dirty clothes, folded them neatly at the foot of his mat, and put on the clean ones. He then went to join Vera for the evening meal.

He ate slowly and quietly. Vera, sensing that he had many things on his mind, did not speak. When they meal was finished, she wished him a good sleep and faded into the trees. Back at his shelter, Pip stripped down to his pants, and lay on his back on the mat. Before he knew it, he was fast asleep.

Charles Ray

Chapter 10

The next morning, Pip woke up completely refreshed, and after eating the morning meal with Vera, informed her that he would find his own way to the glade where he was to meet with Hermes. He asked her to meet him there at midday so they could eat together, and then, unless the training with the troll was to take place somewhere else, he would make his own way to the training ground.

Vera gave him a nod and an approving smile and vanished into the trees. Pip marveled at the way she would be standing there one moment, and a moment later, would be just . . . gone. He determined that he, too, would someday be able to do the same.

He found navigating through the forest easy, and was soon at the glade. Hermes sat in the same spot he'd occupied during the previous training session, as if he had not moved at all, he sat cross-legged, his eyes closed.

Good morrow, Valdar. I trust that thee slept well. His voice echoed in Pip's mind, but his eyes remained closed.

Yes, Hermes. I am refreshed and ready for the next lesson.

For the next several hours, Hermes silently conducted more tests of Pip's powers. In addition to thought transfer, manipulation of water and fire, he discovered that Pip had an affinity for the plants, trees, and other creatures. He informed Pip that he would request Tamara work with him in developing that latter power, while he, Hermes, would work with him on water and air. It would be Vera who would help him with controlling fire and traveling great distances in a heartbeat. The more Pip learned, the more he pressed Hermes for more.

Finally, Hermes sighed and sat slump-shouldered. *Hold, Valdar. Thee has powers that are far beyond my ability to ken. I think thee must grow into them and learn to deal with them as they arise. Of thy ability to do this, I have no doubt, but there is nothing more I can teach thee.*

But, Hermes, does this mean that I will not be able to talk with you anymore?

"Nay, young master, and thee art my master, make no mistake about it, not for the reason that thee art of royal blood, but because thee possesses power superior to mine own. I am always available, however, whenever thee has questions. Thee hast an active, able, and inquiring mind, and I find great pleasure in conversing with thee.

Pip sighed. He, too, enjoyed spending time with the pale teacher. *I do have questions, Hermes, but one above others has me puzzled.*

Ask, Valdar.

You said that in a time long ago, all people of this land were one, but they went their separate ways. What I do not understand is, we are now so different, the people of the Land of Fire and the people of Pandara. We of Pandara share some similarity with the Barbarians, although we are of a different nature. But, we seem, at least the others of Pandara seem to be completely different from you here. How is that possible?

Look around thee, Valdar. Hermes paused. *Now, tell me, what doest thee see?*

I see trees and plants, and now and then, a bird flying high in the sky.

Very good. Now, are the trees the same or different?

They are all different. There are alders, oaks, and pines, and many that I do not recognize.

That is correct, they are all very different from each other, and yet, they stand side by side in the forest. See that tree over there, the tall one with the shiny gray bark? That is an iron tree. It stands next to another of the same species. Are they the same?

Pip saw that one tree was tall and straight, while the other was much shorter, and bent and gnarled. *No, Hermes, they are different one from the other.*

As were, and are, the people of the land. Each is unique, one group from the other, one individual from another. Each tree is different, different species and each individual tree is different from each other tree. Yet, they live peacefully, side by side. With the birds and creatures of the forest, it is much the same. It is true that some feed on others, but only as much as necessary. It seems that it is only the creatures with two legs who seem unable to live with those who are different.

Pip had no problem understanding that. He was different from the other young ones in Lands End, and the other children either taunted or ignored him because of his differences.

So, except for your special abilities . . . our special abilities, Folk of the Land of Fire are the same as the people of Pandara?

That is so. We are also the same as the people of Barbaria, and they are the same as the people of Pandara, with but minor differences. Legend has it that we all came from the same mother and father, but as we grew, we differed one from the other, much as a brother and sister with the same father and mother will have different hair color or personality.

You also said that the legend tells of a child from two people who will reunite us. If people cannot abide difference, how is this to be?

That I cannot tell thee, Valdar. Needs be that thee must find the way thyself, for I know only what the legend has foretold since the earliest of times. I know not the how.

The sound of a throat clearing caused both Pip and Hermes to start. "Forgive my intrusion," Vera said. "But, it is time for the midday meal, and the training that follows immediately thereafter."

Hermes smiled at her. "There is no need for thee to apologize, child," he said. "We were finished, and merely conversing. I fear I have nothing left to teach young Valdar." He turned to Pip. "Go well, my young friend. I think that great adventures await thee, but fear not, I think thee will be ready."

Pip smiled and inclined his head in a gesture of respect, the way he'd seen Vera and Tamara do. Hermes smiled and returned the gesture.

Charles Ray

Chapter 11

After the meal, and despite his protests that he could find his own way, Vera accompanied Pip to the training ground, reminding him that it was her duty to introduce him to his new teacher. Somewhat mollified, he accepted, but insisted that he be allowed to lead the way, so that he could learn his way around.

Waiting for them at the training area was the strangest creature—no, Pip reminded himself, the strangest looking person he had ever seen. He was so strange, he made the ogres look normal. But, as his conversation with Hermes had revealed, the differences that made people strange were often external, different from each other, but, at the same time, quite similar on the inside, or like the Pandarans and Barbarians, similar on the outside, but completely different on the inside—but, all the same, sprung from the same roots. As he neared the center of the area, he kept reminding himself of this.

The troll, for he'd assumed that, since he was to train with a troll on this day, that could be the only answer to the strange person's identity, was half a head shorter than Pip, but with a large, bulbous head and uniformly gray skin. It/he/she had two large eyes, tinged with yellow around a dark, almost black, center, a narrow, hooked nose that curled over fleshy lips. And a fang-like tooth on one side of its mouth, the tip of which protruded up behind the bottom lip. Its clothing consisted of a dingy looking brown coverlet, one of the shoulder straps of which was so frayed it looked as if would fall apart if touched. The gray body was completely hairless, no hair on the head, and no brows or lashes. The arms, which rested on a large club, almost as long as Pip was high, were bony, ending in large hands with long, gnarled fingers. Two bare feet that looked large enough to support someone twice as large, and in sorely in need of washing, protruded from beneath the hem of the coverlet which hung almost to the ground, and ended in bent toes with sharp, downward curling toenails.

Vera walked up to the troll and bowed slightly. "Nork, I have brought thee they pupil. This is Valdar."

Nork the troll looked up at Pip, a sneer on his gray face. "Skinny one, this is. Will not be easy to teach to use weapons."

"Valdar is a quick study. I think he will surprise you."

"Hmph! We see," the troll said. He pointed a finger at Pip. "You, to get club there." He pointed to a twin to the club he was leaning on. It lay on the ground at the edge of the area.

Pip picked it up. It was heavy, and looked as if it had been carved from a small tree trunk.

He walked back, and stood facing Nork.

"I am ready, Teacher Nork," he said.

"Ha! You call that ready? Baby troll kill you in two heartbeats. You not know how to hold club."

He put his own club down and roughly shoved and manipulated Pip, showing him how to hold the club across the front of his body, with a firm grip on the narrow end with his right hand, with the heavy hand resting on his left palm.

"I will return for you at evening meal, Pip," Vera said.

Facing the snarling troll, Pip found himself wishing that she would stay. The ogres had been frightening in appearance, at first, and they were tough teachers, but they had a sense of humor. The angry looking Nork looked all as business, as if he never smiled or laughed.

Before Vera was completely out of sight, the troll set upon Pip, who found himself backpedaling, holding his club up to ward of a series of blows that, he feared, if any connected would crush his skull.

After thoroughly humiliating him, Nork began a series of exercises, showing Pip how to use his club as a defensive weapon, making him repeat each exercise countless times until he could do it perfectly. He then demonstrated a few basic offensive strikes, each of which Pip was able to parry, not perfectly, but at least to Nork's satisfaction.

They went back and forth like this, alternating between defense and offense, and Pip began to get the hang of it. Throughout, Nork cautioned Pop to watch his opponent's eyes rather than his weapon.

"Eyes tell you what enemy do, not weapon," he said. "Always watch eyes to know what enemy plan to do."

Even the dour Nork, though, had to finally admit that Pip was a quick study. He'd been able to get the occasional blow past the shorter man's defenses, and noticed that the sneer on the troll's face had been replaced by a look of grudging respect.

When Nork was satisfied that Pip had mastered at least the basics of the club, he switched to the short sword, two of which he had wrapped in a dingy gray cloth and lying on the ground at the edge of the training ground.

The sword was lighter by half than the club, and was at the same time, easier but harder for Pip. It was easier because, being lighter, he could swing it faster, harder, because, so could his opponent, and Nork was even better with the short sword than he was with the club.

He taught Pip thrusts and parries, offensive and defensive moves, how to use the sword in close quarters, and how to use it in more open space. Again, he stressed the importance of watching an opponent's eyes for clues of planned moves rather than watching the blade.

The sword took Pip longer to get the hang of than did the club, and he fervently hoped that he never had to face an opponent armed with a sword for a long time, in particularly not an opponent with Nork's skill. Had he been engaged in real combat, rather than training, he would have been dead a hundred times over. He was thinking that he would much prefer using his powers, such as the power to manipulate fire, preferably from a distance.

The setting of the sun, and the end of the day's training, were welcomed. Vera returned to the training ground just as Nork nearly knocked Pip's sword from his hand with a flick of his blade.

"Sorry to intrude," she said. "But, it is time for the evening meal."

"And, not a moment too soon," said Pip. "I was just about to get killed for the hundredth time."

Vera laughed, and even Nork made a snorting sound, that was probably as close as he ever came to mirth. "Not worry, Valdar," Nork said. "You not do bad for someone who never hold sword before. Not long, you be almost as good as Nork."

"Never. If I lived a hundred summers, I could never match your skill. I do not think anyone could."

The troll's lips turned up, revealing rows of crooked, yellow—but incredibly sharp—teeth. "Valdar right. You never be good like me. But if you only half as good, you be second best in Land." He turned to Vera. "Vera right. He quick. Learn fast. Never had student learn so fast."

"Did I not tell you. Valdar is special. He is of the Folk and the mundane, and has powers beyond anything that has ever before been seen."

"He one prophecy talk about?"

"It is foretold," she said.

There was that prophecy again, Pip thought. He wished he could share their confidence, or even understand just how he was to go about fulfilling a prophecy that was as old as the land, the details of which no one had yet shared with him.

Charles Ray

Chapter 12

Pip's training went on for three more cycles of the moon. Mornings spent with Hermes, Vera, or Tamara, practicing his newfound powers of manipulating water, air, fire, or plants, or mentally transporting himself, the latter a skill he reckoned would come in handy if he was to get to know all the land, not just Pandara. In the afternoons, he alternated between hand-to-hand fighting with Walu and Wera, and weapons training with Nork, who was joined in the third session by his mate, Nabla, who except for drooping breasts that swelled her coverlet, was his twin. She was every bit as good with club and sword as Nork, and could hold her own in sparring sessions with him.

He discovered that the trolls did have a sense of humor, just that it tended to be based on something bad happening to someone else. When, for instance, Pip swung his sword to wildly during one session, and fell flat on his backside, they rolled on the ground, making cackling sounds until tears well up in their oversized eyes.

Midway through his training he was introduced to Gork and Gollum, two gnomes, shorter even than the trolls, with narrow faces, thing lips, and tiny, almond-shaped eyes. They dressed in bright green tunics and pants, and always wore conical hats atop their pointed heads, which were covered with matted gray hair that was usually filled with cockleburs or twigs. Each had a pointed beard, but a clean shaven upper lip. They were master archers, and with their tiny bows could put an arrow inside a ring no bigger than Pip's hand from a hundred paces. They made a larger bow for him, and soon, he had become a relatively competent archer.

Vera also continued to teach him proper speech, and the instances of pinched ears dropped off to none.

There came a time finally when his teachers all threw up their hands, and admitted that they could teach him no more. He had learned all they had to give, and would now have to improve his skills on his own.

Pip and Vera were sitting on the grassy bank of the stream after the midday meal. He played idly with a blade of grass, staring into the gently flowing water, watching the reflection of light of the undulating surface.

"I sense uneasiness in you, Pip," she said.

"I was thinking about Auric and Ludmilla," he said. "I have been gone for more than four moons. They must be worried sick, especially Aunt Milla. I have never been away from them even for a night before."

"You wish to return to Lands End?"

"Yes," he said. "I miss them. But, I also think that I must return. Something is not right. I can feel it, but I cannot fathom what it is."

She put a hand on his shoulder. "Your powers are developing, cousin. You are becoming one with the land. If you sense trouble, then it is certain, there is trouble. I will inform father, and we will make preparations to return."

He was happy to know that Vera would be going with him. He found that he enjoyed his cousin's companionship.

"At least, with the power to transport, the journey will not take long," he said.

"No, Pip, the journey must be done in the normal way, normal for a mundane, that is. We try to avoid using our powers in a way that they will notice. You must do the same. We will travel as a mundane would; by horse. The trip will take three suns."

"B-but, I have never ridden a horse. I do not think I know how."

"You need not worry. I have already chosen a mount for you. He is gentle, and with your power and skill, you will quickly learn to ride him. Besides, it is fitting that a son of the royal line of Pandara should reenter the city properly mounted and outfitted.

"Okay, cousin," Pip said. "I will trust you."

Charles Ray

Chapter 13

The next morning, after the meal, Pip stood before King Valdun in the amphitheater. He was flanked by Vera on his right and Tamara on his left. Arrayed around him were his teachers, the pale Hermes, attired in a long white robe; Walu and Wera the ogres had combed their fur and placed gold bracelets on their wrists; Nork and Nabla had even put on boots, cracked brown leather that they had even tried to polish; but, Gork and Gellum the gnomes wore the same garb they wore during his training. There was a great gathering of the Folk, including many Pip was seeing for the first time, and many he'd met as he taught himself to navigate around the forest. Hypa, Herma, and Hera, who had skin as pale as Hermes, but with hair so black, it shone blue under sunlight, were from the Folk who had command over water. Pip had only had two sessions with them, and had mastered the power so rapidly they decided that no further training was needed. There were many others, and they all smiled or waved at him, and for the first time in his life, he felt accepted as part of a community. Everyone waited patiently for the king to speak.

Finally, when total silence had fallen over the assemblage, Valdun stood.

"Prince Valdar," he said, his voice soft, but carrying to the very back of the gathering with ease. "Vera has informed me that thee wishes to return to thy place of nurturing. Is this so?"

Pip bowed, dipping his head in the same manner he had seen Vera do. "Yes, King Valdun. I sense that I am needed by my foster parents. With your leave, I would like to return to Pandara." He could not bring himself to calling Pandara the land of the mundane.

"Very well, then," Valdun said. "I can understand thy concern, for I too have sensed a disturbance of unknown origin. But, I would be remiss if I allowed thee to return before thee art fully ready." He scanned the teachers around Pip. "What say ye? Is Prince Valdar fully trained for what he must do?"

Hermes, as the eldest and most senior of the teachers, stepped forward. "Yes, Valdun," he said. "The young prince has powers that are beyond even me. There is nothing more I can teach him."

He stepped back, to be replaced by Walu and Wera. "Valdar good fighter," Walu said. "He even beat Wera." This caused a titter throughout the crowd, and even Wera smiled.

As the ogres moved back into line, Nork moved forward. "King Valdun, young one is good with club and sword. Nork fight with him at side any time."

Gork and Gellum gave a similar assessment of Pip's preparedness, and then Vera stepped in front of all of them.

"Father, Pip, er Valdar, has mastered the proper speech for his station in Pandara, and no longer speaks like a common peasant. His skill at traveling along the power waves rivals my own, and if I may speak for my friend, Tamara." The brown girl beside Pip nodded. "He has an affinity for living things that is unmatched in the Land. Not just the trees and other plants, but the birds and animals. I vow that he is ready."

"Very well," Valdun said. "Prince Valdar, step forward." Pip moved in front of the king and bowed slightly. From his tunic, Valdun pulled a gold chain to which was attached a round, gold amulet with the image of a flame embossed upon it. He placed the chain around Pip's neck. "This is the symbol of our, thy family, Valdar. Wear it always. Thee has my leave to go, and may the spirits guide thy path."

Valdun returned to his throne and sat, regarding Pip with a fatherly expression, part worry and part pride in his half-breed nephew.

Nork and Nabla came to Pip's side.

"Prince need proper weapon when travel," Nork said.

Nabla pulled a short sword from beneath her vest. It was sheathed in a soft leather-like fabric, that while tough as leather, Pip knew had been made from the fibers of the iron tree. The belt to which the sheath was attached had a gold buckle upon which there was engraved the flame symbol to match the emblem around his neck, above which was a circle with rays emanating from it, representing the sun, and the affinity of the Folk with the forces of nature.

Nabla put the belt around Pip's waist and fastened the buckle. Both she and Nork were smiling, showing their sharp teeth in grimaces that Pip had come to recognize as their display of pride in their star pupil. After buckling the belt, Nabla caressed Pip's cheek. He saw a small tear in the corner of her eye, but knew better than to draw attention to it.

Nork gave him a small club, which he hooked into the belt with a cloth loop.

"Now Valdar proper warrior," he said, and the two trolls resumed their places in the line.

Vera stepped up and stood in front of Pip. "I, too, have a gift for you," she said. "But, we must go outside to see it." Outside, of course, meant outside of the pavilion, which was already 'outside,' but, Pip had long since stopped being confused at such distinctions.

The crowd parted and Vera led Pip, King Valdun, and the teachers through the amphitheater's archway.

Standing just outside the exit were two horses, grazing on the thick grass. One was a stallion, a deep ebony color, so black that, like the hair of the water folk, it had a bluish cast. The other, a mare, was also black, but with streaks of gray across her rump and a white blaze on her forehead. As Pip, Valdun, Vera, and Tamara approached, the beasts stopped grazing and stood watching them.

There was something regal in their bearing, especially the stallion. Never before had Pip seen such magnificent animals. Without being told, he knew that this was Vera's gift.

"I only need one, and here there are two," he said to Vera. "Which one is mine?"

The stallion snorted and looked directly at Pip. *By what act of the spirits do you think that a weak two-legged creature such as you could own me?* Pip heard the voice, deep and male, inside his head. He stopped and stared, wide-eyed and mouth agape.

Now, Nightshade. Pip heard a gentle female voice. *He is only a colt. Likely he means no ill will by the statement. Such is only the way of the two-legs.*

The stallion snorted again, causing Pip to take a backward step.

"Pip, what is the matter?" Vera asked.

"I think, I mean, I heard voices," he said. "I believe the horses spoke to me in my mind."

"What did they say?"

The mare walked over to Vera and butted her head gently against her shoulder. Vera's eyes widened.

"He, I mean, they, said that I could not own them," Pip said. "At least, I think that is what the stallion said, for those words sounded like they were uttered by a male voice."

"Well, of course, that is correct. You do not own them. They deign to carry us where we wish to go." She turned and faced both horses. "The lad was but using a figure of speech that is common in the land from whence he comes. He meant no harm."

There, did I not say so! Pip heard the female voice again. It was clear that these were not ordinary horses, and that they were able to communicate, in his language at that. But, then, nothing in the Land of Fire was exactly 'ordinary.' He decided to try his own power.

Forgive me, Nightshade. That is your name, is it not? I truly meant no harm, and would be most grateful if you would allow me to ride you.

The stallion came to Pip and nuzzled his forehead. Pip could feel the hot breath from the flaring nostrils, and smell the sweet grass the animal had just eaten.

Yes, Nightshade said. *I sense no evil in you. I forgive you your ignorance of our customs, two-leg.*

Pip rubbed the stallion's nose. *Here, in the Land of Fire, I am known as Valdar, but in Pandara, the land where I grew up, I am called Pip. It would please me if you would call me Pip.*

Very well, Pip. Nightshade snorted and tossed his head. *I will be your transport when needs you must travel in the ordinary way. You may mount.*

But, you have neither bridle, nor saddle, and I have never ridden before.

That is of no importance. You have but to think of where you wish to go, and I will carry you there. My back is fully as comfortable as any contraption, and I think that you are old enough not to need a child's seat, are you not?

Pip nodded, but he was still apprehensive, having never before in his life done more than rub a horse's muzzle. But, if he was to be a prince of both Pandara and the Land of Fire, he would have to master his fear.

He walked to Nightshade's left side, but again hesitated.

"You only have to grasp his mane and pull yourself up," Vera said.

He dropped his bow and quiver, and grabbed a handful of the black hair, and swung his right leg up and over Nightshade's back. The stallion stood as immobile as a rock until Pip was comfortably settled, and then he did a little prancing step around the area. At first, Pip clung to the mane for his life, but soon settled into the up and down motion as Nightshade did a little trot around the clearing.

You sit well, Pip. It will be an honor to carry you into battle.

Let us hope that we never need do that.

"I fear that is not to be so. I sense a disruption in the harmony of the earth's flow coming from the direction of the land you call Pandara. I think we will see battle soon, and aplenty.

Pip sighed. If it was to be, it was to be. At least, he thought, he had been as well prepared as the teachers here could manage. The rest would be up to him—and fate.

"King Valdun," he said. "I would like to get started as soon as possible, if that meets with your approval."

The king had been silent during Pip's introduction to the horse. Now, he walked forward and put his hand on Pip's knee.

"As thee wish," he said. "But, I will not allow thee to travel alone. Vera and Tamara will accompany thee to Pandara." He turned to the two young women. "Guard him well."

Vera and Tamara bowed.

"Thy wish is my command, father," Vera said. "Tamara, thee should get your own steed, Luna. We leave as soon as you return."

Tamara nodded at Vera, bowed to the king, and hastened off into the trees.

She was quickly back, sitting astride a brown mare, and carrying a small staff laid across the horse's withers.

Vera handed Pip his bow and mounted the mare, whose name, Pip had learned through the mind-to-mind contact he was becoming more comfortable with, was Star.

"Should we not take food?" Pip asked.

"The land will provide," Tamara spoke for the first time. "For those who have affinity with the elements, there is always food."

Pip noticed that, like Vera, she spoke the language of Pandara like a native. While they had never discussed it, he assumed that she must have shared duty with his cousin, watching over him as he grew up. Except for the brown hue of her skin, she would easily pass unnoticed among the people of the rural areas, and would attract scant attention in Lands End itself, if dressed like other people. He was happy to have the two of them as his companions, for he had to come to like both of them, and thought of them as older sisters.

"Very well, then," he said. "I suppose we should be off."

They bowed again to Valdun, and then wheeled their horses, with Vera taking the lead, Pip and Nightshade directly behind her. Tamara followed close behind him.

Chapter 14

The Black Forest

By the time the rumbling of Pip's stomach told him the sun was directly overhead, they were well out of the Land of Fire and into the dim recesses of the Black Forest.

There were no roads, but Vera navigated skillfully along the clear spaces among the towering trees. They saw no other people, and few animals, apart from the occasional herd of short-horned goats, shaggy deer, and a few hares that scattered as they approached.

The overhead branches of the trees did not quite come together, so the path they were on received some sunlight that filtered through the leaves. To either side of their path, though, the darkness was intimidating.

Just when Pip thought his stomach would gnaw through his tunic, they came to a wide clearing with a clear pool in its center, and Vera raised her right hand, signaling for a halt.

They dismounted. Tamara went off into the nearby trees to gather berries and roots for their meal. The horses went immediately to the pool, where they drank noisily from the crystal-clear water. Pip and Vera waited until the animals had slaked their thirsts, and then knelt, using their hands as cups to get at the icy cold water.

Tamara came back with her arms filled with dark blue berries and roots that looked like the potatoes grown by Pandara's farmers. She handed her bundle to Vera and dropped to her knees to get a drink.

Vera separated the berries and roots into three equal piles, one of which she gave to Pip, and another to Tamara.

Pip tried the berries first. The taste was a mixture of sweet and tart, and was quite pleasant. The roots, once he got past the tough skin, tasted like carrots.

As they ate, the horses grazed on the long grass that grew around the perimeter of the clearing.

Once their stomachs were filled, and after drinking once more from the stream, they prepared to resume their journey. Pip picked up his bow and quiver and sent a mental signal to Nightshade. The black stallion started toward them, and then stopped, his broad head coming up and his nostrils flaring. The other horses rushed up, flanking Nightshade, pawing at the ground and staring at a point behind Pip.

Pip felt a lancing throb at the base of his skull. He was not sure how he knew, but he recognized the feeling as awareness of danger, and nearby. He turned slowly, followed by Vera and Tamara, and the three of them became aware of the danger at the same time.

At the edge of the clearing stood a pack of five wolves, dog-like creatures as large as a small colt, with coarse gray hair, pointed ears that lay flat against the sides of their heads, and fangs that looked to Pip to be as thick as his wrist and as sharp as the edge of his sword. They were spread out in a semi-circle, with the largest, a male with narrow yellow eyes, in the middle.

Vera and Tamara came up on either side of him. Tamara held her staff at the ready.

Pip started to take an arrow from his quiver, but then paused. "Wait," he said. "We should not kill them if there is no need."

"What do you mean? If we do not slay them, they will surely slay us," Tamara said.

"But, Tamara, did you not say that I have affinity with all living creatures of the forest and fields?"

She frowned. Then her eyes went wide. "Indeed, I did. Do you think you can convince them to leave us alone?"

The wolves were advancing slowly toward them. Pip sent a sharp thought into the head of the alpha wolf, which caused the entire pack to stop.

What Pip saw in the male wolf's mind was mindless hunger, nothing more.

"If by that you mean reason with them as I would Nightshade," he said. "The answer is no. They are brutes, and at the moment they think only of food, and you can guess what they think of us. I think, though, that I can convince them that we are not an easy meal, and that they would be better off to relocate to another hunting ground with easier prey."

Tamara shrugged and nodded, but kept her staff at the ready. Pip could sense both women's uneasiness as they stood their ground, prepared to do battle with the pack.

He took a deep breath and formed an image of lancing, white-hot flames. He then sent that image in a fan shape, directly at the wolves' heads, with the bulk of it at the alpha male.

When his image hit their primitive brains, the result was instant and explosive. Their ears went up, and the hairs on their bodies stood out stiffly. They yelped loudly, and then spun and fled into the forest, yelping as if they had actually been burned.

When the sound of painful howling had faded the three relaxed and looked at each other. Vera laughed.

"Well, Pip," she said. "I can see that you are not in need of bodyguards. I have never seen anyone who could do that before."

"Did I not tell you that he had powers over the living things of the forest?" Tamara said.

"Yes, but I notice that you kept your staff handy."

Tamara laughed sheepishly. "Well, I was not sure how much control he had over his power, or how much power he had. But, Pip, that was masterful, truly masterful. I think there is no one who is you equal."

Pip took a deep breath and bowed toward them. "Thank you, ladies. I am happy to have been of some small service." Vera pinched his ear. "Ow! Why did you do that. I did not speak wrongly."

"That, my dear cousin, was not for your grammar," Vera said. "But, for your ego. Modesty is the true mark of a hero, Pip, never should you forget that."

"I was but joking. If not for the things you, Tamara, and the others taught me, we would all likely be resting in the bellies of the wolves right now."

"Apology accepted. Consider the pinch a warning for the future."

"It is not right to punish someone for something before they do it."

"You are, of course, correct. I guess that means I owe *you* an apology. But, remember this, except in the Land of Fire, the right way is not always the one followed."

Charles Ray

Chapter 15

Pandara

The rest of their journey through the Black Forest was without incident. On one or two occasions, packs of wolves paced them, running a parallel trail in the trees, but keeping their distance as if sensing that they were not easy prey.

Around midnight, they came out of the forest in the westernmost region of Pandara, a sparsely-populated region with rolling hills and stands of oak and alder scattered about, and with streams that meandered around the hills, running east toward the sea. When they were several hundred paces from the looming forest, they stopped for a few hours of sleep, each of them taking turns standing guard.

Just as the first rays of the sun were beginning to lighten the horizon, they broke their makeshift camp and resumed their journey.

There were few farms in the west; the land was rocky and hard to cultivate, and few of Pandara's people were hardy, or foolhardy enough, to live in such close proximity to the Black Forest. Pip had only met one or two, when they came into Lands End at the end of each harvest to sell their potatoes or other tuber crops, the few things that would grow in the rocky soil, but they seemed friendly enough. He was, therefore, surprised at the reaction they neared the isolated farmsteads.

He would have expected strangers riding in these parts to be greeted at least with a wave or nod of the head. Instead, as they neared each farm house, people stopped what they were doing and went inside. Mothers snatched up their children and hustled them inside, Men went in last, making sure women and children were safely inside, and they glared at Pip and his companions as they rode by.

"Not exactly friendly, are they?" Tamara remarked wryly.

"It is strange," Pip said. "Those from the western region that I met in Lands End were friendly enough. I wonder why they react to us the way they do now."

"It could be related to the feeling of trouble you have sensed," she said.

To that Pip had nothing to add, so they rode on in silence, experiencing the same reaction at each farm they passed.

At the last range of rolling hills, just before the slope that eased down into Lands End, they encountered a young goatherd who was shepherding a flock of twenty, bleating goats across the path.

When the boy, who looked to be about Pip's age, saw the three of them approaching, he stopped in the middle of the path, his staff held across his chest.

They halted the horses fifteen paces from the boy and his herd. Pip sent out a gentle mental probe. The impression he got was a combination of fear and curiosity. The boy didn't seem to be aware of Pip's presence in his mind.

"Wait here," Pip said. "I will approach and talk to him."

He had Nightshade walk forward slowly. The stallion moved in a slow, stately manner, stopping five paces from the boys, who regarded them with wide eyes. His hands shook as they clung tightly to the wooden staff he held across his chest.

"Good morrow, lad," Pip said. "I be Pip from Lands End." Pip had decided to use the peasant mode of speech to put the boy at ease. "My friends and me be returning from a long journey to the west lands. Who be you?"

The boys gaze flicked nervously from Pip to Nightshade. He licked his lips and swallowed several times.

"I-I be D-Derik," he said. "I live just yonder beyond that hill with my ma and pa. You talk like a Pandaran farmer, but I never seen a common man riding such a horse as yours. How be that?"

Pip understood. Even the royal guards, who on occasion rode through the countryside on patrol, did not have horses as fine as Nightshade. Queen Daphne, the few times that she rode, sat astride a snow-white mare, but even her horse would look like a nag standing next to Nightshade. He didn't feel it was the time or place to go into his true identity; that would have to wait until he arrived at the castle in Lands End. "It be a present from a friend who lives far to the west," he said. He could feel Nightshade's flanks quiver in indignation against the inside of his legs, so he sent a mental apology.

Very well, Pip. There was still a tone of indignation in Nightshade's voice. *I can understand your reluctance to tell the young two-legs too much. He would not understand anyway. You are forgiven.*

Thank you, friend Nightshade. To the young farm boy, he said, "Tell me, Derik, as we have ridden through the countryside, folks seem nervous, and have avoided contact with us. This be unlike the normal way of Pandara. What be wrong?"

"Aye," the boy said. "I guess the news not be reaching the far lands. A half moon past, an army of Barbarians rode down upon Pandara. I hear they burned many huts and drove people out. They took livestock and valuables before riding back to Barbaria. So now, people are not trusting strangers."

Nightshade snorted. *I think that was the cause of the unease and trouble I sensed.*

You are right. Pip nodded. *I still sense unease, although not as much as before.* "What news from Lands End?" he asked Derik.

"It be confusing," Derik said. "Some folk fled the town, and one family who spent the night with us said the Barbarians were laying waste to the town."

Pip's stomach lurched. He felt sick, and wondered if Auric and Ludmilla were safe. He felt an urgency to resume his journey to Lands End.

"Thank you, Derik. Be safe. My friends and I must make our way to Lands End."

"It be dangerous there," the boy said. "It be you who should take care."

Vera and Tamara rode up beside him, their expressions showing concern.

"I am sorry," Vera said quietly. "I listened in on your conversation. It sounds as if the Barbarians have decided to turn their attention to Pandara. This is not good for your people."

"No, not good at all," Pip said. "I fear for my foster parents and the other people of the town. They are not capable of defending themselves. If Tenkuk . . . that is the name of the Barbarian commander, if he and his men have set their sights on Lands End, I fear the worst."

"Then," said Tamara. "We must hurry."

The horses were urged into a gallop, over the hill and down the long slope toward the town, scattering Derik's goats across the hillside and leaving him standing, mouth agape, in the middle of the road, staring at the receding backs of the three strangers who rode such fine horses without using bridle or saddle.

They rode flat out for over an hour, and as they came around the last low hill before the town, they saw plumes of wispy smoke curling upwards toward the sky. Far more plumes than the chimneys of Lands End could account for.

As they entered the town, they saw that several houses had been badly damaged, two wooden structures on the edge of town had been reduced to piles of smoldering rubble, and a row of stone houses farther in, including the butcher's shop, were gutted shells. Pip's anxiety over Auric and Ludmilla rose as they rounded the corner on the street where his foster parents' home stood.

The shop next to Auric's tannery showed some damage, smoke stains on the door and walls, and all the front windows had been broken, but his home and workshop appeared undamaged.

They brought the horses to a halt in front of the tannery and dismounted. Pip ran to the door and slammed it open.

Auric was working on a piece of hide at his work bench near the hearth, and Ludmilla stood near him, concern causing her round, usually cheerful, face to crinkle. At the sound of the door banging open, Auric dropped the hide and turned, looking confused. Ludmilla looked up, a puzzled expression on her face at first, and then, when they both recognized Pip, puzzled looks changed to broad smiles.

They rushed forward and embraced him.

"Pip, my baby, I be worried to death about you," Ludmilla said. "We did not know what had happened to you all this time."

Auric released Pip from his embrace and stepped back. "Where have you been all this time, boy? We thought the Barbarians had taken you back to their land."

"It is a long story, uncle," Pip said "I will explain it all in good time, but first, tell me what has happened here in Lands End."

Ludmilla placed her hands upon Pip's shoulders and looked into his eyes. She then glanced at Vera and Tamara, who had followed him into the shop and now stood silently behind him.

"Pip," she said. "You be different somehow." She glanced down at the sword and club at his waist, and the bow he carried. Her eyes narrowed. "Where be you all this time, and who be your companions?"

"Oh, my apologies," Pip said. "This is Vera and Tamara. They are from the Land of Fire. It was they who saved me from Tenkuk and his warriors."

Ludmilla looked long at them, and then smiled, but tentatively. "I know this Land of Fire, or where it be," she said. "But, I thank you for saving my Pip."

"You have my thanks as well," Auric said. He placed a hand on Pip's shoulder. "You seem to have grown, boy. And, these weapons you carry; you be knowing how to use them?"

"He is extremely proficient with them," Vera said. "He was taught by the best teachers in our land, and has surpassed them."

Auric cocked his head to one side. "I be thinking that my boy is no longer a child. You left Lands End a stripling, and return as a man, eh?"

"Not yet fully a man, uncle," Pip said. "But, I have learned things I never knew before."

"You even speak in a different manner," Ludmilla said. You sound like Galen. Did they teach you this, too?"

"And, many other things, Aunt Milla. I have much to tell you, but please, tell me what happened here."

Tears formed in Ludmilla's eyes. Auris put an arm around her shoulder. "The boy be right," he said. "Much has happened in his absence. Pip, just three suns ago, Tenkuk returned. His band was three times larger than it was when he first visited. They marched on the castle, burning the houses of anyone who dared stand in their way. The butcher and his son were slain, and many were injured."

"What about the castle guards? Did they not try to stop them?"

"Aye, they did," Auric said. "But, they be no match for the Barbarians. They were quickly subdued, and Tenkuk entered the castle. Pip, they took Queen

Daphne prisoner, and they left, burning a few houses as they departed."

Pip felt as he had been struck in the chest. The queen was a prisoner of the Barbarians! Such tragedy had never before struck the peaceful people of Pandara.

"Uncle," he said. "I must go immediately to the castle. When I return, I will tell you what has happened to me since I was taken away."

As if this new, assertive Pip was normal, Auric only nodded. "I understand, Pip," he said. "We be here when you return."

Pip spun on his heels and, without waiting for Vera and Tamara to follow, ran outside and leapt upon Nightshade's back. The two women were immediately behind him, and mounted, as he mentally wheeled Nightshade and urged him toward the castle at all the speed he could manage.

Chapter 16

The three riders brought their mounts to a halt in front of the large gates into the castle courtyard, and dismounted. Pip led the way, Vera on his right, Tamara his left.

The two guards at the gate, armed with pikes, eyed them nervously as they approached.

"Halt," the guard on the left said. A middle-aged man, with bowlegs and a slight paunch, he lowered his pike, and, despite the nervous look on his face, did not flinch as Pip walked up to him. "What business do you have here?"

Pip recognized him, a man named Godfred, who, Pip knew, had been a guardsman sine he was not much older than Pip.

"Godfred," he said. "Do you not recognize me? I am Pip, foundling of Auric and Ludmilla. I have many times delivered leather jerkins to you at the guard house."

The guard squinted, staring at Pip. A frown creased his craggy face. "Well, cross my old eyes," he said. "You do look like young Pip, but you do not talk like him."

"I have been away for a while, and have learned to speak differently. But, surely, you recognize me."

Slowly, the frown turned into a weak smile.

"Aye, I do believe you be him. But, I did not recognize you in all that finery, and armed to the teeth, you be. And, that steed you rode up on, that be a horse that belong to royalty. I recall, you be taken by them Barbarians a few moons back. How come you here, and with these two comely wenches?"

Pip sensed both Vera and Tamara tensing at his side. *Hold. He means no harm.* He waited a few heartbeats for their tension to ease. "I must speak with Galen," he said to Godfred. "It is a matter of urgency, and for his ears only."

"I know you to be a favorite of Councilor Galen. I guess it be okay for you to pass."

He resumed his post beside the gate. Both guards' heads swiveled as Pip and his companions passed, looks of curiosity on their faces. As they entered the courtyard, Pip heard the other guard say, "That be young Pip, for sure, but he be changed considerable. He even talk different."

"Mayhap being a captive of the Barbarians be the cause, Godfred said.

As they approached the large wooden doors to the audience chamber, they swung open, and Galen emerged from the dim interior.

He stared down at the three of them, and then his eyes widened, and he smiled.

"Pip, is that you? I hardly recognized you. I see your time with that monster, Tenkuk, did you no harm. By the spirits, lad, you seem to have grown a full inch since I last saw you struggling in that beast's clutches."

Pip bowed slightly. "Yes, Councilor Galen, it is me," he said. "My companions are Vera and Tamara from the Land of Fire. They rescued me from Tenkuk."

"Then, formidable they must be. Only two of them against that band, and you prevailed. You must tell me the story."

"I will tell you, but first, tell me, what of Queen Daphne? I understand the Barbarians came back."

At the mention of the queen's name, a look of immense sadness darkened the elderly man's face. "Yes," he said. "They came back. A full one hundred armed men. They fell upon the town with fierceness, but their main objective was here in the castle. Even had we equal numbers, we could not have stood against them." He wiped a wisp of errant hair from his brow. "Each of them was a hardened warrior, and they were ruthless. They said that since they had lost their guarantee, speaking, I think, of you, they would take the queen herself. When I heard that, I feared that you had perished. They took the queen, and Tenkuk threw her across the pommel of his saddle like a sack of grain. The butcher and his son attempted to stop them, and paid for their bravery with their lives. We also lost two of the guardsmen." A single tear had leaked from his left eye. He wiped at it absently. "I will never, as long as I live, forget the laughter from that madman se he rode off with the queen, never, ever, for as long as I live."

Pip's eyes narrowed, and his facial muscles tightened. "We must rescue the queen," he said.

"Brave words from one so young," Galen said. "But, I fear that we have few in Lands End, in all of Pandara for that matter, who can fight, and we do not have enough time to raise and train an army that would stand a chance against the Barbarians."

"We do not need an army, and we have no time to wait," Pip said. There was steel in his voice.

Are you thinking what I think you are thinking? Vera's voice in his mind sounded incredulous.

Yes. A small force of those with special abilities, and who can also fight, might be able to do what an army cannot do.

He is right. Tamara's voice came into his head. Vera stood silent and still for a few heartbeats, and then she nodded.

Galen watched the three of them as they stood silently, looking back and forth at each other. A knowing expression came upon his face.

"You are familiar to me, young lady," he said to Vera. "Your companion, though, I have not seen before. You say that you are from the Land of Fire?"

"Yes," Vera replied. "And, you have seen me here in Lands End many times. But, I am from the Land of Fire."

"Then, you must be the one Valcan said he would send to watch over Pip as he grew up."

Vera smiled and nodded. "I am one of many over the past summers who has had that responsibility."

Pip shot an incredulous look at Galen. "You knew my father?" he asked.

"Yes, Pip," Galen said. "Or, I suppose I should call you Valdar, since that is the name you were given at birth. Your father brought you to me in the middle of the night when you were but a swaddling. He said that your mother, the Princess Daria, had died, and he made me promise to find you a good home and see that you grew up knowing your mother's people. He said that he would send someone to help watch over you, but from a distance."

"Why? Why, all these summers did you never tell me?"

"You do not know how many times I wanted to do just that." Galen looked old. "But, your father made me promise that I would not. He wanted you to come into wisdom on your own; to know the life of the common folk. Only in that way, he said, could you grow up to be a proper king."

"There is wisdom in what Galen says," Vera said. "A king who does not know the lives of his subjects is but a tyrant."

A part of Pip felt resentful, but he, too, could see the merits of the way he had been brought up. "Well," he said. "the kingfisher has flown the nest. Now, we must rescue Queen Daphne."

"But, what about Pandara?" Galen asked. "It has never been without a sovereign before, and as the son of Daria, you are next in line for the throne. I know this is a heavy burden to place on your young shoulders, but you do have a responsibility to the people."

If choices like this are the lot of the king, Pip thought, I would rather remain a commoner. He was torn between his duty on the one hand, and his love for Daphne—his aunt. There had to be a way, though, to satisfy both.

"Wait," he said. "As acting regent in Queen Daphne's absence, I have the authority to make decisions, do I not?"

"Of course, your highness," Galen said. "Your word is law."

"And, my responsibility to the people is to ensure that there is someone from whom they can seek guidance, and who can provide protection, is that not right?"

"That is a rather simple way of putting it, but, essentially, you are correct."

"Then," said Pip. "My first royal act is to appoint Galen, the councilor, as acting regent. Your authority is mine; your word is mine, until I return with Queen Daphne."

"B-but, that has never been done before."

"There has never before been the need. Unusual circumstances call for unusual actions. You have been the queen's councilor for a long time. There is not another in Pandara with your wisdom or experience, and you truly care for the welfare of the people."

Tears welled up in Galen's eyes. "I see that you have grown more than physically, young prince," he said. "There is much of your mother in you. She was also one to take the path less trod. Am I to assume that you also inherited from your father as well?"

"Pip has all the powers his father possessed, and more," Vera said. "He is the one that the prophecies have foretold will bring our people back together."

Cocking his head to one side, Galen seemed lost in thought. "If that be the case, your plan just might work. Very well, Prince Valdar, I accept appointment as temporary regent, and I wish you the best of fortune in your efforts to rescue the queen."

"Thank you, Galen. Vera can you return and ask King Valdun's permission for any who wish to volunteer?"

"I will stay here with you," she said. She turned to Tamara. "Tamara, return and assemble a force. I think the ogres and trolls will be best."

"Do not forget the gnomes," Pip said. "I think they would resent being left out."

"Fine. The gnomes, too," Vera said. "Meet us on the road near where we rescued Pip."

Tamara nodded. "I will meet you there in two suns." She turned and left.

"It is a long journey to the Land of Fire and back," Galen said. "Can she make it."

"Oh yes," Pip said. "She can make it in even less time if she so wishes. But, it will take some time, no doubt, to assemble volunteers."

Galen shook his head. "I note, Vera, that you call our young prince Pip. Do your people not recognize him as the son of Valcan?"

"Of course, they recognize him. In the Land, he is known as Valdar. But, I have known him as Pip since he began to crawl, and as his cousin, I have to right to use his pet name."

"And, friend Galen, it would please me if you would call me Pip as well," Pip said. "The name Valdar is a heavy coat to wear among those who are close to me."

"Thank you. In private, you will be Pip, but in public, you must be Prince Valdar.

Charles Ray

Chapter 17

"Very well," Pip said. "I have been thinking that I would like one or two of the guardsmen with me in the rescue of the queen. It would be good for the guard morale, and if we are to bring the two people together, this would be a good place to start."

They had moved into a small antechamber off the audience chamber, a room where Galen kept his records and books, shelf upon shelf of bound volumes lined all four walls. A small desk sat in the center of the room, with a high-backed wooden chair for Galen, and two smaller wooden chairs in front of the desk, upon which Pip and Vera sat.

"That is a wise idea," Galen said. "I think Godfred and Melchor are the two most competent men at arms in Pandara, and they are sufficiently brave."

"I saw Godfred at the gate when we arrived. He is truly brave, and I will trust your judgment on the other."

"You have met them both. They always do sentry duty together. They do everything together. They come from the same village in the far west of Pandara, and joined the guard together."

"Then, I shall invite them both to accompany us."

Galen reached for a small silken cord that hung on the wall between two bookshelves, and pulled on it. Pip could hear the sound of a bell from somewhere in the distance. A moment later, one of the castle pages peeked around the door frame.

"Yes, Master Galen," the page said. "You summoned?"

"I want you to go to the captain of the guard," Galen said. "And, tell him to relieve Godfred and Melchor from duty at the gate, and send them to me."

The page nodded, but stood in the door, staring at Pip and the two women. "Yes, Master Galen," he said.

"Well, boy, do it now, and stop standing there with your tongue hanging out."

The young page, turned and fled.

About ten minutes later, there was a knock at the door.

"Enter," Galen said.

The two guards came in and stood at attention to either side of Pip and Vera.

"You wished to see us, Councilor Galen?" Godfred asked.

"Yes, I have a mission for you. But, first, I want to introduce you to someone." Galen nodded at Pip and Vera.

"We already be knowing young Pip," the second guard, Melchor said. "And, the young lady, I be seeing around the town before, although I not be knowing her name."

Galen stood and walked around the desk to stand in front of Godfred. "Yes," he said. "You know him as Pip, foundling of Auric the tanner. But, I am about to disclose to you his true identity. This is Valdar, Prince Valdar, son of Princess Daria of Pandara and Prince Valcan of the Land of Fire."

The guards' eyes widened as they stared at Pip. He and Vera stood.

"Y-your highness," Godfred said. "I not be knowing." He turned back to Galen." He turned back to Galen. "T-that mean, with the queen gone and all, Pip, er Prince Valdar, be the regent, right, sir?"

"That is correct. Prince Valdar is next in line of succession, and in the absence of the queen, he is ruler."

Both men faced Pip and dropped to one knee, their heads bowed.

"Stand, Godfred, stand Melchor," Pip said. "There is no need for that in here."

They stood, but remained stiffly at attention.

"Your highness," they said in unison. "We be ready to serve.

Pip looked at Galen, a question in his eyes. Galen nodded.

"I plan to take a small force into Barbaria to rescue Queen Daphne," Pip said. "I would be honored if the two of you would join me."

Godfred and Melchor looked at each other, and then back at Pip. "What size be the small force you plan to take, your highness?" Godfred asked.

"The four of us," Pip nodded toward Vera. "And, mayhap another six or so from the Land of Fire."

"That be only ten," Godfred said, counting on his fingers. "How can such a small force stand against the Barbarians?"

"I have no plan to confront the Barbarian army directly. My plan involves stealth. The smaller the force, the better we shall be able to move quickly and quietly. Are you will to accompany us?"

Neither man understood what Pip intended, but years of discipline had conditioned them to accept decisive leadership, and, for once in his life, for the first time in his life, Pip was decisive and commanding. Something in his voice, or the hard look in his eyes convinced them that he knew what he was talking about.

"Aye," Melchor said. "We be with you."

"Aye," said Godfred. "We will do anything to get the queen back."

"Good." Pip clapped both on the shoulder. "We leave on the morrow. For now, I want you to go with Vera. She will give you training for our quest."

"I be thinking a mere lass has naught to teach us," Godfred said. "We be ready."

"Mayhap, mayhap not," Pip said. "I would advise strongly against judging Vera by her gender so quickly. I think—I know—there is much she can teach you." He smiled and looked at Vera. *Go easy on them, at least at first.*

She smiled back. *I can only promise not to break any bones.*

Pip smiled as the two puzzled guards followed Vera out.

"Do I sense that two of Lands End's finest are about to get a lesson in humility?" Galen asked.

"Of that you can be sure," Pip said. "But, their pride will heal, and it just might save their lives."

Chapter 18

The next morning, at first light, two completely chastened guardsmen met Pip and Vera in front of the castle. They bowed to Pip, and saluted Vera. Melchor had a blue bruise under his left eye.

Pip smiled at Vera. *I hope you left them in a state to fight if need be.*

Fear not, cousin. They were no match for me, but they are capable fighters, and I am confident they will acquit themselves well.

"Are the two of you ready for our journey?" he asked the two guardsmen.

"We be ready, your highness," Godfred said. "More ready than before, thanks to the Lady Vera."

He did not have to elaborate. Pip could see in both men's eyes looks of respect for Vera. A person who could fight was rare in Pandara. A woman who could fight, and who could best two of the queen's best, was not someone to be taken lightly.

"Very well," he said. "Get your horses, and meet us back here within the hour."

They bowed, saluted Vera again, and scuttled off.

"They would not last a heartbeat against even a stripling from the Land," Vera said. "But, I believe they will do well against the Barbarians."

"The very fact of a Pandaran being willing to do battle should unsettle the Barbarians," Pip said wryly.

The two guardsmen soon came back, mounted upon gray stallions, horses that Pip would have once thought impressive before he met Nightshade.

"We be ready to ride, your highness," Godfred said.

Pip nodded and wheeled Nightshade around, heading south toward the Western Desert, the narrow strip of arid wasteland that lay between Pandara and Barbaria. He had to mentally urge Nightshade to set a slower pace than he usually would so that the guardsmen's horses could keep up, but even then, by the time they neared the point where Pip had made his escape from Tenkuk and his men, the two gray horses were straining.

He called a halt at a bend in the road.

Why are we stopping? Vera asked.

Godfred and Melchor are good and brave men, but I doubt if they have ever heard of an ogre or troll before, let alone seen one. I think we should prepare them. Besides, look at their horses. Even at the slow pace we've been riding, they are already winded.

You are right, of course.

"We will dismount, and rest here for a while," Pip said. The two guardsmen looked relieved. "Godfred, Melchor, come here please. I have something I must tell you before we get to the rendezvous point."

They sat in the shade of a large oak, while the four horses grazed on the short grass that grew at the side of the road. Nightshade and Star ate apart from the other two horses.

"What be it you must tell us?" Melchor asked, as he sat heavily on the ground.

"It is about the group that we are about to meet," Pip said. He then went on to explain the nature of the Folk who be joining them at the meeting place.

"I heard about ogres before," Melchor said. "Ogres be bad. I hear they rip the heads off you before they eat you."

"Aye," Godfred agreed. "But, I hear trolls be even worse. They dig under the houses and steal babies in the dead of night."

Pip rolled his eyes. He, too, had heard such tales from time to time growing up, though not as often as those living in the countryside. But, now, he knew different, so he tried as best he could to explain the Folk.

"If you say so, your highness," Godfred said. "They did save your life, so I reckon they ain't all bad."

"Just remember," Pip said. "They might have a different appearance, but inside, they are no different than you or I. Well . . . except for the powers they have."

"Powers? You mean like magic?" Melchor asked. "I been told ain't no such thing, really, as magic. You mean ogres and trolls have magic, too?"

"Yes, all the Folk of the Land of Fire have some kind of power that mun-, er, people of Pandara do not have."

"You be half them, your highness," Godfred said. "Be that to mean you have powers, too?"

Vera, who had been sitting nearby, quietly enjoying Pip's frustration with the two men, stood and came over.

"Pip, I mean, Prince Valdar, being half Folk and half . . . Pandaran, has powers beyond even the best of the Land of Fire," she said.

"B-but, Pip, er, your highness," Godfred said. "I be seeing you many a time being bullied by the other boys. Why did you never use your powers to fight them?"

"He did not know at the time of his powers. And, it would be wrong to misuse them."

The two men shook their heads, looking nervously at Pip.

"I would use my power in defense of others, or if my life was in danger," Pip said. "I now also know how to fight in the way warriors fight, so should like the bullies of Lands End attack me again, I would have no need of special powers."

"Pip even defeated an ogre in hand to hand combat," Vera said. "An ogre twice his height and three times his weight."

Godfred and Melchor stared at Pip, eyes wide and mouths agape.

"I be thinking there be one young bully in for a nasty surprise," Godfred said, smiling.

Yes, Pip thought, his special tormentors. He had some unfinished business with them.

Vera's thought pushed forcefully into his mind, *That would not be fair combat. They are no match for you, and you know that.*

Pip smiled at her. *I promise not to break their legs.*

Awakening

Charles Ray

Chapter 19

After the horses had rested, they remounted and continued their journey. As they rounded the last bend in the road before the meeting place, Pip was glad that he had taken the time to prepare the guardsmen for the Folk.

Almost all of his teachers were there, standing around on the edge of the road; the ogres, Walu and Wera, were in front of the others, bout it would have scarcely mattered, since they towered over them so; Nork the troll stood just behind them, along with Gork and Gellum, the gnomes, and Hermes, who had shed his scholar's robe for a silver tunic and pants.

When Pip approached, the two ogres sprang forward. Walu reached up and snatched Pip from Nightshade's back.

"Valdar, Walu miss you," he said, as he pulled Pip against his furry chest.

Not to be outdone, Wera clasped her long arms around them both. "Wera miss Valdun, too," she said.

Godfred and Melchor, thinking Pip was being attacked by these two great hairy monsters, moved to defend him, but suddenly found themselves forced to control their horses, that, at the sight of Walu and Wera had begun to whinny and buck, as if someone had placed hot coals under their saddles.

One part of Pip's mind was enjoying the round caresses of his friends, but another part sensed the trouble the guardsmen were having.

Nightshade, Star, please see if you can calm their horses.

A swift kick to the head would do it. Nightshade's voice had a touch of excitement in it.

Without hurting them, please.

Very well, but kicking them would give me pleasure.

The black stallion trotted over to the two gray horses, and nuzzled against the one that seemed the most excited, quickly calming it down, then he moved to the other. Soon, the two horses were calm, and their riders warily watching as the ogres released Pip from their embraces.

"Godfred, Melchor," Pip said. "Come, I want to introduce you to my friends."

"Why you bring mundanes?" Walu asked. "We not need help to rescue your queen."

"The people of the two lands need to start learning to work together," Pip said. "They are going with us."

Walu snorted, but kept his counsel. Nork came forward and clasped hands with Pip. "Valdar, how you fare since leaving us?"

"I have fared well, friend Nork. Where is Nabla? I would have thought she would be the first to volunteer."

"She did. But, she soon have little one. Not good for baby to be in battle before born."

"Congratulations, Nork. Soon you will be a father. Is this your first?" Pip realized that all the time he'd trained with the trolls, he'd never enquired about their family.

Nork cocked his head to one side and laid a finger on his nose. "Nork and Nabla have ten, I think," he said. "Little ones move around so much, sometimes hard to count."

Vera, who had dismounted and made her way to Pip through hellos and shoulder slaps, smiled. "Trolls spend a lot of time underground. When they are not digging for told or other precious metals, there is little else to do. They have large families."

Pip felt his cheeks getting warm. He was spared further embarrassment by Tamara, who had been standing quietly at the back of the group. She came forward and touched hands with Vera before bowing to Pip. "Valdar," she said. "I think this will be army enough to enter Barbaria, rescue your queen and return." She eyed the two guardsmen as if she had doubts about whether or not they were part of the 'army.' "I understand, though, why you must include Pandarans."

"Vera has taught them well," Pip said. "And, they are brave men. They will acquit themselves well if there be battle." He hoped, though, that there would be no battle.

"And, if that be they judgment, it is good enough for me." Hermes said as he stepped forward and touched hands with Pip. "I can see thee has grown since last we met."

Pip looked confused. "But, friend Hermes," he said. "It has only been a few suns since you last saw me."

"I meant not the growth of thy body, Valdar." The gray man smiled. "Thy mind and spirit, though, show much growth. And, thee has grown in wisdom."

The puzzled look on Pip's face remained, but with it was a smile. His old teacher was, as usual, he thought, playing his word games, games that had puzzled Pip during their time in the glade.

"Thank you," he said. "I am surprised, though, that you would come on such a mission."

Now, it was Hermes turn to look puzzled, and a bit offended. "We of the Folk do not shirk when one of ours is in need. And, does thee think that because I spend much of my day in contemplation and teaching that I am unable to do battle?" He gave Pip a wry smile. "I will have you know, young friend, that when I was not thine age, I was one of the best warriors in the Land. All Folk, male and female, as soon as they are weaned from the breast, are taught to defend themselves, with weapons, with hands, and with their powers."

"I meant no insult, friend Hermes," Pip said, his cheeks turning red.

"And, none taken, Valdar. Consider this as merely a continuation of thy lessons."

Chapter 20

The Great Desert

P_{ip} gave the guardsmen and their horses time to become accustomed to their strange new companions. Simple-minded creatures, once they sensed no danger from the new creatures, the horses settled down. It took Godfred and Melchor a bit longer, but, being from Pandara's western region, where fables of magic creatures were common, they soon accepted that the fables that they had thought to be mere fanciful tales were, in fact, true. Hardy men, they found the large hairy ogres only mildly unusual, and the gray, hairless trolls not at all unusual, although their appearance, their small size and knobby features, could cause one to look twice to make sure of what he or she was seeing. Hermes' pale, almost transparent, skin took them somewhat longer, but the old teacher had many summers' experience putting new students at ease, and soon had them captivated by the tales of some of his more unusual students.

Once he was satisfied that everyone in the group was willing to work together, he gave the signal to resume their journey south toward the desert. He took the lead, with Vera riding beside him. The Folk, except for Vera, went on foot. In addition to their ability to move great distances at the blink of an eye, they were also hardy, and could move at a trot, keeping up with horses, without even breathing hard.

Tamara had left her horse behind, preferring to move on foot with her Folk companions. Pip reckoned that he, being a mixture of both worlds, could probably also do the journey on foot, but Vera convinced him that, as leader of the group, he would command more respect, particularly from the two guardians, if he was mounted.

He was feeling more confident in the mission, and his ability to lead it, until he arrived at the stone marker that sat on the border between Pandara and the Great Desert.

He had heard stories about the wasteland called the Great Desert that sat between Pandara and Barbaria, but nothing he had heard prepared him for the sight before his eyes.

His newfound confidence dove into the pit of his stomach. Not even the Folk could easily such an expanse, he thought.

As far as the eye could see, stretching out before him, was a vision that brought to mind what Pip thought the underworld, the place sinners go when they die, would look like.

Stretches of sickly brown, barren earth, littered with rocks, ranging in size from the size of his fist to that of a small house, scrub brush, darker brown than the earth, that was as gnarled and knobby as the trolls' fists, tall, spindly plants with sharp spines as long as Pip's forearms, and interspersed with the flat, dry, rocky ground, were great expanses of yellow sand, some of it flat and undulating like waves on a great, dry ocean, some piled in high, wind-sculpted mounds that were taller than the turrets of the castle in Lands End.

He was convinced that nothing could survive such a place. The Barbarians, he thought, must be hardy folk to be able to cross it to conduct their raids into Pandara.

"What a fool I have been, Pip thought with a sinking heart. There is no way I can prevail over the Barbarians with this small group.

You must have faith in yourself. Vera's voice echoed in his head. *If you expect to fail, you surely will. If you trust in yourself, there is nothing you cannot do.*

She is right, Hermes' voice chimed in. *Thee hast yet to test thy power. Thee must have as much faith in thyself as we have in thee.*

But, look at this place. Nothing can survive here. How can we cross this, rescue Queen Daphne, and then cross back to return home?

The Barbarians do it, and so can we. Vera's voice was adamant. *You must not be conquered by fear, Pip.*

In addition, Hermes said, *Thee art mistaken. Things do survive in this place. Look thee yonder.*

Following Hermes' mental directions, Pip squinted. At first, he saw nothing, and then, a dark brown shape carted across the broken ground. Never had Pip seen or heard of such a creature. It had the head of a snake, with a long pink tongue that darted before it as it scurried over the rocks and dirt, a long, slender body that had lighter brown spots, and four slender legs that ended I long toes that clawed at the ground as it moved. When it stopped, the head raised, and wing-like appendages extended, creating a spiked crown around its head.

Then, Pip saw a shadow moving rapidly across the desert floor toward the creature. Looking up, he saw a yellow and black goshawk swooping down upon the unsuspecting animal. The bird, of a type he had seen occasionally in the fields outside Lands End soaring overhead on the lookout for field mice, seemed to have come out of nowhere. It swooped down and snatched the creature in one of its talons. It then idly flapped away, settling on the top of one of the spiny plants, where it made a quick meal of it.

Godfred rode his horse up next to Vera. "I never seen a creature like that what be a meal for the goshawk," he said. "Bit, if there be goshawks here, there be water, for sure, despite how dry it looks."

"Thee are correct," Hermes said. "Even in the desert, there is water and food, if one knows where to look."

"How long you reckon it take us to cross the desert?" Godfred asked no one in particular.

"the sun is not yet at its highest," Hermes said. "If we do not stop, we can be at the border of Barbaria by night fall."

Everyone looked to Pip for a decision. Despite his misgivings, he had talked them into coming on this mission, and it would be up to him to see it through. He remembered something Hermes had said during one of their sessions together in the glade, *When thee must face a difficult task, it is best to get it done without hesitation. Waiting does not make the task any easier.*

"Very well," he said. "We move on, and at nightfall, we make camp in Barbaria. Tomorrow, we move on to Gondwana and Queen Daphne."

With a jauntiness that was not matched by the gloom he felt, he urged Nightshade forward.

Charles Ray

Chapter 21

Barbaria

They went on at a steady pace, finding an oasis behind one of the dunes when the sun was at its highest. Even Nightshade appreciated the tepid water. Walu showed Pip how to get water from the spiny plants, the heart of which, under the tough exterior, was juicy, and really quite tasty.

They saw other animals, including a green and red snake with a triangular-shaped head, that moved in a sidewise motion over the sand. Its tail ended in little beads that made a rattling sound, like pebbles in a pewter mug, when the horses got close. Hermes cautioned Pip and the guardsmen to give this particular reptile a wide berth. "One bite from this one," he said. "And thee hast but a few heartbeats left to live."

The sun was low in the sky when the ground began to slope downward, and they saw signs of green. Barbaria had no border marker; the sand and parched earth simply stopped as if the gods had drawn a line across the earth. Before them lay rolling hills and copses of trees, with one or two small streams meandering across and around east toward the sea.

Pip pointed at a group of large trees on the bank of a stream.

"I think we should make camp yonder for the night," he said. "There is water and grass for the horses, and it is upon a rise, so that we can see if anyone approaches."

His spirit had lifted. The journey across the desert had not been as arduous as he had feared, even though it had taken its toll on the guardsmen and their mounts. Nightshade and Star hardly seemed to be affected, but Pip knew that even they were thirsty and in need of rest.

They set up camp among the trees, out of sight of casual passersby, and Pip organized sentries, with the guardsmen standing first watch. This way, he figured, they could rest when it got late, and be better prepared for the next morning's journey. In addition, he reckoned the ogres and trolls, with their powers, would be better guards during the late hours.

The ogres found some edible tubers among the trees, which they planned to make a meal of. They would be washed down with cold water from the stream. Godfred and Melchor complained about having no meat, but when they were given a taste of the tubers, found them to their liking, and ate them with gusto before going off to begin their guard duties.

As the sun dipped below the horizon, Pip went to the stream and sat on the bank, gazing into the gently flowing water, watching the glint of the last rays of sunlight bouncing off the water's surface. He sensed Vera's presence as soon as she came up beside him.

She sat next to him. They were silent for a moment. Finally, he turned to her.

"Cousin Vera," he said. "Do you think I am making the right decision, taking such a small force into the heart of Barbaria?"

She laid a hand on his shoulder. "It does not matter what I think, Pip. Look inside yourself. Do you think you are making the right decision?"

"I have thought of little else since this journey started. One part of me says that it is a fool's errand, and that I am likely to get many hurt for no good cause. Another part argues that we have no other choice. We cannot allow the Barbarians to continue to hold Queen Daphne prisoner."

"That we have not turned back tells me that the second part of you has won the argument," she said.

"Yes, I suppose it has. But, not because I believe I have made the right decision. It is because I can think of nothing else to do."

"Pip, you are learning one of the hardest, yet, most important, lessons of command. When a task must be fulfilled, you take the resources available to you, and do the best you can with them. You can do neither more nor less than that. You must learn to trust your inner voice and your instincts. What do they tell you?"

"It would be easier if there was only one inner voice," Pip said. "I have two voices inside my head, arguing opposite sides of the issue, and both argue their points quite loudly."

"In that case, what does your heart say?"

"My heart tells me that we must save the queen, or die trying."

"Then, it is your heart to which you must attend. Sleep well, commander. On the morrow, we will do or we will die."

She clasped his shoulder, then stood and walked away to her chosen sleeping place. Pip sat alone in the deepening night, listening to the chirping of the night insects, the gentle lapping of the water against the banks of the stream, and the voices inside his head.

Vera was right, though. His heart told him that he had but one choice; do his best to rescue his queen, and try to ensure that everyone on his mission returned safely to Pandara. He took her advice and listened to his heart. Soon, that voice overpowered the others.

He walked to the edge of the forest where the guardsmen were just being relieved by the troll. He told them to find a warm place beneath the trees and try to get some sleep, and then found a place not far from Vera, who had already fallen into deep slumber. He envied her ability to face the challenges facing them with such calm. Making a hollow in the soft grass, and pulling up more grass to make a pillow, he lay on his back, staring up at the stars that could be glimpsed through the gaps in the trees.

Just before he drifted off, a voice inside his head rang out loud and clear: *On the morrow, we will do what we must do.*

Chapter 22

At the first sign of sunrise, Pip sat up and stretched the stiffness of sleep from his arms, back and legs. Vera had already risen, and was sitting with her back against a tree, chewing on one of the tubers from the previous evening. He mumbled 'good morning' at her and went down to the stream to wash the sleep from his eyes. His misgivings of the night before were merely a dull feeling at the back of his mind.

He returned and sat next to her, taking one of the tubers from her, and quickly eating it.

After everyone had completed their morning ablutions and eaten, he called the group together to discuss their strategy.

He turned to Hermes who seemed to be more familiar with the territory of Barbaria than anyone else present.

"Friend Hermes, how long to Gondwana from here?"

Hermes closed his eyes and folded his arms across his chest. After a moment, he opened his eyes. "About half a day's journey," he said. "And, we will be on the outskirts of the city. I believe the queen will be held in the castle, which sits on a hill in the center. It is surrounded by the hovels of peasants and shops of merchants, and will be difficult to approach unnoticed."

"Is there any place of concealment outside the town from which we can view the castle?"

"The forest runs along the east and north of town," Hermes said. "If thee wishes to approach the rear of the castle unseen, I believe that would be the best way to go."

"Very well, then," said Pip. "We will stay in the forest and go there. Nork, you go with Hermes and scout the way to make sure we can proceed unobserved. The rest of us will follow. Find a point from which we can observe the castle, and we will join you there and decide our next move."

The troll nodded and trotted off, followed close behind by the pale teacher. When they had disappeared in the trees, Pip gave the order for the others to move. He mounted Nightshade to take the lead. Vera mounted Star and rode up beside him.

"You sounded like a real military commander just now," she said.

"Now, if I can only keep it up, I might even convince myself that I know what I am doing."

She laughed and wheeled Star around to take her place behind him.

Pip instructed Godfred and Melchor to ride behind Vera, and for the rest of the company to follow, with the ogres in the rear to guard against a surprise from that quarter. He then urged Nightshade to move out in a steady canter, following Hermes and Nork.

He set a good, quick pace, but not so fast as to tire the guardsmen's horses, careful to stay well inside the tree line.

At midday, Nork and Hermes rejoined them as they stopped in a clearing to rest and eat.

"Just ahead, no more than an hour's ride, there are people working in the fields," Hermes said. "The peasants are under guard by five armed warriors. It would appear that the people do not work of their own free will."

That news, for some reason, did not surprise Pip after his own experience with Tenkuk and his men. "Will we be able to pass them by without being notices?" he asked.

"Yes, as long as we stay well in the forest, it should not alert them," Hermes responded. "The guards do not seem to be there to protect the workers, but rather, to ensure that they work. Nork and I were able to approach quite close and no one noticed."

"That is good," Pip said. "Now, if only there was a supply of fresh water nearby. It would be good to water our mounts, and I think that Godfred and Melchor could use some as well."

Hermes walked around the clearing, peering at the ground, until he found a level spot that was bare of foliage. Kneeling, he used his hands to scoop earth until he'd made a depression the size of a wash basin. He then waved his hands over the depression, his eyes closed tightly. In a short while, the depression filled with clear water."

"By the gods," Godfred said. "I know not how you did that, but I man like you would be handy to have on guard patrol."

Hermes smiled and nodded his acceptance of the compliment. "Thee may drink now," he said. "After all have slaked their thirst, we can allow the horses to drink."

Why must the two-legs get water first? Nightshade snorted and pawed at the ground.

Pip sent a placating emotion at his horse. *If it makes you feel better, you and the other horses can drink before me. Many in Pandara do not like drinking the same water as their animals. Give them time.*

Nightshade snorted and his flanks quivered.

Star walked over next to him and pushed her nose against his neck. *It matters not. We can go much longer without water than the two-legs, It is only right that they be allowed to slake their thirst first.*

Pip sent a private thanks to the mare. She raised her hade and snorted a horse's version of a laugh at him.

Pip looked up. High above him, he saw a circling goshawk. He could not be sure, but he felt that it was the same bird he'd seen in the desert. Out of curiosity, he sent out a gentle mental probe. The bird's circles grew tighter, and it dropped lower in the sky. In his mind, Pip could see the surrounding countryside for many, many leagues. In the far distance, he could even see the dark spires of the castle of Gondwana.

At first, the images confused him, but in a few moments, he realized that he was seeing through the goshawk's eyes. He increased the power of his probe, and bird went into a tight spiral, ending up gliding to rest on his shoulder.

The bird's talons gripped his shoulder, tight enough to maintain its perch, but not enough to break through the tunic. Pip looked down into the yellow eyes. He could not sense words in the bird's thoughts, but there was a sense of acceptance of this strange four-legged creature with two heads; and more importantly, Pip sensed trust.

"Looks like you have made a new friend." Vera walked up, smiling at him.

"Yes, it would seem so," Pip said. "I can also see through his eyes."

"Amazing," she said. "That gives us an extra pair of eyes. It might prove to be useful."

"That was my thought as well." If I can command him to do it, he can fly ahead of Nork and Hermes. That will give us more warning of any danger that might lie ahead."

He then sent a gentle signal to the bird to fly, and sent it in the direction of the castle. With a squawk, the goshawk spread its wings, and with a spring of its legs took flight. It was soon lost in the distance, but Pip, when he concentrated, could see the land below as clearly as if he was looking with his own eyes. He saw the group that his scouts had reported, twenty peasants hacking away at the hard ground under the watchful eyes of five men in black, who were armed with broadswords and pikes. Their horses were tethered to nearby trees. Just as Hermes had said, the guards were only watching the workers, paying no attention to the surrounding area.

He nodded at Hermes and Nork to resume their scouting, and ordered the others to be prepared to move out.

Charles Ray

Chapter 23

With the goshawk giving him a panoramic view of the land, and the assurances of Hermes and Nork on the ground, Pip began to feel better about his mission. His little troop made good time, seeing only the occasional group of hunters or shepherds, all of whom they were able to evade, thanks to their scouts on the ground and in the air.

The land of Barbaria, though not as desolate as the desert through which they had passed, was, when compared to the Pandaran countryside, or the Land of Fire, like a wasteland. There were large fields, being tended by groups under guard, and the few individual homesteads they saw were but small mud huts with thatched roofs, some with small gardens that looked as if they were barely large food sufficient to keep a small family from starvation. Except for the warriors, who looked well-fed and clothed in neat black uniforms, everyone looked bedraggled and hungry. Even those peasants laboring in the large fields under the watchful eye of guards looked tired and hungry.

"This place looks more like an encampment of slaves than a kingdom," Vera said, after they had passed another group of workers.

"It does appear that Ostro rules through fear rather than loyalty," Pip said. "The people in Pandara have complaints from time to time, but compared to what I see here, they are very happy."

Vera nodded and frowned. "A king who rules through force and fear must not sleep very well at night."

"His men at arms seem to be well cared for," Pip said. "At least, much better than the common folk."

"Loyalty purchased is not to be relied upon. I warrant that his warriors are available to the highest bidder."

"How does a king who is so cruel remain upon the throne? Surely, there must be many who would oppose such treatment, and would rise up against him."

"I think, Pip, that your answer lies in some lonely grave, or perhaps many graves. One who rules is such a manner is also likely to spend much time identifying potential opposition, and then removing that opposition—permanently."

Pi; shook his head. "We have much land in Pandara that is not being used," he said. "Why do the people not just cross the desert? They would be welcomed."

"One who rules through fear, also rules through enforced ignorance," Vera said. "If the people know only Barbaria, they cannot form the will to leave for the unknown. Have you not noticed the guards? This land is but a prison, and the people do not know that freedom lies just beyond the desert."

Once again, Pip shook his head and sighed. He felt great sympathy for the common Barbarians, but he had to push that to the back of his mind. His principal objective was to rescue Queen Daphne for the people of Pandara, his people. The Barbarians would have to wait for another day.

I know what you think, cousin. But, people must be willing to save themselves.

But, everyone can use help. Did you not watch over me as I grew up? Did the people of the Land not teach me what I did not know, even though it was within me all the time?

You are becoming far too wise, my little cousin. What happened to the lost little boy who I had to save from bullies?

You chased that little boy away. I am now what I am, and can be no other. But, fear not, Cousin Vera, I was but thinking. We are here to rescue the queen, and nothing must interfere with that. Another day, mayhap, that is a different matter.

Vera shook her head. *Let us get through one adventure before you undertake another, cousin. One step at a time, one step at a time.*

Pip nodded agreement, but his expression was hard. Vera could not pry too deeply into his mind, but she had no need. The look on his face would tell her that her was warning was unheeded. Pip was planning something. He was not yet sure what he would do, but he knew he would do something.

"Vera," Pip said. "I was told that the Folk and the people of Pandara once lived together. Did the people of Barbaria also not live among us?"

"Yes, a long, long time ago, all of the people of this world lived together in peace. We Folk, though, were the only ones with power, and the others were jealous and afraid of us. The people of Pandara merely wished not to live among us. Others, and among them were those you now know as Barbarians, wished to destroy us. Because of our powers, however, they could not, so they, too, removed themselves. But, the hatred has lasted. They are the sworn enemies, not only of Pandara, but the Land of Fire as well. Only their fear of our power keeps them from invading."

"I wonder why they have not invaded Pandara," Pip said.

"They raid your land and steal your crops and stock, do they not? Mayhap they wish to keep the goose alive that lays the golden eggs so they can continue to steal the eggs. Then again, mayhap they have not had a leader rash enough or brave enough to try it."

"Until now. Ostro, or at least his general, Tenkuk, has enough courage to come into our kingdom and take our ruler hostage. Is that not an invasion?"

"Tenkuk did deliver Ostro's letter of proposal to the queen. Perhaps that was he way of taking over Pandara without invading."

"Queen Daphne would never accept a forced marriage. She would die first."

"I think that would not matter to Ostro. He might even help her die. Without a ruler, Pandara would be like a lamb cut off from its mother. You have no army, and your people would be easy prey."

"Then, that means we must not fail. We must rescue the queen."

Awakening

Charles Ray

Chapter 24

Gondwana

The sun was low in the sky by the time they reached the copse of trees on a hill overlooking the castle of Gondwana.

Everyone crowded to the edge of the trees for a look.

The castle was an imposing structure, constructed with black stones of such a deep hue they showed blue highlights in the fading light of the day. At each corner stood four towers, with outward-facing firing slits. The towers were even higher than the vantage point from which they viewed them. A walled walkway, with firing slits every six paces, connected the towers. In the center of the structure, and even taller tower, capped with a domed roof, stood out.

"The center tower is where Ostro has his quarters and audience chamber," Hermes said. "The guard quarters and cells for prisoners are on the first floor, and Ostro is at the top, above the cells. The center tower is connected to each guard tower by a covered

213

way which thee cannot see from here. There are rumors that there is a tunnel from the central tower to the outside of the castle should Ostro need to flee, but I cannot verify this."

"How is it, Hermes, that you know so much about the castle?"

The pale man sighed. "In my youth, I was impetuous and full of the desire to explore," he said. "I had not yet developed my full powers, and was, I must confess, quite foolish. I decided to explore this land alone, and ended up a guest of Ostro for some ten suns."

"How did you escape?"

"When they were finally convinced that neither torture nor opportuning would force me to reveal the secrets of the Folk, they confined me to a cell on the first level. In my enforced solitude, I was able to meditate and call upon my power to travel. I imagine they were quite surprised to find my cell empty."

"If this happened when *you* were young, Ostro has been on the throne for a long time."

Hermes' brows rose. "I am not *that* old, young Valdar," he said. "But, Ostro was himself a youth at the time. He inherited the throne after his father suffered an unfortunate, and fatal, accident. I believe this is why he himself has not taken a bride from among his own people. The path to Barbaria's throne, I am told, is always a bloody one."

Godfred walked up to the two men. "Prince Valdar, it soon be dark. Will we be making camp until morning?"

"No," Pip said. "We will wait until darkness falls. Under the cover of darkness, we should have the element of surprise."

The guardsman, who had never had to deal with anything more complicated than a small raiding party, with the exception of Tenkuk's raid on Lands End, and then, only in daylight, looked at Pip, his brow furrowed. "You sure that be a good idea, Your Highness?"

Vera walked up behind Godfred. "Pip is correct," she said. "If we try to assault the castle by day, we will have no chance. In darkness, we might be able to get in, get the queen, and get out without having to fight the entire guard."

Where his knowledge of tactics came from, Pip could not say, but it had seemed the prudent course of action. He was glad to see that Vera validated his feeling.

"Godfred, you and Melchor will remain here, and be prepared to defend our backs if need be," he said.

Godfred looked relieved at not having to enter the castle. He saluted and withdrew to talk to Melchor. Just then, the Goshawk appeared out of the darkening sky and lit on Pip's shoulder. The bird made small peeping sounds near Pip's ear.

"You can understand him?" Vera asked.

"Yes. It is not exactly words, more like images, but he is saying that he can get into the castle and locate the queen."

Vera's face brightened. "That will make our task much simpler. I was worried that we would have to waste time searching for the cells."

"I will wait until full dark and send him into the castle to scout," Pip said. "You know, I need to give him a name. I cannot just keep calling him, 'him', now can I?"

The bird nuzzled its beak against Pip's ear, making sounds that were more like a dove than the raptor that it was.

"I think he likes the idea," Vera said.

"I will call him Talus."

The bird let out a squawk, lifted off Pip's shoulder, and flew straight up. It soared in circles for a few moments, and then gently dropped back onto its perch next to Pip's left ear.

"Does that mean he likes the name?" Vera asked.

"Yes, he likes it very much. From now on, you are Talas, then," he said to the bird, which settled down on his shoulder and began preening its feathers.

"What is our plan of assault, Pip?" Vera asked.

"Assemble everyone, and I will explain it."

When everyone was gathered in a circle around him, Pip made eye contact with each before beginning to tell them his plan for the assault upon the castle. "Vera, and I will go directly to the queen's cell once we are inside the castle." He said. "Hermes, Walu, and Nork will cover the entrance to that building in the case the guards are alerted to our presence, while Tamara, Gork and Gellum will cover the front of the castle. If there are reinforcements from outside, it is likely to come from that direction. Godfred and Melchor will cover our rear. Once Talus has located the queen's cell, we will move out."

Everyone agreed that the plan was about the best they could do under the circumstances, and with the help of Talus in locating precisely where Queen Daphne was being held, just might work.

"Bird also useful to let know if guards near any of us," Walu said.

Talus, perched on Pip's shoulder, looked at him and squawked, and then put his beak near Pip's ear and made clucking sounds.

"Bird agree?" Walu asked.

"Yes," Pip said. "And, he expressed surprise that such a hairy one could come up with such a good idea."

Walu grunted. "Bird be careful," he said. "Walu not eat meat, but can make exception."

Charles Ray

Chapter 25

When the sun had finally slipped below the horizon, and the only light piercing the obsidian darkness were the torches high on the castle wall, and the occasional light from lanterns in the hovels and shops that clung to the hillside on three sides of the castle, Hermes walked to Pip's side.

"Valdar," he said. "I know that thee has planned that both of our groups will scale the wall and try to get past the sentries, but I have been thinking, and I would like to offer thee and alternative plan, if thee will."

"Of course, my friend, if you have a better plan, I am willing to listen."

"Since the cells are on the first level, it would be better if thee entered on that level."

"Of course, it would, but I do not think they will open the castle gate to let us enter."

"Yes, I am aware of that. But, there is another way in, and thee will not need permission. Look at yonder wall, about equal distance between the two towers. Doest thee see the dark area at the base of the wall?"

Pip looked at the direction Hermes indicated, and after peering for a while, saw the area he'd described, "Yes," he said. "I see it. What is it?"

Hermes cleared his throat. "That is the outlet for the castle's waste. It is a narrow tunnel that starts at the central tower."

"Waste?" Pip's eyes rounded. "You mean the garbage from the castle kitchen?"

Hermes tried his best to look innocent, but not quite pulling it off. "Well, yes, that also. But, it is the outlet for all waste from the castle, which means it will also connect to the cell area."

"And, you are saying that we should wade through that to get into the castle?" Pip had an incredulous look on his face. "The moment we emerged from the tunnel, we would be discovered because of the odor. Oh, and, how are we to wade through such filth without contracting some deadly disease?"

"Thee would not have to wade *through* it," Hermes said. There is a small ledge which allows workmen to clean it when it becomes stopped up. The inside of the castle smells not much better than the tunnel, so it is doubtful that thy smell will be noticed. There is also little chance of thee becoming infected; the tunnel is less than a hundred paces long from the outside to the central tower, so thee would not be long inside."

Pip wrinkled his nose. "What of the odor? It would be difficult to take for a hundred paces."

Hermes reached into his tunic and removed several small, oval, green leaves.

"If thee holds this under thy nose, it will lessen the odor."

Pip trusted his former teacher, despite his misgivings about entering the waste tunnel. "Okay, Hermes, what you say makes sense. We will enter through the tunnel and rescue the queen, while you and the rest watch the towers. We move out as soon as Talus has found the queen."

Everyone nodded, and Pip signaled the goshawk to begin its search. The bird squawked once and lifted off.

With nothing left to do but wait as the images of the darkened landscape below, as seen by Talus, flashed through Pip's mind, he squatted on the ground. A scowl creased his face.

Vera squatted beside him, and placed a hand on his shoulder. *Worry not, cousin. Follow your instincts. A weak commander would refuse to change his plans or listen to others. You showed wisdom, and handled things well.*

I hope you are right. I just wish there was a better way. I know that Hermes' suggestion is better than mine, but I worry about the way we will have to enter the castle.

Vera pulled a small bunch of the oval leaves from her tunic. *This will help with the odor, and the tunnel is not very long. Just do not breathe deeply, and hold your breath as much as you can.*

Am I the last one to know what is going on here? You knew that Hermes would suggest the tunnel, did you not?

I noticed it earlier, and thought it might be a better way in. I am sure that you would have also when you saw it.

But, these leaves; you and Hermes have them. It is as if you knew in advance that they would be needed.

Oh no, cousin. We always take these with us when we travel. They are useful for more than masking odors. They also heal minor wounds, and repel the bugs that bite in the night.

Why has no one told me of this before? He took two of the leaves from her, and added them to the one in his tunic that he had gotten from Hermes.

Sometimes, even teachers make mistakes. I think that Hermes thought either Tamara or I had told you, and I assumed that he would. Please accept my sincerest apologies, cousin.

Never mind. Better late than never. He mentally summoned Talus, who swooped down out of the gloom and lit on his shoulder, rubbing its beak against Pip's ear.

He instructed the goshawk to fly over the wall and give him a look at the towers and the courtyard, and then to enter the castle's first level and locate Daphne's cell. Talus squawked and flew off into the dark sky.

Through Talus' enhanced vision, Pip could see the castle from above as the goshawk flew a wide circle around the top of the wall. There were two guards in each tower, and they were particularly alert, but their attention was focused on the ground below. It should be easy for Hermes and the others to overpower them, should that become necessary, he thought. The courtyard below was empty, and Talus flew down and into the second level through an open window.

The room he entered was large and rectangular, empty except for a long wooden table with benches down both sides, and a large stove at one end. It was dimly lit by large tallow candles in sconces in each corner. The floor was littered with dust, indicating that it hadn't been swept for a long time. Ludmilla would have a conniption if she saw it, Pip thought.

The door, which was directly opposite the window, was ajar. Talus flew into the hallway. It was unlit, but the goshawk's eyes, used for finding prey by night, enable Pip to see that it too was empty. Talus came to a junction that branched off in three directions. Two of the corridors were unlit, but the third, the one in the center, was lit at intervals by small torches set high in the wall. At the end of this corridor, Pip could see a wooden door with a rectangular opening at head height.

Talus flew down the lit hall and stopped, hovering in front of the opening. Beyond the door was a small antechamber, and inside, Pip could see a corpulent, middle-aged guard, dressed in black, sitting on a wooden bench near another door. The guard, his head intermittently dropping toward his chest, was unaware of Talus at the opening. Talus flew to the rear door, and hovered in front of an opening in it. Beyond the door, Pip could see four cells with iron bars for doors. In the second cell, sitting on a rough-hewn wooden cot, was Daphne. Her dress was smudged with dirt, and her hair had come undone, but she still had a regal expression on her face. Ever the queen, Pip thought, even when a prisoner.

"Talus has found the queen," he said. "Everyone knows what they are to do. When Vera and I have the queen, I will send a signal, and we will rendezvous back here."

Each group moved into the darkness, off to their assigned tasks. Hermes, with the ogres and troll following, went toward the nearest tower. Tamara and the gnomes, went through the trees toward the front of the castle. Godfred and Melchor stood behind revetments they had constructed from boughs and limbs of dead trees they had found, from where they could observe the rear of the castle, and some of the land beyond, without being seen themselves.

Pip took one of the leaves from his tunic. "I hope this works," he said.

Vera took a leaf from her tunic. "Do not worry, cousin," she said. "It will."

"I do not mean the mission," he said. "I mean this leaf." He turned and began trotting toward the opening in the castle wall.

She chuckled as she trotted after him.

When the sun had finally slipped below the horizon, and the only light piercing the obsidian darkness were the torches high on the castle wall, and the occasional light from lanterns in the hovels and shops that clung to the hillside on three sides of the castle, Hermes walked to Pip's side.

"Valdar," he said. "I know that thee has planned that both of our groups will scale the wall and try to get past the sentries, but I have been thinking, and I would like to offer thee and alternative plan, if thee will."

"Of course, my friend, if you have a better plan, I am willing to listen."

"Since the cells are on the first level, it would be better if thee entered on that level."

"Of course, it would, but I do not think they will open the castle gate to let us enter."

"Yes, I am aware of that. But, there is another way in, and thee will not need permission. Look at yonder wall, about equal distance between the two towers. Doest thee see the dark area at the base of the wall?"

Pip looked at the direction Hermes indicated, and after peering for a while, saw the area he'd described, "Yes," he said. "I see it. What is it?"

Hermes cleared his throat. "That is the outlet for the castle's waste. It is a narrow tunnel that starts at the central tower."

"Waste?" Pip's eyes rounded. "You mean the garbage from the castle kitchen?"

Hermes tried his best to look innocent, but not quite pulling it off. "Well, yes, that also. But, it is the outlet for all waste from the castle, which means it will also connect to the cell area."

"And, you are saying that we should wade through that to get into the castle?" Pip had an incredulous look on his face. "The moment we emerged from the tunnel, we would be discovered because of the odor. Oh, and, how are we to wade through such filth without contracting some deadly disease?"

"Thee would not have to wade *through* it," Hermes said. There is a small ledge which allows workmen to clean it when it becomes stopped up. The inside of the castle smells not much better than the tunnel, so it is doubtful that thy smell will be noticed. There is also little chance of thee becoming infected; the tunnel is less than a hundred paces long from the outside to the central tower, so thee would not be long inside."

Pip wrinkled his nose. "What of the odor? It would be difficult to take for a hundred paces."

Hermes reached into his tunic and removed several small, oval, green leaves.

"If thee holds this under thy nose, it will lessen the odor."

Pip trusted his former teacher, despite his misgivings about entering the waste tunnel. "Okay, Hermes, what you say makes sense. We will enter through the tunnel and rescue the queen, while you and the rest watch the towers. We move out as soon as Talus has found the queen."

Everyone nodded, and Pip signaled the goshawk to begin its search. The bird squawked once and lifted off.

With nothing left to do but wait as the images of the darkened landscape below, as seen by Talus, flashed through Pip's mind, he squatted on the ground. A scowl creased his face.

Vera squatted beside him, and placed a hand on his shoulder. *Worry not, cousin. Follow your instincts. A weak commander would refuse to change his plans or listen to others. You showed wisdom, and handled things well.*

I hope you are right. I just wish there was a better way. I know that Hermes' suggestion is better than mine, but I worry about the way we will have to enter the castle.

Vera pulled a small bunch of the oval leaves from her tunic. *This will help with the odor, and the tunnel is not very long. Just do not breathe deeply, and hold your breath as much as you can.*

Am I the last one to know what is going on here? You knew that Hermes would suggest the tunnel, did you not?

I noticed it earlier, and thought it might be a better way in. I am sure that you would have also when you saw it.

But, these leaves; you and Hermes have them. It is as if you knew in advance that they would be needed.

Oh no, cousin. We always take these with us when we travel. They are useful for more than masking odors. They also heal minor wounds, and repel the bugs that bite in the night.

Why has no one told me of this before? He took two of the leaves from her, and added them to the one in his tunic that he had gotten from Hermes.

Sometimes, even teachers make mistakes. I think that Hermes thought either Tamara or I had told you, and I assumed that he would. Please accept my sincerest apologies, cousin.

Never mind. Better late than never. He mentally summoned Talus, who swooped down out of the gloom and lit on his shoulder, rubbing its beak against Pip's ear.

He instructed the goshawk to fly over the wall and give him a look at the towers and the courtyard, and then to enter the castle's first level and locate Daphne's cell. Talus squawked and flew off into the dark sky.

Through Talus' enhanced vision, Pip could see the castle from above as the goshawk flew a wide circle around the top of the wall. There were two guards in each tower, and they were particularly alert, but their attention was focused on the ground below. It should be easy for Hermes and the others to overpower them, should that become necessary, he thought. The courtyard below was empty, and Talus flew down and into the second level through an open window.

The room he entered was large and rectangular, empty except for a long wooden table with benches down both sides, and a large stove at one end. It was dimly lit by large tallow candles in sconces in each corner. The floor was littered with dust, indicating that it hadn't been swept for a long time. Ludmilla would have a conniption if she saw it, Pip thought.

The door, which was directly opposite the window, was ajar. Talus flew into the hallway. It was unlit, but the goshawk's eyes, used for finding prey by night, enable Pip to see that it too was empty. Talus came to a junction that branched off in three directions. Two of the corridors were unlit, but the third, the one in the center, was lit at intervals by small torches set high in the wall. At the end of this corridor, Pip could see a wooden door with a rectangular opening at head height.

Talus flew down the lit hall and stopped, hovering in front of the opening. Beyond the door was a small antechamber, and inside, Pip could see a corpulent, middle-aged guard, dressed in black, sitting on a wooden bench near another door. The guard, his head intermittently dropping toward his chest, was unaware of Talus at the opening. Talus flew to the rear door, and hovered in front of an opening in it. Beyond the door, Pip could see four cells with iron bars for doors. In the second cell, sitting on a rough-hewn wooden cot, was Daphne. Her dress was smudged with dirt, and her hair had come undone, but she still had a regal expression on her face. Ever the queen, Pip thought, even when a prisoner.

"Talus has found the queen," he said. "Everyone knows what they are to do. When Vera and I have the queen, I will send a signal, and we will rendezvous back here."

Each group moved into the darkness, off to their assigned tasks. Hermes, with the ogres and troll following, went toward the nearest tower. Tamara and the gnomes, went through the trees toward the front of the castle. Godfred and Melchor stood behind revetments they had constructed from boughs and limbs of dead trees they had found, from where they could observe the rear of the castle, and some of the land beyond, without being seen themselves.

Pip took one of the leaves from his tunic. "I hope this works," he said.

Vera took a leaf from her tunic. "Do not worry, cousin," she said. "It will."

"I do not mean the mission," he said. "I mean this leaf." He turned and began trotting toward the opening in the castle wall.

She chuckled as she trotted after him.

Chapter 26

It did not take long for them to reach the tunnel entrance. Pip could smell the foul odor, though, long before they arrived. Upon entering the dark entrance in the wall, and seeing the oily, oozing liquid flowing through the tunnel, he had second thoughts, but there was the ledge that Hermes had promised, and, he didn't want to appear hesitant in front of Vera. He held the leaf under his nose, and tried to breathe as little as possible. While the minty smell of the leaf did cut the odor somewhat, it was still strong enough to make his eyes water.

He bent at the waist and entered the tunnel, careful to hug the wall to stay as far from the evil-smelling stream as possible. Vera followed close behind.

He inched along slowly, fearful that he might slip and fall into the noxious water.

Do not worry, Pip. Trust your senses to guide you.

With that part of his mind that was not focused on Talus as he flew from room to room on the first level of the castle, Pip reached out and formed a picture of the tunnel. It surprised him that, even though the tunnel was unlit and as dark as the inside of a cave, he could 'see' the ledge beneath his feet. Reassured, he picked up the pace in order to lessen the time he and Vera would have to spend breathing the fetid fumes.

He was so concentrated on the ledge, he bumped into the gate at the end of the tunnel. Hermes had been correct; it had only been about a hundred paces, but engulfed in the foul smell of the place, it had seemed like a thousand. Pip pushed at the wooden gate, and it swung aside easily. He and Vera crawled through the opening, entering a room that he recognized from Talus' scouting.

He was in the large dining chamber. By the gods, he thought, they dump the waste from chamber pots in the same room in which they feed people. He thought it miraculous that everyone who dined there was not infected with some horrible disease.

They moved away from the opening and nearer the door into the castle interior. Away from the worst of the waste tunnel's odor, they both took deep breaths. While the air in the dining room was dusty, and smelled of stale food and sweat, it was sweet compared to the tunnel.

The door was ajar, and peering through the crack between door and jamb, Pip noticed that the hallway outside was empty. He motioned to Vera and slipped out of the room.

They moved slowly toward a junction in the corridor, on the alert for anyone who might be moving about the castle, but a part of Pip's mind was still focused on Talus. From the view Pip got, he reckoned Talus was up in the rafters looking down. He was looking down at a large room containing many items of gold and silver, clay vases of many colors, and a large number of weapons, swords, lances, and bows, hanging on the walls.

Near the center of the room was a large throne, made of some dark wood, with a high back, and armrests carved in the shape of snakes with gaping maws. In front of the throne were two plain wooden chairs, set so that their occupants were forced to look up to see the occupant of the throne.

Sitting on the throne was the fattest person Pip had ever seen. The man's body seemed to balloon in all directions, draping over the throne and threatening to burst out of the ornate black tunic with gold filigree on collar and sleeves. His head was huge, with protruding ears and a bulbous nose, and small, porcine eyes under bushy brows. The lips were fleshy and pouty above a fleshy chin of three folds of fat. This must be Ostro, Pip thought.

There were two other people in the room. Pip recognized Tenkuk, sitting loosely on one of the chairs, his right leg draped over an armrest. The other man was spindly and curious, hardly bigger than a gnome, hairless as a troll, and dressed in a black robe devoid of any other decoration. He had high, flat cheekbones, a flat nose, and almond-shaped eyes that gazed up adoringly at Ostro.

Pip was able to see everything in the room as Talus swiveled his head, but he signaled the bird to focus on the three figures. Then, he discovered to his surprise, that he could not only see what was happening, he could hear what was being said, as well.

"Has the wench changed her stubborn mind?" Ostro asked, pointing a stubby finger at the smaller man.

"N-no, celestial majesty," the man said. "She remains as stubborn as the day Tenkuk brought her here."

"Kordan, I have given you more than enough time. Why have you failed me?"

"M-most noble and beneficent majesty," the little man said. "I have tried everything I know. She says that she would rather be eaten by rabid wolves than do as you so graciously ask."

"That could be arranged," Tenkuk said. "It would serve her right."

"But, if she is dead, how can I marry her and merge our two kingdoms?" Ostro looked petulant.

"T-that is right," Kordan said. "You cannot expect his supreme majesty to marry a corpse."

Tenkuk snorted. "Of course not, you piece of pig offal. But, your majesty, if Daphne is dead, Pandara has no ruler. I could then take a small army and impose your protection over them. You would have Pandara without having to marry that she-devil."

"My loyal friend and advisor, Tenkuk." Ostro clapped his pudgy hands. "As usual, you have proposed a brilliant strategy. Then, with the population of both kingdoms, I could build an army that would be able to stand against anything."

"This is true, majesty," Tenkuk said. The Land of Fire would not be able to stand against the combined weight of Barbaria and Pandara. I could have an army ready to take the field within six moons of our, I mean, your, assumption of control over Pandara."

"And, we would rid the world once and for all of that race of devil spawn." Ostro rubbed his hands together and smiled evilly. "It is decided then. Daphne will not share the air with the living when the sun rises."

Tenkuk smiled like a wolf sizing up a fat hare. "I shall take care of it immediately, your majesty."

Ostro held up a hand. "No, hold, old friend," he said. "I know how much enjoy doing such things, but I want Kordan to do this job." He looked at the little man who seemed to shrink in upon himself. "You understand me, Kordan? You have failed to bend the wench to my will, but you had best not fail to see that she is dead before the sun rises, or you shall share her fate."

Kordan swallowed hard and bobbed his head up and down. "Y-yes, celestial majesty. It shall be as you commend."

Ostro and Tenkuk laughed and slapped their thighs, enjoying the man's discomfort, but what Pip had heard sent a shudder through his body. He came to a sudden stop, causing Vera to bump into him.

Pip, what is it?

We must hurry. Ostro has ordered Queen Daphne's execution. We have no time to waste.

Uncaring about the noise their passage made, Pip and Vera started running down the corridor toward the door.

When they reached the door, they stood on opposite sides of the opening. Pip eased his head over until he could see through the opening with one eye. The guard was slumped on his chair, his back against the wall, and his chest rising and falling in a regular pattern.

The guard appears to be sleeping.

Vera nodded. *Then we must go in and take his key before he awakes. If you are right, and Ostro has ordered the queen to be killed tonight, we do not have much time.*

Could we be so lucky that this door is not locked?

The only way to know is to try it, Pip. Stop wasting time.

He grasped the curved metal handle and pushed. The door did not budge. *It is locked. We must find another way in.*

Vera had a look of frustration on her face. She pushed his hand away, grasped the handle, and pulled. The door swung outward easily. *Doors can swing in both directions, cousin. If it does not move in one direction, one should always try another.*

Pip's cheeks turned dark, and he looked down at his feet. *Some general I am. I cannot even manage a simple door.*

Vera smiled, shrugged and pushed past him, moving quickly to the sleeping guard's side.

Her body must have moved the air in its passage across the room, for the guard awakened and looked up, wide-eyed, at her standing over him. His mouth opened. "Wha—" he started to say, but Vera cut him off with a sharp blow to the temple. He slumped down until his rump was on the floor. She reached down and removed a ring of keys from his belt, tried three until one fit, and opened the door into the cell chamber.

They walked to Daphne's cell. She was sitting on her cot, looking disheveled, but angry. She stared, wide-eyed, at the two figures standing in front of her cell.

"Who are you?" she asked.

Pip stepped in front of Vera. "Your majesty, we have come to rescue you."

"Young Pip, is that you? I scarcely recognized you in that garb . . . and, are you bearing weapons? You, young lady, your face is familiar. Are you from Lands End?" She stood from the cot and walked to the cell door.

"Your majesty," Pip said curtly. "We will answer your questions later. At the moment, we must leave quickly. Ostro has ordered your death, and I fear the killer will be coming soon."

Vera searched the keys again, tried one, and opened the cell door. "I think I will give the guard a taste of his own medicine," she said.

As Daphne exited the cell, Vera walked back to the guard and grasped his ankles. She dragged him to Daphne's cell, rolled him in and locked the door. She slipped the key into her tunic.

"Now," Pip said. "We must hurry." He led the way to the outer door, opened it and looked outside.

The way was clear. He exited, waving Vera and the queen to follow. They hurried down the corridor in the direction of the dining chamber. When they were but a few paces from the final corridor, Pip heard the sound of booted feet coming from that direction, and drawing near. He motioned them to be quiet and led them down the other, darkened, corridor.

They came to another door. Pip tried the door, pushing and then pulling. It opened on a stairwell leading upward. Four torches, two at the bottom of the stairs and two at the top, illuminated the stairwell, showing a closed door at the top. Once the three of them were inside the stairwell, Pip closed the door and motioned them to go ahead of him up the stairs.

At the top, Vera opened the door and she and the queen walked through and out of Pip's view. When he joined them, he found them standing in a small space, just big enough to hold the three of them, with a closed door opposite the stairwell.

Pip looked at the door. *We do not know what lies beyond this door.*

True. Vera laid a hand on the door handle. *But, we do know what lies down the stairs, people who would be willing to kill us and the queen. We can only find out what lies beyond the door by opening it.*

Daphne looked from one to the other, her eyes wide. Before she could ask them what was going on, Pip reached over, put his hand on Vera's and opened the door.

They slipped quietly through the door, and found themselves in a large bedchamber. Across from the door through which they had entered was another door. A candle burned feebly on a table next to the large canopied bed against the center of the wall to their left. In the center of the bed, on his back with his arms splayed to the sides, lay Ostro, ruler of Barbaria. He looked dead to Pip until he began to snore loudly.

He motioned for the women to keep quiet, and started leading them across the room.

They had almost made it to the door, when there was a loud snorting sound and then a squeak.

"Who are you, and what are you doing in my bedchamber?" a querulous voice asked.

They turned to see Ostro sitting up in the bed, clutching the sheet and coverlet over his massive belly.

He was staring at them, panic in his tiny eyes. He squinted at them, his eyes going wide when he recognized Daphne. "You! You, wench, how did you get out of your cell? Who are these people with you?"

"Are you surprised that I am not dead, Ostro?" Daphne asked.

"That is a condition that will be remedied very shortly." He reached up and pulled on a long silken cord hanging at the head of the bed. They could hear a ringing sound from somewhere in the distance. "In a moment," Ostro said. "My guards will be here, and you will all be dead."

"In that case," Vera said. "We might as well kill you first." She advanced toward the bed.

Ostro scrambled away from her approach, his eyes wide with panic and fear. "Guards! Guards! Come quickly. Assassins have invaded my chambers," he shouted. "Please, do not kill me . . . please." He cowered and pulled the coverlet over his head.

But not for the mortal danger they faced, Pip would have laughed at this mountain of quivering flesh, a man who could calmly order the death of another person, cowering in fear from an unarmed woman, for Vera had not removed the club from her waist, and was approaching his bed empty handed.

"As much as he deserves to die," Pip said, straining to hold back the laughter. "We have no time. We must leave here immediately."

The sound of the door banging into the wall startled them all.

"Unfortunately, you have left that too long, and you will not leave alive," Tenkuk's voice said.

Pip whirled. The Barbarian warrior, his sword drawn, was standing in the doorway.

"Tenkuk, my loyal friend and supporter," Ostro said from underneath the coverlet. "They were about to kill me. Kill them, immediately!"

Tenkuk looked at Pip, his left brow arched. "I recognize you, do I not? You are the young warrior who came to the queen's rescue before, and who managed to escape my men in the forest. You cost me two good men. I had them gutted on the spot for allowing you to escape." He frowned at Vera. "And, I suppose you are the female witch who frightened my men so?"

"I am not a witch," Vera said coldly. "But, yes I am the one who sent them running like the frightened dogs they were."

"You will find that I am not so easily frightened by your little parlor tricks. I warrant that I will be able to run you through before you can do anything."

Pip drew his sword. "First, you will have to go through me, Tenkuk," he said.

"Very well," Tenkuk said. "The little pup has grown fangs. Oh well, I will make short work of you, and then I will take care of the girl and the queen." He raised his sword and move toward the bed. "But, there is something else I must do first."

Ostro, who had pulled the coverlet off his head, watched with a puzzled look on his face.

"Why do you not go ahead and kill them, Tenkuk?"

"Oh, I will, your majesty. But, first, I must right a great wrong that has been done to the kingdom of Barbaria. For too long, we have had a weak and ineffective ruler. One who is afraid of his own shadow, and who could not even kill his own father to take the throne, but instead had to hire someone else to do it. Barbaria needs a strong and resolute hand, and our friends here have given me the way to make that happen."

"I-I d-do not understand."

"Of course, you do not, you great fat warthog. Without someone to explain things to you, you understand nothing."

"Y-you cannot speak to me like that. You c-cannot mean what I think you mean."

"Oh, but I do mean it," Tenkuk said. There was steel in his voice. "Only a strong man should rule Barbaria, and eventually Pandara and the rest of the world as well. There will be a great ceremony, and much rending of garments and tears for the Great Ostro. I, Tenkuk, will be among the lead mourners, for it was I who arrived too late to save him. The intruders, helped the prisoner to escape, and came to your chamber and slew you before I arrived. I, of course, slew them as punishment for their great crime. I will be hailed as a hero. Oh yes, in case you are thinking of fleeing, I have men posted at the stairs back to the first level."

The three of them watched, mouths agape, as Tenkuk whirled around and thrust his sword into Ostro's fat throat. A great fountain of blood spurted like a geyser from the wound, and, when he opened his mouth, more blood poured forth. He grabbed at his throat, but the light of life was already leaving his eyes. The fat body sank back onto the bed, the sheet turning crimson from the blood that had flowed from his torn throat. As his heart stopped beating, the flow slowed to a treacle-like trickle.

Tenkuk withdrew the blade, and turned to Pip. "Now, young warrior, it is your turn."

He thrust his sword viciously at . . . where Pip was. Using what he'd been taught by Vera, Pip transported himself two paces to the left, leaving Tenkuk stabbing empty air with a surprised look on his face. At the same time, Pip swung his own weapon, slashing Tenkuk's sword arm. The dark-clad warrior gasped in pain, and grabbed at the wound with his free hand.

As Tenkuk tried to bring his sword up for another thrust, Pip moved again. One moment, he was standing in front of Tenkuk, slightly off center, and the next, he was behind him. The warrior spun around just as Pip's sword nicked his lower back, just above the buttocks. He grunted in pain and dropped his sword. Pip kicked him in the face. His eyes turned up in their sockets, and he flopped back, out cold.

Pip stood over his unconscious body, his sword at Tenkuk's throat.

Vera laid a hand on his sword arm. "No Pip," she said. "It would be wrong to kill a defenseless man, even one as evil as this. Leave him to the jackals down below. We must get out of here."

"I agree with your companion, Pip," Daphne said. "We cannot go down the way that he came, but we could go back through dungeon."

"That means we will have to go back the same way we came in. I beg your forgiveness in advance, your majesty."

"For what must I forgive you?"

He took the extra leaf from his tunic and handed it to her.

"You will know in a short while. Take this and stay close to me. Place it over your nose when Vera tells you to do so."

Charles Ray

Chapter 27

When they had cleared the tunnel, and were nearly back to the trees, Pip mentally signaled for the other teams to rejoin them.

Daphne was gasping in the night air, and waving her hands in front of her face. "I . . . wee what you asked forgiveness for," she said. "The two of you came through that to rescue me?"

Pip nodded.

"Well, then, you surely are forgiven," she said. "You made that journcy twice. Once is more than enough for me. I owe the two of you a debt that can never be fully repaid."

"You owe me nothing," Pip said. "I was but doing my duty."

"Young Pip, you sound so different. My, my, you *are* different. I suppose I must call you Valdar now, eh?"

Pip stopped and stared at her. "You know my birth name?"

"Yes, nephew," she said. "When I came to the throne, Galen told me, and swore me to secrecy. All those summers watching you grow up, and wanting to tell you . . . well, tell me, though, how did you come to know it?"

As they walked, Pip described his rescue from Tenkuk and his warriors by Vera and Tamara, and his stay in the Land of Fire. "So, you see," he concluded. "I had the power within me all the time, but did not know it. Vera and the others helped me to learn."

"From what I witnessed in Ostro's bedchamber, you were a good student, and they were very good teachers. They even taught you to speak properly. How long were you with them?"

"Not very long, your majesty," Vera said. "Pip, or Valdar, is a very quick learner. He was an excellent student, and he surpassed his instructors, myself included, in a very short time."

"He obviously inherited the best from both parents," Daphne said.

"I have heard that the Princess Daria was intelligent as well as beautiful," Vera said. "And, my uncle Valcan, was the greatest of the Folk. He would have been king, but he gave it up to marry your sister."

"So, you and Valdar, no, Pip is how I have known him all his life, and as his aunt, I feel entitled to a pet name." She and Vera smiled at each other. "So, the two of you are cousins, then. I guess that makes us family of a sort, eh?"

Pip had stood quietly listening to the two women talk about him as if he was not present. He was beginning to feel left out. "Your majesty," he said. "Galen said that my father swore him to secrecy. Why did he tell you?"

"Yes, it is true that your father swore Galen to secrecy, but I am sure he understood that such things should not be withheld from the king and queen, so when I took the throne, Galen told me. He knew that, even though it was difficult, I could keep the secret."

"Things would have been so much better for me," Pip said. "If you or Galen had told me."

"I think not, young man. Your father was wise. He knew that growing up as you did among common folk, you would have their interests in your heart when you matured. Too many of the royalty have no understanding or sympathy for their subjects. Trust me, Pip, growing up in a castle, with retainers watching you from the rising of the sun, and even as you sleep, might sound like a wonderful life, but as my sister and I learned, it is not much different than being imprisoned."

"But, you never had bullies like Sandrin waiting at every corner to beat you, either."

"That is true, but it has made you stronger, and you know the evil of taking advantage of those who are weaker than you. That is an important lesson which you might not have learned if you had grown up in the castle."

"But, you grew up there, and you are kind and compassionate," Pip said.

Daphne's eyes widened, and twin blossoms of red appeared on her cheeks. She was saved from having to address his comment by their arrival at the revetment. Godfred and Melchor ran forward and dropped to their knees in front of her.

"Your majesty," they said in unison. "We be so glad to see you safe, and we get your forgiveness for our inability to protect you against that madman, Tenkuk."

"These two stalwarts are Godfred and Melchor," Pip said. "Two of your most valiant guardsmen. They volunteered to accompany me on this rescue mission."

Daphne smiled down at them. "Rise Godfred, rise Melchor," she said. "There is nothing to forgive. You did your best, and you have acquitted yourself well by coming on such a dangerous mission as this."

"It be not all that dangerous," Godfred said. "Them faeries did all the real dangerous stuff."

It was the first time Pip had heard the name the country people used to describe the Folk of the Land of Fire, but in his mind, it seemed appropriate for beings who had magical powers. He wondered, though, what name they would give to one such as he; half faery and half mundane.

"Why do you call them that, Godfred?" he asked.

"I be not knowing, highness," the guardsman said. "Just that it be the name the old people used for those who live in the land of the *fae*; I reckon that be the Land of Fire the Lady Vera talk about; and what can do magic. I be not intending any insult by it."

"No insult taken, my friend," Pip said. In fact, I think I like it. The Faeries of Fire, Water Faeries, and Wood Faeries. I am not sure which I am, being half mundane, but I do not think Vera and the other Folk would take offense." He looked at his cousin.

"No," she said. "We are aware that some of the mundane call us faeries, which we believe comes from their mispronunciation of 'fire.' It matters not what we are called. We are what we are, and a name will not change that."

The others arrived, and Pip noticed that the guardsmen welcomed them as warmly as they had the queen, albeit without bowing. They had truly become comrades in arms.

"Now that we are all here," Pip said. "I think we should make our exit from Barbaria as hastily as possible. When Tenkuk awakens, he will not be happy that I kicked him in the face."

Everyone laughed. Walu slapped Pip on the back. "Walu like see that," he said. "Valdar knock out?"

"Completely," Pip said. "He fell like a tree, and I believe that when he awakens, he will have quite the headache for some time."

There was more laughter as they prepared to depart. Pip requested Nightshade's permission for Daphne to ride, which the black stallion granted immediately, and without his usual huffiness. Pip decided to test his stamina by 'walking' with Tamara and the others. He instructed Vera to ride near Daphne and keep an eye on her, and then set out to join the others.

Having had the evening to rest, the guardsmen's horses were well rested, enabling them to set a good pace. Pip was pleased to discover that he could travel great distances on foot at the pace of a horse's canter without tiring. He was also happy to have to opportunity to get to know Tamara and the others better, as they engaged in friendly banter as they walked. This, he found, was completely different from the conversations he'd had with them during his training.

By sunrise, they had crossed the desert without incident, and were at Pandara's border.

Pip halted them once they were well inside Pandara. "I suppose all of you will want to go home from here," he said to the Folk.

"I would be honored if you would escort me to my castle, and be my guests at a banquet," said Daphne. "You did, after all, rescue me, and you are due some reward."

"And, it be a chance to show the rest of the guard how to really fight," Godfred said.

There was a brief huddle of the Folk, with Tamara in the middle, and then they all agreed to go to Lands End.

Pip shrugged. *Well, I have already begun the process of bringing our two people together. Might as well keep going. This, though, will be an interesting banquet.*

Chapter 28

Pandara

The sky was still dark, but beginning to turn pink at the horizon, signaling the imminent arrival of dawn. Pip suggested that they rest in a field beside the road just outside Lands End, going into town at sunrise rather than skulking in under cover of darkness.

Hermes dug a small trench behind a stand of acacia bushes and filled it with clear water to allow the women to refresh themselves out of sight of the males, and found another spot behind some trees, where he constructed a trench for the men.

After everyone had washed and cleaned off as much of the dust of travel from their clothing as they could, they ate some of the tubers that Walu found just inside the fringe of the Black Forest, washed down with a third pool that Hermes had dug to provide drinking water.

"It will be dawn soon," Pip said. "I suggest that we get some sleep until sunrise."

Everyone dropped where they stood and stretched out on the grass. Pip lay on his back, looking up at the fading stars, but could not sleep. He gave up trying, got up and walked over to the small stand of trees, and sat with his back against one of the trunks, watching the others in their various poses, some so still it was as if they were dead, while others tossed and turned on the grass.

He didn't sense Vera's approach until moments before she sat down beside him, her shoulder brushing against his.

"Could not sleep, eh?"

"No, I do not feel tired, though I should," Pip said. "I was just thinking about our entry into Lands End."

"Do you worry about the reception our Folk will get from the people?"

"A bit," he replied. "But, I think they will be so happy to see Queen Daphne return, they will scarce notice at first. No, I was thinking on our entrance into the city, and how we should do it."

"You are becoming a true commander, cousin. Always thinking about the next mission, and worrying about the smallest things, while lesser beings are content to wait to be told what to do. What do you have in mind, then?"

"I thought to have Queen Daphne ride in on Nightshade, with me leading the procession afoot. You would follow on Star, flanked by Godfred and Melchor, and the Folk would follow in twos directly behind. What do you think?"

"I think, dear cousin, that you have a flair for the dramatic, but it does indeed sound like a good plan."

The sky was still dark, but beginning to turn pink at the horizon, signaling the imminent arrival of dawn. Pip suggested that they rest in a field beside the road just outside Lands End, going into town at sunrise rather than skulking in under cover of darkness.

Hermes dug a small trench behind a stand of acacia bushes and filled it with clear water to allow the women to refresh themselves out of sight of the males, and found another spot behind some trees, where he constructed a trench for the men.

After everyone had washed and cleaned off as much of the dust of travel from their clothing as they could, they ate some of the tubers that Walu found just inside the fringe of the Black Forest, washed down with a third pool that Hermes had dug to provide drinking water.

"It will be dawn soon," Pip said. "I suggest that we get some sleep until sunrise."

Everyone dropped where they stood and stretched out on the grass. Pip lay on his back, looking up at the fading stars, but could not sleep. He gave up trying, got up and walked over to the small stand of trees, and sat with his back against one of the trunks, watching the others in their various poses, some so still it was as if they were dead, while others tossed and turned on the grass.

He didn't sense Vera's approach until moments before she sat down beside him, her shoulder brushing against his.

"Could not sleep, eh?"

"No, I do not feel tired, though I should," Pip said. "I was just thinking about our entry into Lands End."

"Do you worry about the reception our Folk will get from the people?"

"A bit," he replied. "But, I think they will be so happy to see Queen Daphne return, they will scarce notice at first. No, I was thinking on our entrance into the city, and how we should do it."

"You are becoming a true commander, cousin. Always thinking about the next mission, and worrying about the smallest things, while lesser beings are content to wait to be told what to do. What do you have in mind, then?"

"I thought to have Queen Daphne ride in on Nightshade, with me leading the procession afoot. You would follow on Star, flanked by Godfred and Melchor, and the Folk would follow in twos directly behind. What do you think?"

"I think, dear cousin, that you have a flair for the dramatic, but it does indeed sound like a good plan."

Chapter 29

When the first rays of the sun pierced the sky at the horizon, and the sky was beginning to turn from pink to grayish-blue, Pip woke the others and explained his plan.

"Nephew, you are not only a superb warrior," Daphne said. "But, you also have a fine grasp of regal display. That sounds like a wonderful plan."

With the queen in agreement, no one could—or cared to—argue against Pip's plan. So, after a quick meal of tubers and some freshening up, he lined them up.

When he was satisfied that everyone looked presentable, he took his position in front of Nightshade, mentally urging the stallion to put on his best strut when he entered the town, and then strode off, his bow in his left hand, and his sword and club swinging at his side.

They entered the outskirts of Lands End just at the end of the morning meal hour, when there were not many people about the streets. The first to see them was Mordan, the old baker. He was standing in front of his shop, and when he saw Pip come around the corner, followed by a magnificent black stallion upon whose back Queen Daphne sat, his mouth flew open, snapped shut, and gaped open again.

"Gor!" he said to himself. "If that not be young Pip. And, it be the queen herself. Oh my." He whirled and stuck his head inside the shop. "Wife, come and see. Pip be back with the queen, and a strange bunch as I ever seen."

He was joined by a portly woman wearing an apron over her smock, her arms covered in the white dust of flour.

"Oh, my goodness," she said. "You be right. It be the queen and Pip."

They ran off in different directions, knocking on doors and arousing the townspeople.

By the time they reached the street leading to the castle, a crowd had gathered around them, and was keeping pace.

There was much shouting and pointing, and many 'huzzahs', as more and more people caught sight of them.

"Glory be, it be the queen done escaped from the Barbarians!"

"Huzzah! Be that Pip, Auric's boy? He got weapons. Look at how he strut."

"Gor! What be them creatures walking behind the queen?"

And, on it went. Pip kept his head high, and his gaze focused on the street ahead. The others followed his example, except for Wera, who could not resist teasing some of the bystanders.

"You cute one," she said to one young man as she passed him. "But, too skinny, and not got enough hair." She stuck a huge pink tongue out at him, causing him to stumble backwards, trip, and land on his backside, much to the delight of his two companions.

"What be the matter, Merrick," one said. "Be she too much woman for you?"

The two guardsmen and Nork laughed. Pip, without breaking his stride, looked over his shoulder with a disapproving glare, and their laughter cut off abruptly.

When they neared the castle gate, Pip halted. Nightshade stopped behind him, so close that Pip could feel the stallion's breath on the back of his neck. Vera and the two guardsmen came up to flank Queen Daphne.

The two guards, one on either side of the closed gate, stood, open-mouthed and staring.

"Here, now," Pip said. "Will you not admit the queen and her entourage?"

"Why is the gate closed?" Daphne asked. "We have never closed it before except at night."

"Your majesty," one of the guards said. "The commander ordered it closed after the Barbarian raid."

"That is closing the barn door after the cows have gone," Pip said.

"We will not be ruled by fear," said Daphne. "Open the gate immediately, and keep it open. The citizens of Pandara will not have to face a locked gate when they come to the castle."

The guards hastily obeyed, throwing the gate open and resuming their post. They saluted as Pip led Nightshade through the arched opening and into the courtyard, and then looked goggle-eyed at those who followed him and the queen.

As he passed, Godfred looked down at them. "Look sharp, and stop your gawking. This be the best band of warriors I ever been with, and you be paying them proper respect." He then kneed his horse and continued through the archway, leaving the guards gape-mouthed, but standing at respectful attention, saluting the rest of the group as it passed them.

As they entered the courtyard, a door at the far end swung open, and Galen emerged. He looked only a little less frazzled than he had on the day bade him farewell and left on the mission to rescue the queen.

When he saw the queen astride the black stallion, he smiled broadly and bowed. "Your majesty, welcome home," he said. He turned his gaze to Pip. "Well, young prince, I see your quest was successful."

Pip nodded his head in acknowledgement, and turned to help Daphne dismount. She walked up to the gray-haired Galen and embraced him. "Galen, old friend," she said. It is good to be home. I wish to go to my chambers and freshen up, and I want you to find suitable quarters for this valiant band. Oh, and as for Pip, Prince Valdar, give him quarters near my own."

"It will be done," Galen said.

"And, on this night, I want to host a feast to thank and honor my rescuers. The entire town is to be invited."

Galen smiled and bowed. He stepped aside for her to enter the castle. As Pip started to follow, Galen leaned in toward him. "Prince Valdar," he said. "I assumed that the queen would want you near, so allow me to show you the new chambers I have chosen for you." He turned to a young boy who had been standing in the shadows just beyond the door, gaping at them. "You, boy, show the others to the chambers on the second level, and see to their needs."

"Galen, friend and teacher," Pip said. "You have known me as Pip for many summers. It would please me if you would continue to address me as such. I must, however, beg leave now to see to Auric and Ludmilla."

"I also assumed that you would wish to do that, Pip. You can see them as soon as you have freshened and changed into suitable attire. I took the liberty of moving them into the castle. After all, they did foster the queen's nephew. Having them near is something I thought you would wish, and it is little enough reward for their service."

Pip laughed. "I imagine that Aunt Milla has already taken over the cleaning of the castle?"

"With a vengeance, my boy, with a vengeance," Galen said. "She has even taken charge of cleaning my private office. She said that I could not think proper thoughts in such clutter, but I have not been able to find anything since her arrival."

"Trust me, old friend. You will become accustomed to it in time. I find that with Aunt Milla, it is best to just do as she says."

Galen shrugged. "There is, I fear, no alternative. The woman is a force of nature, and like a force of nature, is not to be denied. The castle has not been the same since she arrived, though, I must confess, it is cleaner and neater than I have ever seen it."

Charles Ray

Chapter 30

The chambers that Galen had chosen for Pip were larger than Auric's shop, with an antechamber for bathing that contained a large wooden tub. His closet contained more clothing than he had ever imagined owning, with silk tunics in many colors, and pants in blue, and green cloth, and some of black leather, along with black and brown leather shoes with large brass buckles.

A manservant, one of many serving in the castle, was available for his every need. He asked for the tub to be filled with hot water, and a green tunic and pants laid out.

While Pip had thoroughly enjoyed his baths in the stream in the Land of Fire, he had never experienced such luxury indoors. The tub was large enough for him to stretch out his entire length, and unlike the harsh smelling soap made from animal fat that Ludmilla made him use, there was a vial of crystals that made the water foamy as the area under a waterfall, and that smelled like a field of flowers in fresh bloom. He lay on his back, with only his nose above water, for a long time, enjoying the relaxing feel of the warm water.

After scrubbing away the dust of his travels, he dried off with a large towel made of some soft cloth that felt warm and gentle against his skin.

The clothing that had been laid out for him was emerald green. The tunic had gold buttons with the seal of the royal family engraved upon them, and his pants had a soft leather belt made from calfskin. The boots were also calfskin, stained black, with gold buckles. Clothing and boots felt soft against his skin.

After dressing, he noticed a writing desk in the corner of the chamber. Upon it was a large inkwell with a quill pen, and a stack of writing paper.

While the bath had relaxed him, he didn't feel sleepy, so he went to the desk, took out the pen and a sheet of paper, and began drawing a map of the world based upon his travels, and what he'd been told by his teachers in the Land of Fire. Although he was not the most competent draftsman, his memory of the places he had seen or heard about was good, and in a short time, he had a rough sketch showing Pandara, the Black Forest, the Land of Fire, the desert, and Barbaria. Beyond Barbaria the lands were unknown.

As he was admiring his handiwork, there was a soft knock on the door.

"Enter," he said.

The manservant entered. "Sire, the queen requests your presence in her chambers."

Pip pushed the map aside and stood. He followed the manservant down the long corridor to a large set of wooden doors at the end, about fifty paces from the door to his own rooms.

The man knocked softly on the door.

"Enter," the queen's voice said from behind the door.

The manservant opened the door and stood aside.

The room that he entered was three times larger than his own, with a huge canopied bed dominating the center. Daphne, Vera, and Tamara sat on three cloth-covered chairs around a low carved wooden table in the corner to the right of the head of the bed near a large window that gave a vied onto the castle garden. There was an ornate porcelain pitcher and four crystal goblets on the table. An empty chair sat opposite the queen.

"Please come and join us," Daphne said. "We were just having some jasmine tea, and the girls were telling me of your adventures."

Pip sat in the empty chair and poured himself a goblet of the steaming brown liquid. He took a sip. The tea had been sweetened with honey, and the taste and aroma caused him to lean back and sigh. Then, his stomach rumbled.

"Oh, forgive me," he said. "The tea is delicious, but I think my stomach is reminding me that I have not eaten since the morning."

"I can have some cakes brought in," the queen said. "But, I would not want you to spoil your appetite for the night's banquet."

"I suppose I can wait, as long as you ladies can abide the sounds that will be coming from my stomach."

They all laughed. "I have heard much worse," said Vera.

"Pardon me for intruding on such pleasant conversation with business," Daphne said. "But, I have a proposal for each of you, and I wanted you to all hear it at the same time."

"I have no objections," Pip said. "I fear that if I am not in the room when you talk to these two, things will be said about me that I would rather you not hear."

"Oh, cousin, fear not," Vera said. "I will not tell the queen how many times Nork knocked you down when you were learning to use the club."

Pip's face turned a bright red. "Precisely the kind of story I would rather the queen not hear."

"But, you quickly mastered the club, and you put Nork on his backside an equal number of times."

"Oh, you must tell me more," Daphne said, smiling. "It would be most amusing. But, now to business." She turned to Pip. "Nephew, I think that recent experience has shown that Pandara can no longer be without an army to defend itself."

"I agree, your majesty. I fear that we will now face dangers far greater than the occasional raid."

"It pleases me to hear you say that. That is why I wish to raise an army, and I want you to command it."

"B-but, your majesty, Aunt Daphne," Pip said, raising his hands in protest. "I am but a boy. How can I command an army?"

"Your grandfather commanded the guard when he was two summers younger than you are. And, you have proven yourself capable of leadership. Nephew, your experience in battle is already greater than anyone in Pandara. You are also a member of the royal family, and must have assigned duties. I believe that this is the duty for which you are best fitted."

Pip inclined his head. "If that is your wish."

"It is," she said. "And, I would like Vera and Tamara to serve as your advisors."

The two women stared open-mouthed at the queen. "Would your people accept us?" Vera asked.

"I think they will. I saw the respect the guardsmen gave you."

"Your majesty," Pip said. "Do I have your leave to make a suggestion?"

"Of course, Pip. As of now, you are my army commander. You may always speak your mind."

"I would like to make Vera my second in command, and have Tamara in charge of training and supply."

Daphne smiled, and turned to the two women. "I know that you might have to ask your king's permission," she said. "But, I believe that would be a wonderful idea."

"I have no doubt that my father would approve," Vera said. She looked at Tamara, who nodded. "I would like to offer an additional suggestion. I believe that we should also raise a contingent of Folk willing to serve in this army. That would give us an added advantage against any Barbarian force, and further cement relations between our people."

"That would be a great idea," Pip said. "I would also like to promote Godfred and Melchor to captains, and put them in charge of units within the army. They have proven themselves brave and adaptable, and I think they would make excellent commanders."

"As commander," Daphne said. "You are free to make any decisions you feel necessary. I take it we are agreed that you will be my commander, then?"

"Yes, your majesty. I will certainly do my best."

"As will I," said Vera.

"And, I," Tamara added.

"Very well," Daphne said. "It would appear that Pandara has an army. I wish each of you well in your tasks. Now, we must go and prepare for the evening's festivities."

The three stood, bowed respectfully, and left for their chambers, each lost in his or her own thoughts of what lay ahead.

The chambers that Galen had chosen for Pip were larger than Auric's shop, with an antechamber for bathing that contained a large wooden tub. His closet contained more clothing than he had ever imagined owning, with silk tunics in many colors, and pants in blue, and green cloth, and some of black leather, along with black and brown leather shoes with large brass buckles.

A manservant, one of many serving in the castle, was available for his every need. He asked for the tub to be filled with hot water, and a green tunic and pants laid out.

While Pip had thoroughly enjoyed his baths in the stream in the Land of Fire, he had never experienced such luxury indoors. The tub was large enough for him to stretch out his entire length, and unlike the harsh smelling soap made from animal fat that Ludmilla made him use, there was a vial of crystals that made the water foamy as the area under a waterfall, and that smelled like a field of flowers in fresh bloom. He lay on his back, with only his nose above water, for a long time, enjoying the relaxing feel of the warm water.

After scrubbing away the dust of his travels, he dried off with a large towel made of some soft cloth that felt warm and gentle against his skin.

The clothing that had been laid out for him was emerald green. The tunic had gold buttons with the seal of the royal family engraved upon them, and his pants had a soft leather belt made from calfskin. The boots were also calfskin, stained black, with gold buckles. Clothing and boots felt soft against his skin.

After dressing, he noticed a writing desk in the corner of the chamber. Upon it was a large inkwell with a quill pen, and a stack of writing paper.

While the bath had relaxed him, he didn't feel sleepy, so he went to the desk, took out the pen and a sheet of paper, and began drawing a map of the world based upon his travels, and what he'd been told by his teachers in the Land of Fire. Although he was not the most competent draftsman, his memory of the places he had seen or heard about was good, and in a short time, he had a rough sketch showing Pandara, the Black Forest, the Land of Fire, the desert, and Barbaria. Beyond Barbaria the lands were unknown.

As he was admiring his handiwork, there was a soft knock on the door.

"Enter," he said.

The manservant entered. "Sire, the queen requests your presence in her chambers."

Pip pushed the map aside and stood. He followed the manservant down the long corridor to a large set of wooden doors at the end, about fifty paces from the door to his own rooms.

The man knocked softly on the door.

"Enter," the queen's voice said from behind the door.

The manservant opened the door and stood aside.

The room that he entered was three times larger than his own, with a huge canopied bed dominating the center. Daphne, Vera, and Tamara sat on three cloth-covered chairs around a low carved wooden table in the corner to the right of the head of the bed near a large window that gave a vied onto the castle garden. There was an ornate porcelain pitcher and four crystal goblets on the table. An empty chair sat opposite the queen.

"Please come and join us," Daphne said. "We were just having some jasmine tea, and the girls were telling me of your adventures."

Pip sat in the empty chair and poured himself a goblet of the steaming brown liquid. He took a sip. The tea had been sweetened with honey, and the taste and aroma caused him to lean back and sigh. Then, his stomach rumbled.

"Oh, forgive me," he said. "The tea is delicious, but I think my stomach is reminding me that I have not eaten since the morning."

"I can have some cakes brought in," the queen said. "But, I would not want you to spoil your appetite for the night's banquet."

"I suppose I can wait, as long as you ladies can abide the sounds that will be coming from my stomach."

They all laughed. "I have heard much worse," said Vera.

"Pardon me for intruding on such pleasant conversation with business," Daphne said. "But, I have a proposal for each of you, and I wanted you to all hear it at the same time."

"I have no objections," Pip said. "I fear that if I am not in the room when you talk to these two, things will be said about me that I would rather you not hear."

"Oh, cousin, fear not," Vera said. "I will not tell the queen how many times Nork knocked you down when you were learning to use the club."

Pip's face turned a bright red. "Precisely the kind of story I would rather the queen not hear."

"But, you quickly mastered the club, and you put Nork on his backside an equal number of times."

"Oh, you must tell me more," Daphne said, smiling. "It would be most amusing. But, now to business." She turned to Pip. "Nephew, I think that recent experience has shown that Pandara can no longer be without an army to defend itself."

"I agree, your majesty. I fear that we will now face dangers far greater than the occasional raid."

"It pleases me to hear you say that. That is why I wish to raise an army, and I want you to command it."

"B-but, your majesty, Aunt Daphne," Pip said, raising his hands in protest. "I am but a boy. How can I command an army?"

"Your grandfather commanded the guard when he was two summers younger than you are. And, you have proven yourself capable of leadership. Nephew, your experience in battle is already greater than anyone in Pandara. You are also a member of the royal family, and must have assigned duties. I believe that this is the duty for which you are best fitted."

Pip inclined his head. "If that is your wish."

"It is," she said. "And, I would like Vera and Tamara to serve as your advisors."

The two women stared open-mouthed at the queen. "Would your people accept us?" Vera asked.

"I think they will. I saw the respect the guardsmen gave you."

"Your majesty," Pip said. "Do I have your leave to make a suggestion?"

"Of course, Pip. As of now, you are my army commander. You may always speak your mind."

"I would like to make Vera my second in command, and have Tamara in charge of training and supply."

Daphne smiled, and turned to the two women. "I know that you might have to ask your king's permission," she said. "But, I believe that would be a wonderful idea."

"I have no doubt that my father would approve," Vera said. She looked at Tamara, who nodded. "I would like to offer an additional suggestion. I believe that we should also raise a contingent of Folk willing to serve in this army. That would give us an added advantage against any Barbarian force, and further cement relations between our people."

"That would be a great idea," Pip said. "I would also like to promote Godfred and Melchor to captains, and put them in charge of units within the army. They have proven themselves brave and adaptable, and I think they would make excellent commanders."

"As commander," Daphne said. "You are free to make any decisions you feel necessary. I take it we are agreed that you will be my commander, then?"

"Yes, your majesty. I will certainly do my best."

"As will I," said Vera.

"And, I," Tamara added.

"Very well," Daphne said. "It would appear that Pandara has an army. I wish each of you well in your tasks. Now, we must go and prepare for the evening's festivities."

The three stood, bowed respectfully, and left for their chambers, each lost in his or her own thoughts of what lay ahead.

Charles Ray

Chapter 31

People began arriving at the castle as the sun was sinking below the far hills. Queen Daphne sent pages to Pip and the others, but with a special message for Pip, Vera, and Tamara, asking that they join her in the throne room to watch people arrive, and await the start of the evening's ceremonies.

She was waiting, seated in a plain wooden chair while two pages prepared her throne to be moved to the stage outside the room.

"Welcome, Pip. Come and sit beside me." She pointed to another plain chair at her side.

From where he sat, Pip could see the area in front of the state, and as far back as the entrance to the courtyard. A crowd was already starting to gather in front of the opening. Near the gate, Pip saw Sandrin and three of his friends, standing around picking on the younger children, and making faces at the adults who tried to ignore them.

"If I may have your leave, your majesty," he said. "There is something that I must attend to."

I know what you are thinking, Pip. Vera's voice echoed in his head, as she and Tamara entered the room. *Must you do this?*

Yes, there is one ghost of the past that must be finally laid to rest.

But, must you do it in this particular way?

Unfortunately, it is the only way that Sandrin and his friends will understand.

Daphne had been sitting, quietly watching the byplay between Pip and Vera, and from the looks on their faces, and the way Pip kept looking toward the entrance, she intuited the conversation. She, too, had seen Sandrin and his friends, and knew of Pip's past history with them. "If you must go, Pip," she said. "Please be back here in time for the ceremony. You are an important part of what is planned."

"I promise that this will not take long." Pip turned to Vera. *I also promise that I will not break anything. Mayhap a bruise or two; that much I owe to myself.*

Vera shrugged. *Do what you must, cousin. I guess the mundane half of you demands it. We Folk are above such things.*

As if she had been able to listen to the private communication between Pip and Vera, Daphne stood and placed a hand on Vera's shoulder. "My dear," she said. "There are things about the male of our species that you do not understand. There is a void in Pip's psyche, caused by his past experience, and he must address it if his mind is to be at ease. I trust that the heritage he has inherited from his father will at least curb his actions somewhat."

Pip saw no need to stay and argue further. Vera would never understand, but the queen did, and that was enough for him. He walked to the entrance to the courtyard, and looked outside. Sandrin was huddled with his friends, looking to Pip like they were planning some special mischief for the evening.

He eased out of the courtyard and walked along the side of the building, staying in the shadows as much as possible, a difficult task, given the number of torches that had been set into the walls. A few people in the front of the crowd saw him and waved. He waved back, but said nothing, and kept moving along the wall toward the trio.

A small boy, about ten summers old, approached them from the opposite direction, and passed very near Sandrin. He was carrying a basket of tomatoes.

Sandrin stuck out his foot and tripped the boy, sending the ripe tomatoes flying in all directions. The boy tried to get up, and retrieved the spilled food, but Sandrin put a foot in the small of his back, pressing him against the stones. Pip could see the tears of frustration beginning to well up in the boy's eyes, and hear the harsh laughter of Sandrin's friends.

He was able to get within five paces of them before they noticed him.

"Let the lad be," he said. "You should pick fights with someone who is more your equal."

Sandrin took his foot off the boy's back and turned to face Pip. "I suppose you think that be you, little girl," he said. Then, he noticed the sword and club at Pip's waist. "Oh, I see the runt now be carrying a man's weapons. Do you know how to use them?" He sneered at Pip.

"I have no need of them," Pip said. "Now, once again, I say, let the boy be."

"That be strong language you be using," said Sandrin. "You think without your toys you be a match for me?"

Pip kept his voice low. "Let us go around the side of the castle and see, shall we?"

"Listen to him," one of the boys said. "He be talking funny, like a toff."

"I am not be caring how the little sissy talk," Sandrin said. "Okay, little girl. We go around the side and see what you can do."

Forgotten by the bullies, the little boy quickly gathered his spilled tomatoes and scurried off toward a group of adults near the archway.

Sandrin and his friends went around the corner of the castle and waited for Pip. When he came around the wall, they moved near the spot where that had beaten Pip earlier. The significance wasn't lost on Pip. He followed them.

They gathered in a group near the wall.

"He got that sword," a boy said. "Ain't fair if he use it. We got no weapons, just our hands."

Pip unbuckled the belt holding his weapons, and placed them on the ground near his feet. "There," he said. "Now, I have no weapons."

As he turned, the four boys rushed at him. Sandrin, in the lead, threw a wild punch at Pip's head, while two dove at his waist to knock him over. Using the techniques taught to him by Walu and Wera, Pip dodged his head to one side, causing Sandrin's fist to whistle past. At the same time, he spun around, and using his left hand, pushed the closest boy aside and into his companion. With his right hand, he grabbed

Sandrin's fist, and pulled, and brought his knee up and rammed it into the boy's midsection.

The fourth boy went for Pip's discarded club. He kicked him in the head, flattening him on the ground, all of the fight gone out of him for the moment. His move had caused Sandrin to fall flat on his face as well, and the other two boys were lying in a tangle on the ground, moaning. As Sandrin started to rise, Pip cuffed him behind the ear, stunning him and causing him to fall again. When the other two untangled themselves and rose, he turned to face them, relaxed but alert, his hands at his side.

They looked at their two companions lying stunned on the ground, and hesitated.

"Where you be learning to fight like that?" one asked.

"It does not matter. You only need to know that I shall be able to defeat you, one at a time, or all together. If you wish to avoid a beating, you will go back inside the castle, and behave in a proper manner."

On the ground, Sandrin moaned and tried to rise, but was still too dazed. The other boy stirred, but stayed down. The two facing Pip looked down at their friends, and back at him. His return gaze was steely. That look made up their minds. They dashed past him, leaving their companions to fend for themselves.

Sandrin finally managed to get himself up into a sitting position. He looked up at Pip, a dazed look on his face. Nonchalantly, Pip leaned over and retrieved all his weapons. As he put them on, Sandra started the slow process of standing. When he was finally erect, he faced Pip. "Who taught you to fight like that?" he asked.

"The best fighters in the world," Pip said. "And, by the end of my training, I could best them. Would you like another demonstration?"

Sandrin shook his head. "No, I wish nothing more to do with you."

Pip smiled. "Good. Now, help your friend there up, and go back inside. And, be warned. I will be keeping an eye on the four of you this night. If you cause any more mischief, we will have another . . . talk."

Sandrin was sullen, but silent, as he helped his friend stand. The two of them limped away, casting furtive glances over their shoulders at Pip.

Pip maintained a stony expression, but inside he was smiling. That, he thought, was not so bad, and I only bruised them a little. Vera should be pleased.

When he returned to the courtyard, Queen Daphne had already taken her place on the stage. Vera and Tamara stood at her side. When she saw Pip, she beckoned him to join her. Vera moved to allow him to stand next to the throne.

As Pip stepped up onto the stage there were shocked whispers from the crowd.

Daphne held a hand up for silence.

"People of Pandara," she said. "You all know of the calamity that befell our peaceful kingdom. Many were injured, and some were slain. I was taken prisoner by the Barbarians, and taken to their capital of Gondwana." She waved a hand, taking in Pip, Vera, Tamara, and the others who were standing at the side of the stage. "But for the gallant actions of these who stand before you, I would still languish in the dungeon of the castle in Gondwana."

A loud cheer arose from the crowd. Godfred and Melchor, standing among the Folk, smiled and tried to look modest. The ogres, Walu and Wera, smiled and waved, while Nork merely frowned. The gnomes looked confused. Hermes, standing somewhat apart from the group, and deep in a whispered conversation with Galen, paid the proceedings no mind.

Daphne put a hand on Pip's wrist. "This young man led the gallant ban that rescued me."

The crowd cheered again. Pip's face felt hot.

"Huzzah for Pip," someone yelled

"That be my boy," Auric's voice came from somewhere near Galen and Hermes.

"That be *our* boy," Ludmilla's voice, from close by, corrected him. "And, you best not be forgetting it."

Daphne once again signaled for silence. "You know him as Pip," she said. "And, Pip he will always be to most of us. But, he is also Valdar, son of my sister Daria and Valcan, a prince from the Land of Fire."

Gasps could be heard from throughout the crowd. "That mean he be the nephew of the queen," a fat man in the front row said. "He be a prince."

"That is correct," Daphne said. "He is Prince Valdar, next in line to the throne of Pandara, and henceforth, he is to be addressed as such."

She no longer had to call for silence. A hush fell over the crowd. In the back of the crowd, Pip could see Sandrin and his friends, looks of astonishment on their faces. He allowed a small smile to play on his face.

"From this day," Daphne continued. "He is also the commander of the army of Pandora."

"Army? What army?" someone in the crowd asked. "Pandara has no army."

"Oh, we have an army," Daphne said. "Or, we will have as soon as we get recruits. Any man who volunteers will receive a summer's pay in advance. I want the word to go out all over Pandara. Never again shall we be defenseless against the predations of such as Barbaria."

Auric stepped from behind Galen. "I be the first to volunteer," he said.

Pip gaped in astonishment, and was about to protest, but Daphne laid a hand on his wrist. "Thank you, Auric," she said. "But, I have another task for you. You will be the royal tanner, responsible for uniforms, shields, and other equipment for the army."

Ludmilla squealed and grabbed Auric in a hug that threatened to smother him. "Oh, husband mine, this be such a great appointment."

"Over her head, Auric smiled at Pip. "Thank you, your majesty," he said. "I will do my best for you, I swear."

"Thank you, Auric. And now, good lady Ludmilla, if you will kindly release your husband and step forward."

With a puzzled look on her round face, Ludmilla turned. She stepped tentatively forward and curtsied. "Yes, your majesty. I beg your pardon for such an unseemly display."

"There is no need for apologies, good lady. I understand that since your arrival, the castle has never looked neater?"

Ludmilla's face turned red, and she looked down at her feet. "W-well, it not be that it was not already neat, your majesty. But, there do be a few changes I made. If they not be to your liking, I will put them back the way they were before."

"Not at all, good lady. They please me very much. So much, in fact, that I am appointing you head of chambers. You will supervise all castle staff. Are you willing to take on that responsibility?"

Ludmilla looked flustered, and for the first time in Pip's live, he feared that she might be at a loss for words. She gulped, though, and found her voice. "Your majesty," she said. "I know not what to say."

"You might try merely saying, yes," Daphne said.

"Oh, yes, your majesty, and I swear that I will do you proud."

"Thank you," said Daphne. "I have no doubt you will. Now, guardsmen Godfred and Melchor, would you kindly step forward."

The two guardsmen stepped forward and bowed.

"Godfred and Melchor, you are hereby relieved of duty as guardsmen."

Their mouths fell open and they looked as if they'd just been struck in the stomach. After seeing Auric and Ludmilla rewarded, they had no doubt expected some kind of small token, but, to be tooted from the guard hit them like a thunderbolt.

"B-but, your majesty," Godfred said. "We have served you loyally almost since we were striplings. Have we not performed our duties properly?"

"You have, and admirably," Daphne said. "And, that is precisely why I am promoting the two of you as captains in Pandara's new army."

They looked puzzled, but her words finally sank in and they smiled broadly. "Thank you, your majesty," they chimed together.

She inclined her head. "Very well. And now, Commander Valdar, would assemble your group in front of the stage?"

Pip sent a mental signal to the Folk. To the newly-promoted captains, he said, "Captain Godfred, Captain Melchor, as my new subunit commanders, your first duty is to assemble the team."

Melchor deferred to Godfred, as he often did, and they set about getting Hermes, the ogres, the troll, and the gnomes into a line facing the stage, and then position themselves in front of that line. "The troops are assembled, sir," Godfred said.

Pip nodded, and with Vera and Tamara flanking him, took his place in front of his two captains.

"Your majesty," he said. "The troops are assembled."

Daphne smiled and nodded. She then turned to Councilor Galen. "Councilor, would you bring me the box I gave you?"

Galen presented her with a box covered in purple velvet, bowed and then moved to stand behind her.

Daphne opened the box, looked inside, and nodded. She moved to stand in front of Pip, who had a puzzled look on his face. "I felt that there had to be more than mere words to recognize the great service all of you have done for Pandara," she said aloud, and then, in a quieter voice to Pip, "Galen had the metalsmiths and seamstresses working on this since our arrival."

A loud squawk echoed around the courtyard, causing Daphne to flinch and look up. Talus swooped down from atop the wall and lit on Pip's left shoulder. The goshawk cocked its head to one side, looking at the queen with one eye. She smiled and winked at Pip. "I see now that your entire team is actually assembled, commander. I think this one would have resented being left out.

Talus squawked again, and then nuzzled his beak against Pip's ear. "Yes, your majesty," Pip said quietly. "If not for Talus, your rescue would have been much more difficult. He is indeed an important part of our team."

Daphne reached into the box and removed a medallion that was suspended from a green, blue, and red ribbon. The medallion was a gold circle with the image of a goshawk etched on it. The words, 'For Conspicuous Bravery,' encircled the bird.

She placed the ribbon around Pip's neck. The medallion rested on his chest, giving him a warm feeling in both his chest and face. She then repeated the process with the others, beginning with Vera. After draping the last one, she paused. Talus squawked loudly, and she smiled. From the box, she withdrew a smaller version of the one she'd given Pip, and draped it around Talus' neck. As if understanding the significance of her action, Talus kept his head high, and when the medallion dropped against his feathered chest, he threw his head back and squawked.

"I think he likes it," Pip said quietly.

Talus spread his wings and soared up, circling the courtyard. The gold disk reflected the light from the torches on the wall as he circled.

"He is something of a showoff," Daphne said.

The crowd cheered lustily as Talus flew, causing him to swoop and loop even more. Finally, Pip sent him a mental command, *Enough!* Talus did one final circuit of the courtyard and then flew back and landed on Pip's shoulder.

"Your majesty," Galen said, clearing his throat. "I believe our guests are anxious to sample the viands we have prepared for them." With a wave of his arms, he indicated the four large tables laden with food that lined two side of the courtyard walls.

"Of course," Daphne said. "Good people of Lands End, please avail yourselves of the food. We will have entertainment as we eat."

At those words, people began a semi-orderly movement toward the tables, filling their arms, aprons, and whatever else they use as a container, with fruits, bread, pies, and meat. A group of musicians, who had been waiting in a corner behind the stage, mounted the platform and began playing 'Maiden on the Green,' Pip's favorite song, but, on this occasion, he was not really listening.

He stood quietly, stroking Talus' head. He was too excited to eat, and felt that even if he was not so overcome with emotion by events, it would be unseemly for him, as commander of the army, to eat before everyone else. Except for Vera, who stood at his side, and Daphne, who stood in front of him, smiling at the people, the rest of his team joined the crowd at the tables.

I see that your former enemies have been well-behaved, and, true to your word, nothing seems to have been broken.

Pip smiled at Vera. *Well, I think I might have broken them of their bad habits. And, Sandrin and one other will have headaches for a few suns.*

Vera shrugged and made a face. *I have been watching over you since you were still a stripling, and I was a mere sixteen summers myself. And, still, I do not understand the mundane side of you. But, that, I suppose, is how it must be. Shall we get something to eat before we swoon from lack of nourishment?*

Yes, cousin, we should. But, then we must busy ourselves with the planning for Pandara's new army, and more the challenge, how we will create a combined army of Folk and my mundane fellows.

Pip, you have already demonstrated that the two people can work together when there is a common purpose. I should think that a threat from the army of Barbaria, and doubt not that it will happen, should make our task less difficult.

Pip put his hands behind his back and crossed his fingers. *Of course, you are correct.* At least, he thought, I pray that you are correct. Here I am, not yet I the summer of my majority, and I have to learn how to rally people who are so different from each other to work and fight together. He knew that Tenkuk would not let the insult to his honor go unanswered, and would show Pandara no mercy when he invaded again—and, that he would invade again, Pip had no doubt.

As he followed Vera to the food tables, accepting congratulations from everyone he passed, he nodded politely and absently stroked Talus' head. In Auric and Ludmilla's household, there had never been any kind of observance of obeisance to the unseen gods that many in the countryside believed in, but as he walked, he prayed silently for guidance, and the grace of those gods that he had never before thought much of. If, as people thought, the gods of the land were the gods of all, on whose side would they stand?

People began arriving at the castle as the sun was sinking below the far hills. Queen Daphne sent pages to Pip and the others, but with a special message for Pip, Vera, and Tamara, asking that they join her in the throne room to watch people arrive, and await the start of the evening's ceremonies.

She was waiting, seated in a plain wooden chair while two pages prepared her throne to be moved to the stage outside the room.

"Welcome, Pip. Come and sit beside me." She pointed to another plain chair at her side.

From where he sat, Pip could see the area in front of the state, and as far back as the entrance to the courtyard. A crowd was already starting to gather in front of the opening. Near the gate, Pip saw Sandrin and three of his friends, standing around picking on the younger children, and making faces at the adults who tried to ignore them.

"If I may have your leave, your majesty," he said. "There is something that I must attend to."

I know what you are thinking, Pip. Vera's voice echoed in his head, as she and Tamara entered the room. *Must you do this?*

Yes, there is one ghost of the past that must be finally laid to rest.

But, must you do it in this particular way?

Unfortunately, it is the only way that Sandrin and his friends will understand.

Daphne had been sitting, quietly watching the byplay between Pip and Vera, and from the looks on their faces, and the way Pip kept looking toward the entrance, she intuited the conversation. She, too, had seen Sandrin and his friends, and knew of Pip's past history with them. "If you must go, Pip," she said. "Please be back here in time for the ceremony. You are an important part of what is planned."

"I promise that this will not take long." Pip turned to Vera. *I also promise that I will not break anything. Mayhap a bruise or two; that much I owe to myself.*

Vera shrugged. *Do what you must, cousin. I guess the mundane half of you demands it. We Folk are above such things.*

As if she had been able to listen to the private communication between Pip and Vera, Daphne stood and placed a hand on Vera's shoulder. "My dear," she said. "There are things about the male of our species that you do not understand. There is a void in Pip's psyche, caused by his past experience, and he must address it if his mind is to be at ease. I trust that the heritage he has inherited from his father will at least curb his actions somewhat."

Pip saw no need to stay and argue further. Vera would never understand, but the queen did, and that was enough for him. He walked to the entrance to the courtyard, and looked outside. Sandrin was huddled with his friends, looking to Pip like they were planning some special mischief for the evening.

He eased out of the courtyard and walked along the side of the building, staying in the shadows as much as possible, a difficult task, given the number of torches that had been set into the walls. A few people in the front of the crowd saw him and waved. He waved back, but said nothing, and kept moving along the wall toward the trio.

A small boy, about ten summers old, approached them from the opposite direction, and passed very near Sandrin. He was carrying a basket of tomatoes.

Sandrin stuck out his foot and tripped the boy, sending the ripe tomatoes flying in all directions. The boy tried to get up, and retrieved the spilled food, but Sandrin put a foot in the small of his back, pressing him against the stones. Pip could see the tears of frustration beginning to well up in the boy's eyes, and hear the harsh laughter of Sandrin's friends.

He was able to get within five paces of them before they noticed him.

"Let the lad be," he said. "You should pick fights with someone who is more your equal."

Sandrin took his foot off the boy's back and turned to face Pip. "I suppose you think that be you, little girl," he said. Then, he noticed the sword and club at Pip's waist. "Oh, I see the runt now be carrying a man's weapons. Do you know how to use them?" He sneered at Pip.

"I have no need of them," Pip said. "Now, once again, I say, let the boy be."

"That be strong language you be using," said Sandrin. "You think without your toys you be a match for me?"

Pip kept his voice low. "Let us go around the side of the castle and see, shall we?"

"Listen to him," one of the boys said. "He be talking funny, like a toff."

"I am not be caring how the little sissy talk," Sandrin said. "Okay, little girl. We go around the side and see what you can do."

Forgotten by the bullies, the little boy quickly gathered his spilled tomatoes and scurried off toward a group of adults near the archway.

Sandrin and his friends went around the corner of the castle and waited for Pip. When he came around the wall, they moved near the spot where that had beaten Pip earlier. The significance wasn't lost on Pip. He followed them.

They gathered in a group near the wall.

"He got that sword," a boy said. "Ain't fair if he use it. We got no weapons, just our hands."

Pip unbuckled the belt holding his weapons, and placed them on the ground near his feet. "There," he said. "Now, I have no weapons."

As he turned, the four boys rushed at him. Sandrin, in the lead, threw a wild punch at Pip's head, while two dove at his waist to knock him over. Using the techniques taught to him by Walu and Wera, Pip dodged his head to one side, causing Sandrin's fist to whistle past. At the same time, he spun around, and using his left hand, pushed the closest boy aside and into his companion. With his right hand, he grabbed Sandrin's fist, and pulled, and brought his knee up and rammed it into the boy's midsection.

The fourth boy went for Pip's discarded club. He kicked him in the head, flattening him on the ground, all of the fight gone out of him for the moment. His move had caused Sandrin to fall flat on his face as well, and the other two boys were lying in a tangle on the ground, moaning. As Sandrin started to rise, Pip cuffed him behind the ear, stunning him and causing him to fall again. When the other two untangled themselves and rose, he turned to face them, relaxed but alert, his hands at his side.

They looked at their two companions lying stunned on the ground, and hesitated.

"Where you be learning to fight like that?" one asked.

"It does not matter. You only need to know that I shall be able to defeat you, one at a time, or all together. If you wish to avoid a beating, you will go back inside the castle, and behave in a proper manner."

On the ground, Sandrin moaned and tried to rise, but was still too dazed. The other boy stirred, but stayed down. The two facing Pip looked down at their friends, and back at him. His return gaze was steely. That look made up their minds. They dashed past him, leaving their companions to fend for themselves.

Sandrin finally managed to get himself up into a sitting position. He looked up at Pip, a dazed look on his face. Nonchalantly, Pip leaned over and retrieved all his weapons. As he put them on, Sandra started the slow process of standing. When he was finally erect, he faced Pip. "Who taught you to fight like that?" he asked.

"The best fighters in the world," Pip said. "And, by the end of my training, I could best them. Would you like another demonstration?"

Sandrin shook his head. "No, I wish nothing more to do with you."

Pip smiled. "Good. Now, help your friend there up, and go back inside. And, be warned. I will be keeping an eye on the four of you this night. If you cause any more mischief, we will have another . . . talk."

Sandrin was sullen, but silent, as he helped his friend stand. The two of them limped away, casting furtive glances over their shoulders at Pip.

Pip maintained a stony expression, but inside he was smiling. *That, he thought, was not so bad, and I only bruised them a little. Vera should be pleased.*

When he returned to the courtyard, Queen Daphne had already taken her place on the stage. Vera and Tamara stood at her side. When she saw Pip, she beckoned him to join her. Vera moved to allow him to stand next to the throne.

As Pip stepped up onto the stage there were shocked whispers from the crowd.

Daphne held a hand up for silence.

"People of Pandara," she said. "You all know of the calamity that befell our peaceful kingdom. Many were injured, and some were slain. I was taken prisoner by the Barbarians, and taken to their capital of Gondwana." She waved a hand, taking in Pip, Vera, Tamara, and the others who were standing at the side of the stage. "But for the gallant actions of these who stand before you, I would still languish in the dungeon of the castle in Gondwana."

A loud cheer arose from the crowd. Godfred and Melchor, standing among the Folk, smiled and tried to look modest. The ogres, Walu and Wera, smiled and waved, while Nork merely frowned. The gnomes looked confused. Hermes, standing somewhat apart from the group, and deep in a whispered conversation with Galen, paid the proceedings no mind.

Daphne put a hand on Pip's wrist. "This young man led the gallant ban that rescued me."

The crowd cheered again. Pip's face felt hot.

"Huzzah for Pip," someone yelled

"That be my boy," Auric's voice came from somewhere near Galen and Hermes.

"That be *our* boy," Ludmilla's voice, from close by, corrected him. "And, you best not be forgetting it."

Daphne once again signaled for silence. "You know him as Pip," she said. "And, Pip he will always be to most of us. But, he is also Valdar, son of my sister Daria and Valcan, a prince from the Land of Fire."

Gasps could be heard from throughout the crowd. "That mean he be the nephew of the queen," a fat man in the front row said. "He be a prince."

"That is correct," Daphne said. "He is Prince Valdar, next in line to the throne of Pandara, and henceforth, he is to be addressed as such."

She no longer had to call for silence. A hush fell over the crowd. In the back of the crowd, Pip could see Sandrin and his friends, looks of astonishment on their faces. He allowed a small smile to play on his face.

"From this day," Daphne continued. "He is also the commander of the army of Pandora."

"Army? What army?" someone in the crowd asked. "Pandara has no army."

"Oh, we have an army," Daphne said. "Or, we will have as soon as we get recruits. Any man who volunteers will receive a summer's pay in advance. I want the word to go out all over Pandara. Never again shall we be defenseless against the predations of such as Barbaria."

Auric stepped from behind Galen. "I be the first to volunteer," he said.

Pip gaped in astonishment, and was about to protest, but Daphne laid a hand on his wrist. "Thank you, Auric," she said. "But, I have another task for you. You will be the royal tanner, responsible for uniforms, shields, and other equipment for the army."

Ludmilla squealed and grabbed Auric in a hug that threatened to smother him. "Oh, husband mine, this be such a great appointment."

"Over her head, Auric smiled at Pip. "Thank you, your majesty," he said. "I will do my best for you, I swear."

"Thank you, Auric. And now, good lady Ludmilla, if you will kindly release your husband and step forward."

With a puzzled look on her round face, Ludmilla turned. She stepped tentatively forward and curtsied. "Yes, your majesty. I beg your pardon for such an unseemly display."

"There is no need for apologies, good lady. I understand that since your arrival, the castle has never looked neater?"

Ludmilla's face turned red, and she looked down at her feet. "W-well, it not be that it was not already neat, your majesty. But, there do be a few changes I made. If they not be to your liking, I will put them back the way they were before."

"Not at all, good lady. They please me very much. So much, in fact, that I am appointing you head of chambers. You will supervise all castle staff. Are you willing to take on that responsibility?"

Ludmilla looked flustered, and for the first time in Pip's live, he feared that she might be at a loss for words. She gulped, though, and found her voice. "Your majesty," she said. "I know not what to say."

"You might try merely saying, yes," Daphne said.

"Oh, yes, your majesty, and I swear that I will do you proud."

"Thank you," said Daphne. "I have no doubt you will. Now, guardsmen Godfred and Melchor, would you kindly step forward."

The two guardsmen stepped forward and bowed.

"Godfred and Melchor, you are hereby relieved of duty as guardsmen."

Their mouths fell open and they looked as if they'd just been struck in the stomach. After seeing Auric and Ludmilla rewarded, they had no doubt expected some kind of small token, but, to be tooted from the guard hit them like a thunderbolt.

"B-but, your majesty," Godfred said. "We have served you loyally almost since we were striplings. Have we not performed our duties properly?"

"You have, and admirably," Daphne said. "And, that is precisely why I am promoting the two of you as captains in Pandara's new army."

They looked puzzled, but her words finally sank in and they smiled broadly. "Thank you, your majesty," they chimed together.

She inclined her head. "Very well. And now, Commander Valdar, would assemble your group in front of the stage?"

Pip sent a mental signal to the Folk. To the newly-promoted captains, he said, "Captain Godfred, Captain

Melchor, as my new subunit commanders, your first duty is to assemble the team."

Melchor deferred to Godfred, as he often did, and they set about getting Hermes, the ogres, the troll, and the gnomes into a line facing the stage, and then position themselves in front of that line. "The troops are assembled, sir," Godfred said.

Pip nodded, and with Vera and Tamara flanking him, took his place in front of his two captains.

"Your majesty," he said. "The troops are assembled."

Daphne smiled and nodded. She then turned to Councilor Galen. "Councilor, would you bring me the box I gave you?"

Galen presented her with a box covered in purple velvet, bowed and then moved to stand behind her.

Daphne opened the box, looked inside, and nodded. She moved to stand in front of Pip, who had a puzzled look on his face. "I felt that there had to be more than mere words to recognize the great service all of you have done for Pandara," she said aloud, and then, in a quieter voice to Pip, "Galen had the metalsmiths and seamstresses working on this since our arrival."

A loud squawk echoed around the courtyard, causing Daphne to flinch and look up. Talus swooped down from atop the wall and lit on Pip's left shoulder. The goshawk cocked its head to one side, looking at the queen with one eye. She smiled and winked at Pip. "I see now that your entire team is actually assembled, commander. I think this one would have resented being left out.

Talus squawked again, and then nuzzled his beak against Pip's ear. "Yes, your majesty," Pip said quietly.

"If not for Talus, your rescue would have been much more difficult. He is indeed an important part of our team."

Daphne reached into the box and removed a medallion that was suspended from a green, blue, and red ribbon. The medallion was a gold circle with the image of a goshawk etched on it. The words, 'For Conspicuous Bravery,' encircled the bird.

She placed the ribbon around Pip's neck. The medallion rested on his chest, giving him a warm feeling in both his chest and face. She then repeated the process with the others, beginning with Vera. After draping the last one, she paused. Talus squawked loudly, and she smiled. From the box, she withdrew a smaller version of the one she'd given Pip, and draped it around Talus' neck. As if understanding the significance of her action, Talus kept his head high, and when the medallion dropped against his feathered chest, he threw his head back and squawked.

"I think he likes it," Pip said quietly.

Talus spread his wings and soared up, circling the courtyard. The gold disk reflected the light from the torches on the wall as he circled.

"He is something of a showoff," Daphne said.

The crowd cheered lustily as Talus flew, causing him to swoop and loop even more. Finally, Pip sent him a mental command, *Enough!* Talus did one final circuit of the courtyard and then flew back and landed on Pip's shoulder.

"Your majesty," Galen said, clearing his throat. "I believe our guests are anxious to sample the viands we have prepared for them." With a wave of his arms, he indicated the four large tables laden with food that lined two side of the courtyard walls.

"Of course," Daphne said. "Good people of Lands End, please avail yourselves of the food. We will have entertainment as we eat."

At those words, people began a semi-orderly movement toward the tables, filling their arms, aprons, and whatever else they use as a container, with fruits, bread, pies, and meat. A group of musicians, who had been waiting in a corner behind the stage, mounted the platform and began playing 'Maiden on the Green,' Pip's favorite song, but, on this occasion, he was not really listening.

He stood quietly, stroking Talus' head. He was too excited to eat, and felt that even if he was not so overcome with emotion by events, it would be unseemly for him, as commander of the army, to eat before everyone else. Except for Vera, who stood at his side, and Daphne, who stood in front of him, smiling at the people, the rest of his team joined the crowd at the tables.

I see that your former enemies have been well-behaved, and, true to your word, nothing seems to have been broken.

Pip smiled at Vera. *Well, I think I might have broken them of their bad habits. And, Sandrin and one other will have headaches for a few suns.*

Vera shrugged and made a face. *I have been watching over you since you were still a stripling, and I was a mere sixteen summers myself. And, still, I do not understand the mundane side of you. But, that, I suppose, is how it must be. Shall we get something to eat before we swoon from lack of nourishment?*

Yes, cousin, we should. But, then we must busy ourselves with the planning for Pandara's new army, and more the challenge, how we will create a combined army of Folk and my mundane fellows.

Pip, you have already demonstrated that the two people can work together when there is a common purpose. I should think that a threat from the army of Barbaria, and doubt not that it will happen, should make our task less difficult.

Pip put his hands behind his back and crossed his fingers. *Of course, you are correct.* At least, he thought, I pray that you are correct. Here I am, not yet I the summer of my majority, and I have to learn how to rally people who are so different from each other to work and fight together. He knew that Tenkuk would not let the insult to his honor go unanswered, and would show Pandara no mercy when he invaded again—and, that he would invade again, Pip had no doubt.

As he followed Vera to the food tables, accepting congratulations from everyone he passed, he nodded politely and absently stroked Talus' head. In Auric and Ludmilla's household, there had never been any kind of observance of obeisance to the unseen gods that many in the countryside believed in, but as he walked, he prayed silently for guidance, and the grace of those gods that he had never before thought much of. If, as people thought, the gods of the land were the gods of all, on whose side would they stand?

Charles Ray

Epilogue

Tenkuk sat on the carved throne, in the throne of Castle Gondwana. He was dressed in his usual black uniform, but around his neck he wore the seal of the sovereign, a golden circle with a star inscribed in the center, on a gold chain. Kordan, the former advisor to Ostro, still dressed in his drab robe, and now serving as Tenkuk's advisor, stood before him, twisting his hands together. Tenkuk regarded the little man with the same disdain as always.

"Have you issued the commands as I instructed," Tenkuk said in a voice that was as cold as ice.

"Y-yes, Ten-, er, your celestial majesty," Kordan said. "It is as you have commanded. All the nobles of Barbaria will assemble this evening to crown you as the regent of Barbaria."

Tenkuk toyed with one end of his drooping mustache. "And, the instructions to assemble an army?"

Kordan was shaking so, his robe quivered as if blown by the wind. "Uh, well . . . there will be some delay in that, my lord. A few of the nobles question the wisdom of invading Pandara. They are afraid the

Pandarans will ally with our enemies to the west, and we might be overwhelmed."

Tenkuk's eyes blazed cold fire, and the muscles of his jaw tightened.

"Fools," he said, and spat. "Do they not see the wisdom of striking before there is time for such an alliance to be formed? If we delay, that is what they are certain to do. The only way to avoid that is to invade before they have time to organize. Which nobles have expressed disagreement?"

"Coltar of the southern province has been the most vocal in opposition. He is the leader, and a few of the others follow him."

"Ah, yes. Baron Coltar. I am not surprised. He fancies himself as more fit to rule than I," Tenkuk said. "I shall arrange that he does not leave the ceremony this night. If we cut off the head of the beast, we will own the body."

Like most Barbarians, Kordan was not averse to the shedding of blood, but he found Tenkuk's relish of it a reason to shiver. He remained still, though, fearing that any sign of hesitation on his part would invite Tenkuk's wrath, and thus earn him the same fate as the unfortunate, soon to lie in an unmarked grave, Baron Coltar. Mayhap, he thought, if I serve him well and please him, he will award me Coltar's lands.

"You are absolutely correct, beneficent one," he said. "Those who are not loyal deserve no other fate."

Tenkuk looked down at the cowering, groveling little man. He was not fooled by his toadying and obsequious language. But, as long as Kordan served his purposes, he would keep him around. As distasteful as that was, he realized that the little weasel did have his uses.

"If you will convey this order to the captain of my guard, Kordan," he said. "There will be a special reward for you. What would you say to being named baron of the southern province to replace Coltar?"

"Celestial majesty." Kordan's eyes gleamed, and the knot below his chin bobbed up and down. "I do not know if I am worthy . . . but, of course, it is my honor to serve in whatever capacity you think appropriate, and I gladly accept whatever reward you think fit." He rubbed his hands together and licked his lips.

"Very well, then. See that it is done." Tenkuk paused. "And, Kordan . . . do not fail me as you failed that fool Ostro in eliminating that wench, Daphne."

There was no mistaking the menace in his voice.

"It will be done, oh glorious one."

Of course, it will, you slimy little toad, Tenkuk thought, because I will personally check with the captain of the guard to ensure you have given him my orders. And, there is the added motivation; you know that if you fail me, there will be two meals for the wolves this night. He nodded curtly, and dismissed Kordan with a wave of his hand.

When Kordan had gone, he sat back on the throne, feeling the power from that seat course through his body. None in the castle had questioned his version of events. He had arrived at Ostro's bedchamber, but too late to save him. The boy, Pip, had killed him, and as Tenkuk entered the room, Pip and his allies had overpowered him. The purple bruise on his face from Pip's kick, now faded, had added credibility to his story. Except for that fool, Baron Coltar, none of the nobles really questioned his decision to invade Pandara to punish them for killing Ostro. There were the fools from the outer provinces who slavishly followed Coltar, who had been jealous of his relationship with Ostro, and who would have been happy had he also perished during the Pandaran raid on the castle; only they had the temerity to express doubts about the advisability of an invasion. No matter, he thought. After Pandara was conquered, he would take care of any remaining rivals, or even potential rivals, and then he would form a combined army of Barbarians and Pandarans to invade and conquer the lands to the west.

That had always been his aim, and something he had urged on Ostro on a daily basis. But, his reasons differed from the fat man's. While Ostro, like many a Barbarian, feared the people of the west because of their powers, and wanted to erase them from existence, Tenkuk had no such fears. Far from it. He did not want to eliminate the powers possessed by the mutants who inhabited the land of the fire-breathing mountain. He wanted to possess those powers for himself.

With a combined army, he was confident that he could overpower the devil spawn and bend them to his will. With that power behind him, he could then turn his attention to the unknown lands to the south, a land where power even greater than that of the west was rumored to exist. One day, he vowed, that power would be his to command. He would not be content to be king, and that was how he would insist his new subjects addressed him, of a semi-arid kingdom where the peasants had to be guarded by armed warriors to get them to raise crops. He would have the fertile lands of Pandara, and the magic-infused lands of the west. And, from there, he would conquer the mysterious south, and be the emperor of the world.

He leaned back on the throne, his eyes half closed, and with a leering smile on his vulpine face.

Yes, he thought, that did sound good; Tenkuk the Magnificent, Emperor of the World.

Charles Ray

Original Author's Note

Child of the Flame got its start about ten years ago as a short story about a child who grew up different and struggled to learn that being different does not mean being inferior. It was based in large part on my own experience as a step-child growing up with half-siblings with whom I shared only one parent's blood, and little else, and the tribulations of adjusting to that lack of shared traits.

After many false starts, I realized that there was just too much to cover to do it justice in a short story, but at the same time, even I would have trouble reading a long non-fiction work on the subject. At some point, and I no longer recall what triggered the realization, it became a novel, and in a mythic setting with magic and medieval customs (of a sort).

As it went through successive drafts, I toned the magic down a bit, but added the ability of the 'special' people to communicate without words. The smart-aleck animals sort of crept into the draft as I was working, and I didn't have the heart to send them back to the forest or stable.

This, dear reader, is just the beginning. Pip's world is much larger than Pandara, Barbaria, and the Land of Fire, and there are many more people, creatures, and adventures awaiting him.

Charles Ray, Harare, Zimbabwe

Charles Ray

Books by this author:

Al Pennyback mysteries
Color Me Dead
Memorial to the Dead
Deadline
Dead, White, and Blue
A Good Day to Die
The Day the Music Died
Die, Sinner
Deadly Intentions
Death by Design
Till Death Do Us Part
Deadly Dose
Dead Man's Cove
Dead Men Don't Answer
Deadly Paradise
Kiss of Death
Death in White Satin
Death and Taxis
Deadbeat
A Deadly Wind Blows
Death Wish
Deadly Vendetta
A Time to Kill, A Time to Die
Dead Ringer
Death of Innocence
Dead Reckoning
Murder on the Menu
Over My Dead Body

The Buffalo Soldier series:
Buffalo Soldier: Trial by Fire
Buffalo Soldier: Homecoming
Buffalo Soldier: Incident at Cactus Junction
Buffalo Soldier: Peacekeepers
Buffalo Soldier: Renegade

Charles Ray

Buffalo Soldier: Escort Duty
Buffalo Soldier: Battle at Dead Man's Gulch
Buffalo Soldier: Yosemite
Buffalo Soldier: Comanchero
Buffalo Soldier: Range War
Buffalo Soldier: Mob Justice
Buffalo Soldier: Chasing Ghosts
Buffalo Soldier: The Piano
Buffalo Soldier: Family Feud

Ed Lazenby mysteries
Butterfly Effect
Coriolis Effect
The Cat in the Hatbox
Murder is as Easy as ABC

Other fiction
Angel on His Shoulder
She's No Angel
Child of the Flame
Pip's Revenge
Wallace in Underland
Further Adventures of Wallace in Underland
Dead Letter and Other Tales
The White Dragons
The Dragon's Lair
Dragon Slayer
The Last Gunfighters
The Culling
*Frontier Justice: Bass Reeves, Deputy
   U.S. Marshal*
Angel on His Shoulder-Revised Edition
Battle at the Galactic Junkyard
Mountain Man
Devil's Lake
Wagons West: Daniel's Journey
Wagons West: Trinity

Vixen
Awakening

Nonfiction

*Things I Learned from My Grandmother About
   Leadership and Life*
*Taking Charge: Effective Leadership for the
   Twenty-first Century*
Grab the Brass Ring
*African Places: A Photographic Journey
   Through Zimbabwe and southern Africa*
A Portrait of Africa
There's Always a Plan B
*In the Line of Fire: American Diplomats in
   the Trenches*
Advice for the Insecure Writer
Looking at Life Through My Lens
Ethical Dilemmas and the Practice of Diplomacy
Making America Grate Again

Children's books

The Yak and the Yeti
Samantha and the Bully
Molly Learns to Share
Where is Teddy?
Catie and Mister Hop-Hop
Tommy Learns to Count
Catie Goes to School

Charles Ray

ABOUT THE AUTHOR

Charles Ray served 30 years in the Foreign Service (from 1982 to 2012), after completing a 20-year career in the U.S. Army. His first Foreign Service assignment was as a consular officer at the U.S. Consulate General in Guangzhou, China. He then served as the sole consular officer at the newly-opened consulate general in Shenyang, China, where he achieved tenure and was reassigned to the Consulate General in Chiang Mai, Thailand, as the administrative officer and acting deputy principal officer.

After three consecutive overseas tours, he returned to Washington where he served as the Special Assistant to the Director of PM Bureau's Office of Defense Trade Controls. After Washington, he went to Freetown, Sierra Leone as Deputy Chief of Mission.

In 1998, he became the first American consul general in Ho Chi Minh City, Vietnam, with consular responsibility for Vietnam from Hue to Phu Quoc Island. In 2002, he became ambassador to Cambodia, serving for three years. During the 2005-2006 academic year he served as diplomat-in-residence at the University of Houston. After leaving that job, he was appointed deputy assistant secretary of defense for Prisoners of War/Missing Personnel Affairs in the Office of the Secretary of Defense, responsible for the recovery, repatriation and identification of personnel missing from World War II to current conflicts.

His final assignment before retiring from the Foreign Service was as ambassador to Zimbabwe, from 2009 to 2012.

He holds a B.S. in business administration from Benedictine College, Atchison, KS; an M.S. in systems management from the University of Southern California; and an M.S. in national security management from the National War College. Ray is also a graduate of the U.S. Army Command and General Staff College (resident/non-resident program), the Army War College's Land Forces Commander Course, and the Defense Intelligence School's Postgraduate Intelligence Course.

His military awards include two Bronze Stars, the Joint Service Commendation Medal, Army Commendation Medal, National Defense Service Medal, Armed Forces Reserve Medal, and the Humanitarian Service Medal among others. He received a Superior Honor and a Meritorious Honor Award from the Department of State, and the Distinguished Civilian Service Award from the Department of Defense.

A native of Texas, Ray now leaves in suburban Maryland, just outside Washington, DC, with his wife, Myung.